ALSO BY BEHCET KAYA

NOVELS
Voice of Conscience
Murder on the Naval Base
Road to Siran

Treacherous Estate

By

Behcet Kaya

The events and characters in this book are fictitious. Certain real locations are mentioned, but all the characters and events described in the book are totally imaginary.

Copyright @ 2018 Behcet Kaya. All rights reserved.

No part of this book may be reproduced, stored in a retrieval system, or transmitted by any means without the written permission of the author.

www.hollywoodturk.com

To my wife, Nancy

Edited
By
Lisa J. Jackson

"Behind every great fortune lies a great crime."
Honore de Balzac

Chapter 1

Bayside Restaurant is a well-known, popular eatery situated on Santa Rosaria Sound in the small beach town of the same name. Due to its central location in the Panhandle of Northwest Florida, its regular customers number in the hundreds, with people traveling from as far east as Panama City, as far west as Mobile, and some as far away as New Orleans.

Friday nights are always filled with families and single people alike; all enjoying their meals. The atmosphere is that of a big log house with sturdy wooden tables and chairs. The restaurant has open patio dining and a bar looking over the marina which is the favorite spot of most diners. Across the sound one can see the high-rise condominiums situated along the thin strip of Santa Rosaria Island and in the distance the beginning of the pristine nine-mile Gulf Islands National Seashore. The condos and homes along the Gulf are owned by a wealthy clientele, with homes priced into the millions.

In the evenings, even when there is no moonlight, how beautiful the landscape is. The twinkling lights of cars look like kindling-light crossing over Santa Rosaria Bridge on the horizon. There is that luxuriant influence passing on like a celestial presence, with the bright and colorful lights from the high-rises reflecting in the waters of the sound, reminding one of a Disney dreamland. From the vantage point of the restaurant patio, it looks as if night and day are intermingled into one. In reality, it is neither day nor night; yet beyond the deep darkness, the night is smiling.

On this particular late July Friday night, I was among the throng of diners sitting outside on the patio, enjoying a cooler than usual summer evening. After my dinner of barbecued ribs, baked beans, and Cole slaw, I settled my bill, moved to the patio bar and ordered a Samuel Adams.

As I was taking a gulp from the large glass mug, I noticed a woman walk up to the stool next to me and sit down heavily. I glanced over, never missing an opportunity to check out a beautiful woman.

For some reason, my mind went into full alert. In a mere second, I took in the basic facts. She couldn't have been more than five-foot tall, slender, with pale skin, symmetrical face, petite nose, dark eyes, and raven black hair. I couldn't discern whether she was Asian or not. It seemed to me that she might have had surgery on her eyes to hide her ancestry.

She was dressed simply, but eloquently in a blue blouse, white pants which were rolled up to her knees, and a white lightweight sweater. There were diamond earrings in her earlobes, and a gold ring on her wedding finger along with a large diamond engagement ring. Her hands were delicate with long, slender fingers, and her fingernails were perfectly manicured indicating to me that she has never done a day's work; all adding up in my mind to a woman of class and wealth.

She looked over at me with pleading eyes and discretely pushed a brown envelope she was carrying towards my hand.

"Can you help me, Mr. Ludef…?"

Before she could finish saying my name, she slipped off the stool and onto the floor.

Everything began to happen in rapid fire. The bartender rushed around the bar, knelt down, and placed his fingers on the woman's neck to try and find a pulse. He looked up at me, shaking his head. A second before calling 911, I folded and slipped the brown envelope into the inside pocket of my sweat-jacket. I dialed, gave the police my name, location, brief pertinent facts, and then took a picture of the woman with my cell phone.

As the other diners realized the seriousness of what had just happened, the shouting and screaming began and parents tried to shield their children from the dead woman sprawled on the wooden deck. It seemed only minutes before the police and ambulance sirens could be heard above all the noise.

Along with the paramedics wheeling in a stretcher, a Santa Rosaria Deputy Sheriff strode out onto the patio, his voice booming over all the noise and chaos.

"Folks, please calm down! I want everyone to cooperate. The sooner we take everyone's statement the sooner you all can go home."

He walked over to the bar where I sat, somehow not surprised to see me in the midst of the chaos.

"Ludicrous? Seems like wherever you go, trouble follows you."

Deputy Erik Lawson stood in front of me, staring down from his six-foot-four, slender frame. He was clean-shaven, with a broad face and a wide nose that had been broken in his youth, and his hands were perpetually calloused. His Scandinavian heritage was reflected in his sandy brown hair. He was a man who found it difficult to say he was sorry, or even to say thank you; partially his way of camouflaging his true feelings. Above all he was a man of character.

How did I know all this? Lawson and I had served together in the navy for a good number of years, lost contact for a few more, then reunited after I'd moved to Santa Rosaria.

"Look, Deputy Lawson. I had nothing to do with all this. I was just having a beer and minding my own business until this woman sat down next to me and said,

'Can you help me, Mr. Ludef…' She didn't even finish the sentence. The next thing I know she's laying on the deck. I don't know who she is or why she sought me out."

"Seems I've heard this story before. You have a nasty reputation of people dying around you."

"You know better. That comes with the occupation."

"And, you know the drill. Don't leave town until we get to the bottom of this."

Chapter 2

As for me? My given name is Jacques Ludefance, Jack for short. If I had to describe myself? I'm 44, six-foot-two, with a long face, high cheek bones, dark hair and mustache, and deep green eyes, which have always been a hit with the ladies. On the down-side there is a deep scar on my right cheek, the slash extending from my eye to my lip that not even my deep tan can hide; which is definitely not a hit with the ladies. At first glance, they either back off, or are curious as to how it happened. My standard answer is short and simple, alligator bite. Growing up in Louisiana, I did some crazy things as a kid. Tangling with alligators was one of them.

Currently I live aboard a vintage 57-foot Hatteras, THE LUNA SEA. After purchasing her in what was definitely rough condition, I spent over eight months refurbishing her. Then, a little over a year ago, I moved her from New Orleans to her current home at the marina behind Bayside Restaurant soon after my wife and I divorced. Restoring the mahogany was my greatest satisfaction. She has a salon, a good-sized galley, two staterooms each with their own head, and on the large back deck there are comfortable cushions for sitting, along my fishing chair.

The locals call me alligator man, not only because of my scar, but because I keep an alligator by the name of Emma on my boat. I caught her as a young'un back in Louisiana. She's small and doesn't take up much room. So far, I've had no complaints, although I have no illusions that at some point I will be forced to give her up. For now, what better watch dog could I have? No alarm system needed, I simply post my sign, "Beware of Alligator" on the dock.

In my previous life, I was a navy pilot by career. It was a hard-fought battle. After failing several flight tests for FA/18 Hornet, I was permitted to finish flight school as a pilot on the Prowler. To this day, I must remind myself I'm not alone in the failure, as only a few succeed at becoming FA/18 pilots. Life is all about how you look at things. Never thinking of myself as one of the unlucky ones, I accepted the fact that I just was not cut out to be a Hornet pilot.

After the service, I did the usual that is expected of any red-blooded American male. I returned to my small home town near New Orleans, married my high school sweetheart who was the proverbial "girl next door," and tried out several career occupations before getting a respectable job working at a manufacturing company, Thomson Air Products, as a supervisor.

Enduring several years of what I considered tedious, monotonous days, my boss approached me about finding out who was stealing company parts and selling them. It didn't take me long to ferret out the suspects. As a reward, the CEO of the company compensated me with fifty-thousand for what he considered my ingenious way of catching the thieves. I was tempted to blow it all, but, for once, let caution rule my decision. I invested it, thinking it might come to good use one day.

Flush with my success at catching the thieves at Thomson, I decided to leave the company. It seemed only logical to get my PI license. Although I took whatever cases came my way, my specialty became working for wealthy women whose husbands were cheating on them. After getting into trouble on one of my cases, my wife, Sarah, left me. She found out I had slept with the secretary of the man I was hired to investigate. I can't blame her. It was a stupid thing to do, and I will regret it until the day I die.

By this time, my investments afforded me the luxury of taking some time off. I purchased my current floating home, rented dock space, and bought a townhouse to live in while I worked on the boat full time.

Sarah and I stayed separated for several years, but the divorce was inevitable and painful. I still haven't been able to completely let go of my bitterness, both at her and myself. We did manage to part without too much legal hassle. There were no children to muddy up the agreement. She got the house. I got my unwanted freedom. Not wanting to live in the same town, I moved the boat to Santa Rosaria.

After completing my 40-hour Florida Private Investigator "CC" *Intern* Training Course, I was given my license to practice in Florida, and have the distinction of being the only private investigator in the area. I still do PI work when the right job comes along. The sheriff's department, for some reason, has given me the nickname of 'Ludicrous.'

That brings us back to Friday night and a dead woman. After Lawson and the paramedics did what they needed to do, and the poor woman was taken away, I quietly slipped out the side entrance and returned to my boat. Opening the brown envelope the mystery women had given me, I found a smaller envelope with two bundles of crisp, brand new 100-dollar bills. All told, both stacks added up to twenty-grand.

Among the other items were birth certificates for two boys, a marriage certificate, and copies of off-shore Cayman Island bank account numbers. The last item I pulled was a photo that almost made me vomit. In the picture was an Asian girl whose throat had been slashed and a heavy-set man standing over her body, his back to the camera.

Grabbing a Samuel Adams from the fridge, I sat down and took a deep breath. Who was this mystery woman? Who were the boys? Who was the dead woman in the picture? And, who was the man standing over her body? Lastly, how did the now-dead woman find me? I debated with myself whether to turn all this evidence over to the police. It only took me seconds to decide against it.

Not able to ignore either my investigative instincts or my curiosity, I knew I wanted to find out what happened without the police knowing. Besides, this woman sought me out and had come to me with this evidence and money to pay me for my services. Although, I had no idea for what, I was not about to turn her down.

Later that night as I watched the local news, the incident was splashed across the screen. Not much was said about who she was. Either the police didn't have any information or, if they did, they were keeping it under wraps.

Chapter 3

The next morning on the local news, the dead woman was identified as Lillian Holler, the wife of Jonathan Holler, an import-export company owner, trading in Southeast Asia. According to the reports, he exported used machinery from the US, but no information was given as to what he imported from Asian countries. As for the woman, her given name was Hieu Nguyen from Vietnam. The autopsy results indicated she died of natural causes; a bleeding ulcer that had gone undetected and untreated. There would be no further investigation by the police.

Bleeding ulcers? It could happen. I'd experienced it myself.

When I was still in New Orleans and refurbishing *THE LUNA SEA*, I'd taken some time off from PI work. But, when a seminar was offered in Pensacola, I decided to attend. After driving over, I couldn't find a hotel with an available room. I drove east until I reached Santa Rosaria and found a motel right on the sound. Quiet, peaceful, and friendly people. I was, like so many others, instantly hooked on the area.

Back in Pensacola, during one of the meetings, I started to feel dizzy. I quietly left the room and laid down on a sofa in the hotel lobby. When I tried to stand up, I started sweating, pissed in my pants, and keeled over. The next thing I knew, a hotel security guard was helping me sit up and asking for my ID. I handed my driver's license to him as two medics approached with a stretcher and took me out to a waiting ambulance.

As the one of the medics started an intravenous in my arm, I remembered that the security guard had not returned my driver's license. After a moment of panic, and some additional confusion, the guard came out and handed back by ID.

I must have passed out again, because the next thing I remembered was waking up in a hospital ER. The ER doc told me that I was bleeding internally from ulcers and was blunt enough to tell me my blood count was so low that in another hour I would have been dead. I had bleeding ulcers and never knew.

How easily I could've ended up like Lillian Holler.

I've also heard of Holler Enterprises. Everyone in Santa Rosaria knows about it. His company is the largest and most influential in the area, employing hundreds of people. In my experience, import-export companies always raise questions. Add to that a Vietnamese wife? Too many questions kept popping in and out of my head.

I wouldn't be surprised if, in the near future, Holler didn't own the city council. He has a way of putting his people in councilman positions, two so far. What better way to expand his empire, which also includes a slew of massage salons, all supposedly legit.

But, I know one thing for sure. He couldn't and wouldn't own the sheriff's department. The current sheriff is planning on retiring in November and Deputy Lawson is running for the position. My intention is to help him in any way I can, knowing that Holler could never own Lawson. A man of character can never be bought.

Suspicious of Holler on several levels, but not sure where to start, I did a little snooping around on the internet. First stop was his website. Impressive and well-done. Several pages on the business itself, job opportunities, and a rather interesting biography on Holler. It was glaringly sketchy on his early life, with only a brief mention of his stint in the military and working in Southeast Asia. It was, however, quite heavy on a list of his current accomplishments, and his "good works" in the community. In addition, it listed the various national charities he was involved with. After reading it, most anyone would come away with the impression his was a stellar member of society.

Not buying it, I wanted to go deeper. Military and Southeast Asia gave me a starting point. It took a while, and I'm still not sure how or why I ended up finding it, but I watched a YouTube video made specifically for American service men for when they did their tours to countries such as Malaysia, Taiwan, Vietnam, and Thailand. In those countries girls were for sale and loved anyone in uniform. They either worked the streets themselves to get their clients for the night, or, many of the very good-looking girls had their own pimps to acquire clientele for them. In addition to servicemen, wealthy men would willingly pay these girls for several nights or weeks, or whatever arrangement was worked out between them. On the surface it appeared legal, as they are working as a "maid," when, in actuality, it was pure and simple prostitution.

Was it possible that at some point Lillian Holler could have been one of these girls? If she was, she ended up being one of the lucky ones to marry Holler and come to the US. But, just how did Holler meet her? And, more importantly, when, and under what circumstances? I immediately threw out the scenario that Holler had been in Vietnam. Lillian Holler was in her mid-thirties and the Vietnam War ended over forty years ago. I made the decision to concentrate on the Malaysia scenario.

Taking the contents out of the brown envelope Lillian had given me, I looked at them again. Knowing now who she was also settled the question of the birth certificates, both with the last name of Holler. Her children. However, the dead woman in the photograph remained a mystery. Could the man standing over her body be Jonathan Holler?

It was easy to make the obvious leap that the money was supposed to be my fee for whatever Lillian Holler wanted to expose. Sometimes my clients come with prepayment. I still questioned why she had picked me and how she had found me. But she was a wealthy woman and wealthy women have ways of finding out whatever it is they want to know.

Since the police had closed the case, I was free to move ahead. But, I knew whatever I did, there might have issues with Deputy Lawson. Lawson and I have a tendency to butt heads. Might be because in our past dealings, I somehow have, at times, managed to embarrass him.

As I said, Lawson and I go way back to our navy years. Both of us failed our F/18 Hornet training, both of us were ECMO officers on the Prowler, and we even served in the same unit. After the navy, he married and took a job at the sheriff's department in Santa Rosaria. I tried to pursue several different careers, ended up becoming a PI, and settled in Santa Rosaria after my divorce.

It has become a personal satisfaction to come out ahead of him, but sometimes this kind of rivalry isn't good between a PI and an officer of the law.

Chapter 4

The next evening, I had no interest in returning to Bayside Restaurant for dinner. To think clearly about my next steps, I needed to separate myself from all that had happened and the recurring vision of Lillian Holler lying dead on the deck. Taking my time on the half-hour drive over to Destin gave me the space I needed, and Harry T's at Destin Harbor, afforded me the luxury of enjoying a good bottle of Italian wine and a well-made shrimp Alfredo, all the while staring out at Destin Pass.

If I intended to find out more about Holler's dirty business without revealing who I was, if, indeed there was dirty business, I needed a well-planned strategy. Finishing my dinner, I opened my laptop and Googled Holler's company website again. Scanning the various pages, I selected "Job Openings." Several were listed, including a position for an experienced shipping-handling clerk. Sometimes in PI work, the simplest solution works the best. My simple solution? Should I apply for a job in Jonathan Holler's company? Obviously, it would be best to work for Holler as one of his shipping clerks. What better way to know what he was exporting and importing. Now, all I needed was a new resume detailing my so-called shipping and handling experience and list a few references.

As quickly as I had come up with it, I immediately discarded the idea of writing a phony resume. It could easily backfire and get me into a lot of trouble. Besides, I didn't really want to be in that close of a proximity to Holler. If not me, who? I immediately thought of Katy. She was eighteen at the time she had come to me early last year with a problem she was having with her boyfriend. Cute little Katy Ozener from Ohio, all of five-foot-two, with dark hair and green eyes she inherited from her mom. I know this because she brought her mother when she came to meet with me. Katy is humorous, a quick thinker, has as a fiery personality, and is unafraid to say whatever comes into her mind.

Ended up her boyfriend was jealous of her working in a restaurant and having all the guys hit on her. When he started beating her, she walked out. When she arrived on my doorstep with a black-eye and her mother in tow, my heart melted. Who would do such a thing? Even though I never had any kids, my paternal instincts kicked in and my immediate reaction was to protect her. Her mother, a flighty, fidgety woman, was of no help.

Long story short, I took Katy in for a couple of weeks until she found a job in the shipping department of a local NAPA store and her own apartment with another girl. In addition, I got a restraining order slapped on her boyfriend, who ended up arrested and jailed for forging bad checks. Perhaps she would consider giving me a hand. And no time like the present to give her a call. It didn't surprise me when her roommate answered.

"Is Katy there?"

"She's at work. This is her roommate, Jocelyne. Can I take a message for her?"

"Thanks. This is Jack Ludefance. Can you tell her to call me back?"

"Sure. She talks a lot about you."

"I hope all good?"

"Absolutely. I'll give her the message."

Katy returned my call later that night, worried that I had some bad news for her.

"No, nothing like that Katy."

"What then?"

"I have a proposal for you for a full-time, good-paying job. Can you come by my boat tomorrow morning? We can discuss the details."

"Sure, Jack. I can be there about eight."

Next morning, I walked up to McDonald's and picked up three bacon, egg and cheese bagels, hash browns, a large coffee with lots of cream, orange juice and tea. Great thing about living in a beach town is the convenience of stores and restaurants. Santa Rosaria is still small enough that just about everybody knows everybody and everybody pretty much comes from somewhere else. Many come down from the northern parts of the US for vacation, love it so much they end up buying property and settling in, either as part-time or full-time residents.

On the way back, Katy drove by, stopped, and picked me up. After finishing off breakfast, it was time to get present my plan.

"Okay, Jack. I am intrigued. What kind of job do you have for me?"

"First off, where are you working now?

"Not at NAPA anymore. I'm working part-time at Macy's at the mall."

"I think I can get you a full-time job at Jonathan Holler's company."

"Jonathan Holler? The guy whose wife just died? But why?"

"I want to find out what Holler's business encompasses. You already have some experience in shipping and handling from the job at NAPA. That can help us to get you a position at Holler Enterprises. The job pays $10.44 an hour with five years of experience. If they pay you less, I'll make up the difference."

"Wow! That's more than I make at Macy's. I'm definitely in. But I still don't understand. Why do you want me to work at Jonathan Holler's company? What's going on, Jack?"

"Katy, what I'm going to tell you must stay between us. This wasn't in the papers or on the news. Lillian Holler came to that restaurant and sat down next to me. She asked for my help and then she died. I'm still not sure why she came to me, but I want to help her. I want to know what kind of business her husband runs. I know on the surface he exports used machinery to Southeast Asia. Your job will be to find out exactly what he ships to Southeast Asia, what he imports in return, and anything else you can find out about his background. Are you interested?"

"Sure. It sounds simple enough."

We worked on Katy's resume, adding a few more years of experience at "Custom Apparatus Company," listing my telephone number and my fake name of Greg Foster as her supervisor.

Piece of cake. Katy aced her interview and within a week started work at Holler Enterprises.

Was this too easy?

Chapter 5

While Katy settled in to her first work week at Holler's company, I was busy strategizing how to stalk him. I wanted to know everything there was to know about him and his company. Of course, I didn't want to get too close to Jonathan Holler too soon. When you stalk your game, it is nice to know what it eats, where it drinks and where it beds down, and if it has any particular nasty habits, like circling back and pursuing the pursuer.

I didn't know all the questions to ask, but I had an idea about where to start. A friend of mine by the name of Logan works at the Santa Rosaria Country Club. It was a long shot, but it was worth trying, and it seemed the most logical place to start.

I paid a visit to the country club, settled myself at the piano bar overlooking the golf course, and checked out the surroundings. Logan was off for the next several days, so I left a message at the desk for him to call me when he returned.

Katy called during her second week working at Holler's.

"Jack, I think I may have something for you. I've been writing up shipping statements for parts to something called a C130. I don't really know what that means, but I thought I'd let you know. I'll text you the pictures I took."

"Katy, my girl, I think you may be on to something. A C130 is a military cargo plane. Good work and keep it up."

Katy sent the texts of the pages she had photographed. Is Holler still dealing with the military?

Before I went in the direction, I wanted to talk to Logan. I called the country club again.

"Santa Rosaria Country Club. How may I direct you call?"

"Logan? Jack here. I was there last week to talk to you."

"Yeah! I had a message that you wanted me to call you, but you know how it is. I was going to call you tonight. What's up?"

"Logan, is Jonathan Holler a member of the club?"

"He's in here all the time for drinks and holds meetings several times a month."

"Meetings? What kind of meetings?"

"I don't know the details, but I think they're military people."

"Why do you think that?"

"They call one another with their military titles, although they dress civilian. I heard one-time Holler called another one of his colleagues, 'colonel.' Actually, another time, the same man came here dressed in his uniform."

"Anything else you can tell me about him?"

"He's one of the club's charter members, very involved with the activities, and well-respected."

"Thanks, Logan."

"Anytime. And, of course, I won't ask why you want to know."

With a starting point I could work both backwards and forwards. From his company website, I already knew he was ex-military, and I assumed he must have been a ranked officer to be associating with 'colonels.' From his picture in the news, he looked to be in his late 50s to early 60s. So, going back 30 or so years would put him in the military in the late 1980's to the early 1990's.

What I like about research is that Google can provide all kinds of information on just about anything. I wanted to find out as much as possible before calling on a friend who works at the Pentagon. I also didn't have to approach Holler's buddies at the county club as it would be suspicious. Like I said, I'm stalking him without his knowledge.

On one of my Google searches, I came across Holler's name along with Bosnia. What I came up with was utterly fascinating. Holler was a lieutenant during the time of the '94 Balkan Wars between Bosnia and Serbia. The puzzling piece to this picture was the fact that the US was not involved in those conflicts other than NATO's involvement.

His name was also linked to a company called, Lightening Speed Services, Inc. Their motto was, "Providing effective responses to emergencies, conflicts and post-conflicts transitions around the world." So, was Lightening Speed Services a private company? Googling that name, their website came up. They're still in business doing service to both the army and navy in the form of maintenance of motorized vehicles and aircraft, as well as providing medical support to the troops. They also train foreign armies.

How did Holler fit into all this?

There was no avoiding the fact I needed to call Colonel Jeffery Scott, my ex-wife's uncle, who worked at the Pentagon. Thankfully, I've managed to maintain a good relationship with him. I pulled out his card with his direct number he had given me, dialed, and heard his familiar voice.

"Colonel Scott."

After the pleasantries, I asked him if there was a way for him to find out about Jonathan Holler. I gave him what information I had, and that he had been an active duty officer during the time of the Bosnian War.

"I take it this is important, Jack?"

"Yes, sir. Very important. A favor to a deceased friend."

"I see. My condolences. Let me do some digging and see what I can come up with. Give me your e-mail address. Give me a day or two. If I find anything I'll send it to you."

"Thank you, sir."

"You take care. I'll be in touch one way or the other."

Chapter 6

Keeping an alligator on board requires she be fed. Although alligators can go months without eating, I prefer to feed Emma often. Keeps her and me both happy. Since Publix roasted chickens are her favorite meal, I made a quick trip to pick up several. Most of the deli counter clerks know me and set aside roasted chickens that are out of date, so feeding her is free of charge.

When I returned, Katy was standing on the dock, pacing back and forth.

"Katy? Everything Okay?"

"Jack, evidently someone saw me when I took those pictures of the invoices last week and called me on it. I made up an excuse and tried to explain that's what I do. I take pictures so I can write it up later. I know it didn't make any sense, but it's all I could come up with. I promised I wouldn't do it again, but they're accusing me of spying on the company. You know I don't scare easily, but these guys are creepy as hell."

"Katy, I understand you're upset, but we need more information. Try and hang in there for just a little while longer?"

Katy paced some more. "Okay, but after this, we're even."

"Katy, you don't owe me anything. Give it another couple of weeks and if you want to quit, I'll go with what you've found."

I didn't want Katy to bug out now. Too much was riding on her getting more information, if she could. It was Friday night, so I treated her to dinner at Bayside, although it took a few beers before she calmed down. Yeah, I know. Bad parenting, letting her drink underage.

Saturday, I put the top down on my RX7 and we drove over to Destin for lunch. Sunday, we drove through the National Seashore to Pensacola Beach and did some swimming. A weekend of relaxing and Katy was ready for another week at Holler's company.

On Monday my inbox was filled with e-mails from Colonel Scott. Seven separate e-mails to be exact. All declassified. What he sent gave me a lot to digest and not just on Holler and his company, but he also included information on government outsourcing in general. It seems that there are numerous private intelligence services that not only our government, but the governments of many nations and political groups around the world, outsource to. And, from here on, it appears that the private intelligence sub-sector is at its initial stage of a huge boom.

Besides working for Lightning Speed Services, Inc., Holler also worked for one called, Outsourcing Intelligence, or OI. Turns out that OI and the CIA entered a competition on intelligence gathering and OI won.

According to their website, OI was founded in 1988 by a General Braydon Wyette, and was a part of the South African Civil Cooperation Bureau. It was one of the most elite combat strike forces in the South African Bush wars, with the highest kill ratio. OI also made a reputation for itself in Sierra Leone, Africa. They were most effective in what they agreed to do and were finally accused of being "a mercenary army of racist killers." Even Google searches substantiated this information that the company had been accused of egregious human rights violations.

This Holler was turning out to be a real piece of work. After he was dishonorably discharged from the military for stealing and secretly selling bazookas to Indonesian rebels, he worked as a crew member on C130 cargo planes where he was eventually caught altering the parts on the plane. The way he did it was pure genius. He and one of his buddies would buy gold on the black market in Turkey, then melt the gold down and make it into a solid block. At a little machine shop in, the city of Adana where the Incirlik American base is located, they made structural parts for the C130 out of the gold and painted them with aluminum paint. They then would change out the actual parts with the gold parts. When the plane landed back on US soil, they would change the gold parts back to the original parts. Long story short, they brought untold ounces of gold back into the US.

Holler was also an expert in demolitions, having being trained for secret combat duties. He was the preverbal Jack of all trades. As for OI, the Pentagon stopped giving contracts to Outsourcing Intelligence after it was discovered the company was involved in human trafficking. During their work for the Bosnian government, they would bring young girls and boys to the US from Eastern Europe and they were led into prostitution and porno films. Holler got his hands dirty in this operation as well and ended up serving five years in prison.

Seems Mr. Holler had stellar reputations with every job he took, and each job he held had more infamous reputations. He may currently be an upstanding member of our community, and run a supposedly above board and legitimate company, but with everything I'd just read, he had a much darker, sinister side.

The more I researched, the more questions there were.

Just how did he find and marry the lovely Hieu Nguyen, aka Lillian Holler, and just how did she end up with a bleeding ulcer that took her life?

Just how big were Holler's holdings? Were they all legitimate businesses? Or were they hideous tax shelters hiding nefarious and dirty dealings?

Chapter 7

An idea came to me. A crazy idea. I wanted to sneak into Holler's estate located behind Holler Enterprises and find out more about what he had going on. I wanted to know about all those other buildings that could be seen stretching back into a heavily wooded area. Did it go all the way back to Santa Rosaria Sound?

Checking Google maps, an aerial showed just how vast Holler's complex was. It had to be at least a half-mile fronting Highway 88 and included the large warehouse buildings and corporate offices of Holler Enterprises, along with several other smaller businesses. As I had suspected, from there it did stretch all the way back to the sound. Had to be well over a dozen acres. Scattered throughout the property were various sized buildings, none of which I could discern the purpose for, but had every intention of finding out. There was also a race track, barns for horses, a gun range, and a large lake. When I zoomed in on the Google map, I could see several large alligators lying on the bank. At the very back of the property, his mansion fronted the shoreline of the sound with a dock and several nice size boats.

I studied the map until I was comfortable with the location of each building. What I needed now was another person to have radio communication with while I was inside.

Katy? Of course. Katy would be perfect.

I just hoped I could persuade her to help me after her experience at Holler's. After a trip to the mall and the purchase of two walkie-talkies, I called her.

"Katy, how are you? Everything going okay at Holler's?"

"I'm okay, Jack. I would've called you if it wasn't. What's up?"

"I have another job for you. I'll pay you $200 bucks."

"For what?"

"I'm going inside Holler's estate. You're going to wait on the outside and keep watch for me and we'll communicate with walkie-talkies."

"Isn't that dangerous?"

"It is for me, but you'll be safe on the outside. We'll touch base every fifteen minutes, so in case I have trouble, you can call the sheriff's office. I've got to know what all those buildings are for inside Holler's property."

"What about the Dobermans?"

"Dogs. Of course. He has dogs. Yeah, I'll have to think of something."

"When do you want to do this?"

"Saturday night. Be here at the marina around midnight."

I went up to Publix, bought some steak for the dogs, cut it up into small chunks, and marinated it hot pepper sauce. Problem solved.

Saturday night. Midnight. Katy arrived on time. I had my gear ready. My cell phone was fully charged and purged of any other pictures. I put a flashlight in one pocket and the meat for the dogs in another pocket. My gun was secure in my shoulder holster, my knife taped to my leg. Wire cutters were nice and sharp. We tested and adjusted the volume on the walkie-talkies. Time to do this.

Pulling off into a vacant lot overgrown with brush, I parked at the very end of Holler's complex. The car wouldn't be seen from the highway, nor would I be noticed as I approached the barbed wire fence enclosing that side of the complex. I took my wire cutters and cut a hole just big enough to squeeze through, and I was in.

"In." I whispered to Katy.

"Okay. Be careful, Jack."

"I'll call you in fifteen minutes. If you don't hear from me within a half-hour, call the sheriff's office."

"Wait! What do I say?"

"Tell them they've got Jack inside Holler's estate. Over and out."

The first building was easy. Locked doors are never a problem for a PI. Once inside the cavernous space, I flipped on my flashlight and kept it low where no one could see from the outside. To the right I found a room with dozens of storage shelves filled with bottles of drugs labeled in what looked like Chinese lettering. I pulled out my cell phone and took photos of the drugs, then moved back out into the warehouse area. The more I looked the more I saw; military hardware including bazookas, machine guns, AK-47's, grenades, even Czech-made mines. Further back, were used machinery, milling machines, Lathes, saws, welding torches, and parts I don't know what for. Pulling out my cell phone again, I took as many pictures as I could.

I was way over my fifteen minutes.

"Katy, all clear."

"Jack, you had me scared."

"Over and out."

Exiting and re-locking the door, I moved on to the next building, and was surprised to find the door wasn't locked. I slowly opened it, crouched and moved in. With my flashlight on, what I saw confounded me. The space was spit-polish clean, sectioned off with couches, beds, tall professional light stands, and cameras. There were several dressing rooms obviously used for makeup and hair. No guessing what this was used for. As in the first building, I took as many pictures as I could.

Once again, I was way over my fifteen minutes and checked in with Katy. I knew I was pushing it, but I wanted to see more. I moved back through the property and closer to the house, ducking as I heard noises coming towards me. It was too dark to tell who they were, but before reaching where I was, they turned and headed back to the house. I passed the garage, headed toward the boat dock, but before I could get close, I heard voices talking in a language I wasn't familiar with. It sounded like a party of some kind, and then a loud argument broke out.

Along with that, I heard the dogs barking and knew they must have caught my scent. I also knew the Holler's men wouldn't be far behind. I began a crouching, zig-zag run back to the fence and my escape, managing at the same time to pull out the meat. Just before reaching the fence, I threw it at the dogs. They stopped, gobbled it up and started howling. I turned and slipped back through to other side.

"Katy! You there?"

"I'm here Jack! I heard the dogs!"

"Start the car. I'm almost there!"

When I reached the car, Katy had it running, and we were out of there. It was too close a call, but what I had seen was invaluable. Picture proof of that Holler was selling military equipment. Picture proof he produced porno movies. The drugs were another matter. What were they, and what were they used for?

Chapter 8

Sunday morning, after a short sleep, the first thing on my list was to transfer the photos from my cell phone to my laptop. In addition, I made copies which I added to the envelope Lillian had given me. I then erased all the photos off my phone. I couldn't be too careful with this critical evidence.

Frustration set in, along with anger. How did Holler keep operating under the radar? Illegal arms sales, drugs, porno movies and no one suspected anything?

That night I drove over to Destin, cruised around for a while, and decided to stop at Harry T's and enjoyed a dinner of shrimp Alfredo, lots of garlic bread and a bottle of wine. I kept telling myself I should cut down on the eating, perhaps the drinking too, but somehow eating my favorite dinner was a kind of substitute for my frustration.

Finishing the last glass of wine, I tried to clear my mind. It suddenly occurred to me how I could find out more about Hieu Nguyen; Lillian Holler. From Panama City to Pensacola, the majority of the massage salons, although operated by Asians, were owned by Holler. If, if I could make contact with just one girl who knew of Lillian, or actually knew her, maybe I could find out more about what had happened to her.

I've had massages at several of these salons, and knew the girls were not supposed to have conversations with the clients. But, it was worth the chance. There are other kinds of massages called Tantra massages and Holler owned these as well. But, they were much more exclusive places, where one must be a member. I'm sure it's more than just a massage; more like a high-class brothel house. I discounted those. Too expensive, and I wasn't interested in what they were selling.

Over the next two weeks, I tried several salons and finally found one where I was sure the girl really liked me. I've always preferred a hard massage, and her hands were as strong as a vice-grip. I gave her a big tip. Her name was Sofia, obviously a fake name, but she told me whenever I wanted a massage, to call ahead and ask for her.

A week later, I called and made an appointment with Sofia. About a half hour into the message she directed me to turn over onto my stomach. But, it came out, "Tun oveh."

I did as she instructed and indicated with my finger for her to come close.

She put her ear in front of my mouth and whispered that I would like to speak with her.

"No speak," she whispered back.

Reaching over into my backpack, I pulled out a small notebook and pen and wrote a quick note. *I want to see you outside.* I slipped it into her hand.

She quickly wrote back. *No leave. Too dangerous. We stay here.*

It made sense. They'd been brought in illegally and been lectured that 'out there' was no life for them. This building was their safe place. I could understand that. If they're not here legally and don't know the language well, outside their comfort zone was no place for them.

Did you know Hieu Nguyen, Lillian Holler?

She shook her head; her eyes took on a look of suspicion.

I'm not police. I need to talk to someone who works in the Holler household.

She looked at me as if to ask why I wanted to know. I wrote, *Lillian Holler asked for my help, then died. Why did she need my help?* Then I indicated for her to come close.

Once again, she brought her ear to my mouth, and. I whispered to her.

"Let's talk this way. Where are you from?" then I turned my ear to her mouth.

"Vietnam."

It turns out she was a university graduate but couldn't find a decent job. To survive, she and the other girls got involved in escort dating, and soon became nothing more than sex slaves. Long story short, she ended up here.

As she was finishing my massage, I felt she was beginning to trust me, and I took a chance and asked her again if she knew someone in the Holler household.

"Lillian had Vietnamese old lady for cook." She wrote a name on a piece of paper and handed it to me.

Looking at the note I couldn't read the name. I moved slightly and dropped the note on the basket where my clothes were.

"How do I get in touch with her?"

"When she goes groceries but need someone interpret her."

"Okay. Do you know anybody who can help interpret? I'll pay them well."

I watched as she debated with herself. Money always talks. Sofia's English wasn't the best, but it would have to suffice. If she could pull the meeting off.

"I might can do. Sometime I drive her. But I work."

"Sofia, I'll pay for your time."

"I call you when we go groceries."

"Okay. Thank you."

"May be next week."

After she finished wiping me off, I dressed and met her at the front desk. She giggled when I handed her my cell phone number and a hundred-dollar tip. It was worth every penny.

Sofia contacted me a week later to meet her and the Vietnamese cook at a Taiwanese grocery store over in Ft. Williams. Interesting that she had initially told me she couldn't go 'outside,' yet, not only had she left the massage salon, she was driving the Vietnamese cook to the grocery store.

When I arrived, Sofia waved and pointed to a bench where we could sit and talk.

"Sofia, ask her how long she worked for Lillian."

They bantered back and forth in Vietnamese.

"Five years."

I pulled out the picture of the dead girl with her throat slashed.

"Does she know who this is?"

The old woman gasped, clutched her throat and babbled on almost incoherently.

"Lillian's cousin, Duyen. She fight with Holler. She try go to police. He kill her."

It took me a moment to process what she had just said. Holler killed Lillian's cousin? I let it sink in and continued with my questions, not sure of how much time I had before Sofia called a halt to our meeting.

"What about the building on the estate where they film porno movies?"

Sofia looked at me in shock. "You there?"

I nodded.

"Girls come through Malaysia. All Chinese girls. Come over on boats. If get sick on boats and die, they tied to concrete blocks and dumped overboard. Girls who survive work in massage place. Go there to make movies."

She turned back to the old woman and spoke to her.

"Two girls die on estate."
"Two girls died? On the estate? What happened?"
"Drugged."
"Sofia, what do you mean drugged."
The old lady kept on with her gibberish.
"They give drug to girls and men. Make them happy. Then some girls die. Buried there. She know where. One buried faah corner. Late. Must go now."

After Sofia and the old woman left, I sat there unable to move. To say I was stunned would be an understatement. Girls are brought over on boats and, if they die during the transit, their bodies are thrown overboard? Lillian's cousin murdered by Holler? Drugs, porno movies, and two more dead girls?

Where was all this leading?

I could end it right now and turn everything over to the police, or follow my instincts and continue to whatever end it took me.

Chapter 9

Among the voluminous info that Colonel Scott had e-mailed me were the names and pictures of the two "buddies" of Holler who worked with him on the C130. One was Kevin Bradford, currently living in Kansas City and the other was DeAngelo Gonzales, currently living in Dallas Texas. Time to make some visits.

It was easy to locate Kevin Bradford's address and phone number in Kansas City from a service I subscribe to and I decided to pay him a visit.

I called Katy, got her voice mail, and left her a message. "Katy, I'm going to be out of town for a few days and asking a favor from you to watch over the boat. I'll explain when you return my call."

After a few hours, I began to worry. It was not like Katy to ignore my message. I tried again and this time she picked up. I started to explain the situation about the boat and not having to feed Emma.

"Jack...Jack...slow down. Jocelyne just moved out on me. I can't afford to pay the rent myself, even working full-time at Hollers. Is it okay if I stay on the boat for a few days?"

"You know you can stay as long as you need to."

"Thanks, Jack. I'll take good care of the boat. I'll even feed Emma."

"You don't have to do that. Just take care of yourself and be careful at Hollers."

"I'm being careful after what happened a few weeks ago. Everything seems to have quieted down. But, I haven't come up with anything else for you."

"Katy, if by the time I get back, you haven't found out anything else, you can quit."

"That sounds good, Jack. When do you want me there?"

"Tomorrow?"

"What time?"

"I'll let you know as soon as I've booked my flights."

After hanging up with Katy, I called Kevin Bradford's number and an elderly woman answered.

"Good evening. My name is Jack Ludefance. May I speak to Mr. Kevin Bradford?"

"I regret to say that Mr. Bradford passed away last October. October 11, 2016, to be exact."

"May I speak to Mrs. Bradford?"

"That would be me. I'm his widow."

"I'm sorry for your loss, ma'am."

"Oh, thank you. But it was a blessing. I prayed for his transition."

"I just wonder if he was the Mr. Bradford I'm trying to locate. Was he a pilot during the Bosnian war back in 1990s?"

"Oh, heavens no! My husband was 94 years old. You must mean my son."

"Is there any way I can get in touch with your son, Mrs. Bradford?"

"If you'd been here last week you could have talked to him yourself. He was here for a nice long visit."

"Where can I reach him now?"

"I'm sorry. You sound like you're calling from out of state. You keep cutting in and out."

"Apologize for that. I'm calling on my cell phone from Florida. Ma'am, let me call you right back from a landline."

I rushed up to Bayside to use their landline phone. Since I eat there so often, they know me well and simple requests are always accommodated.

"Mrs. Bradford, this is Jack Ludefance again. Can you hear me any better?"

"Yes! Thank you, young man."

"As I said, I'd like to reach your son."

"His home is in West Virginia, but he's at a convention in Los Angeles this week. Just a moment, I have it written down here somewhere."

She put the phone down with a clunk and there was nearly a minute of silence before I heard her voice again.

"Here we are. I have here that he's staying at the Americana Hotel. I suppose you can reach him there. But, I do remember he said he was going to be very busy."

"Thank you very much, Mrs. Bradford. By the way, where was your son's overseas duty?"

"Other than Bosnia, he was stationed in Turkey, Indonesia, and India. He liked Turkey and he's always wanted to go back to visit."

"Thank you again, Mrs. Bradford."

After booking my flights on Delta departing tomorrow afternoon and a room at the Americana Hotel, I called Katy to come by on her lunch break. I ordered a mug of Samuel Adams and contemplated my questions to Mr. Kevin Bradford.

Although Katy was happy to have a place to stay, she wasn't pleased that I was going to be out of town for a few days. She didn't like living on the boat by herself. I kept reassuring her she would be fine. No one dares to come near the boat with an alligator on it.

Before leaving, I had her write down things that needed to be done, such as collecting my mail and a few things to do in case of emergency. Even though she had lived aboard for a time last year, I gave her a refresher in how to use the fire extinguisher, the manual switch to kick the air conditioner back on, how to lock up, and a few small items of standard marine maintenance.

I packed a small roll-aboard with a few essentials, made sure the charger was in my laptop bag, and retrieved my credit cards from my safe. For most in-town business I use cash. But on a trip, it's impossible to do everything without credit cards. It can be done, but then I'd have to carry a lot of cash and that can be risky. Credit cards are handy, but downside is that they make me visible to whoever may be looking.

Katy wanted to drive me to the airport, but I declined her offer, preferring to keep my car at Pensacola Airport. Even though her car was parked at Bayside, she knew she wouldn't be using it much except to get to and from work at Hollers. Everything else she needed was within walking distance, Publix and McDonald's were right down the street, and the beach was less than a mile across the Santa Rosaria Bridge.

Chapter 10

My Tuesday, September 12th flight from Pensacola to Atlanta lasted a mere 50 minutes. My connection was tight, and I hurried from Concourse B to Concourse A, gate 21. The walk did feel good, though. A chance to stretch my legs before the four-hour flight to LA.

Landing at LAX, I turned my watch back two hours. Walking outside the terminal, my ears were assaulted with a cacophony of screeching brakes and blaring horns. What a difference from quiet Pensacola.

I didn't have to wait long for the shuttle to the Americana Hotel. But, traffic? That was another matter. It's my belief that there's a perpetual rush hour in LA. Traffic barely crawled on the 405 as we headed towards Beverly Hills. It was after 7 pm before the shuttle finally reached the hotel and I was able to check in.

Although the outside temperature was a very hot 95 degrees, inside the hotel, the air was chilled and refreshing. Large posters on tri-pods advertised three conventions currently going on. I scanned the luxurious lobby filled with conventioneers and it seemed as though everyone was trying to make their voices heard above everyone else.

Kevin Bradford was not listed under his own name, but listed as Bradford Inc., occupying Suites 1018 -1024. I asked reception which convention that was and was told Aluminum Foundry. In addition, I asked which suite I needed to call to reach Mr. Bradford directly. Using one of the numerous house phones, I dialed and a woman with a young earnest voice answered. When I asked to speak with Kevin Bradford, she said she would check his schedule.

After a minute, she was back and said in a hushed voice, "Sir, Mr. Bradford is in a meeting with his staff."

"Will he be there long?"

"I would think at least a half hour, sir, and then he is meeting a few people at the piano bar in the lobby."

Thanking her, I hung up, and took the elevator up to the 15th floor. After locating my room, I tossed my roll-aboard and laptop bag on one of the two double beds. A quick shower helped lift the jet-lag. I'd packed my one good suit; a conservative, deep brown pin-stripe, along with a beige shirt and tie. With my deep tan, clothes can be a tricky thing. I certainly didn't want to look like an out of touch salesman. Add to that my scar which makes for an unforgettable face, and dressing to impress has its challenges.

Checking myself in the full-length mirror, I practiced my business smile. A quick shine on the shoes, and it was like, 'get out of here and sell whatever the hell I'm selling.' Smile and look people straight in the eye. Shake hands firmly as if I mean it. And, above all, remember names.

The piano bar was filled with dozens of men in suits. They all had confident voices and big laughs, holding beers, glasses of wine, some with bourbon, and lots of bottled waters. Thankfully, I've been around long enough to be able to tell junior executives from CEOs. One of the juniors told me Mr. Bradford was the one with a mustache and a glass of bourbon in his hand sitting over by the big window.

Before walking over, I quickly sized him up. Kevin Bradford was in his fifties, impeccably dressed, black hair and mustache, and small, deep, dark eyes behind big glasses with black frames. He was talking with two other men. They stopped abruptly when I was six feet away and they all stared at me.

"Excuse me, Mr. Bradford? At your earliest convenient, I'd like to have a word with you."

"Are you one of the Bureau people?" One of the men asked.

"No. My name is Jack Ludefance. It's a personal matter."

"If it's about that opening, this isn't the time or the place, Mr. Ludefance," Bradford replied.

"No, I'm not looking for an opening. As a matter of fact, other people work for me. I'll wait in the hall, Mr. Bradford."

I knew that would shake his curiosity. They always want to know where you fit into the corporate world. With their shrewd managerial instincts, they can look at a man and guess his salary within a couple of thousand dollars. They are the high executives and CEOs of major companies, and their life span in a corporation is usually not that long.

As soon as they are retained they are looking for their next position. Rarely are they fired, normally resigning when their contracts are up. It's a survival reaction. They are planted high on the hill. They like to know what is coming at them and how fast.

I waited in the hallway for a little over five minutes before Bradford appeared.

He walked toward me and said, "Personal matter, ha?"

"I came out from Florida this afternoon just to see you."

"You could have phoned. I would've told you I have a very busy schedule here."

"Mr. Bradford, it's not easy to reach a busy executive like yourself. This won't take long. Do you remember a crew chief named Jonathan Holler?"

The mention of the name snapped him out of his present train of thought and it changed the look in his eyes.

"Yes, I remember him, but I was never friends with him."

"He lives in Florida and operates an import-export company."

"Does he really! He didn't seem the type of man."

"What do you mean?"

"I didn't have that impression of him. Quite simply, he was a nasty man and a loner. Didn't talk much. Thought he'd make a bodyguard of some executive. I just can't picture him a business man."

"People change."

"I guess so, I didn't really know him. Like I said, he was not a sociable man. That's all I can remember of him. What do you think I've got to do with him?"

"Nothing much. All I need is some information about him."

"Why is that so important to you?"

"Mr. Bradford, as you yourself said, Jonathan Holler isn't a nice man." I pulled out the photo of Lillian's cousin with her throat slashed and Holler standing over her body.

"Good Lord!" His face turned pale. "But what has that got to do with me?"

"I'm trying to help Holler's deceased wife, Mr. Bradford. She came to me and handed me an envelope with some very damning information and then she dropped dead. I think she was trying expose her husband. I'm trying to get down to the truth of this and have Jonathan Holler put away."

"Are you a lawyer, Mr. Ludefance?"

"No, but I feel morally obligated to help both these dead women."

"Like I said I wasn't close to him and I didn't know him very well, or for very long."

"Anything you can remember and tell me could help."

He shook his head and said, "It was a long time ago really I have no time for this right now. Can you come back at, say, eleven tonight?"

"I'm registered here."

"That's even better. I'll come to your room as near eleven as I can make it."

"Room 1591, Mr. Bradford."

Chapter 11

It was 11:15 before he knocked on my door. He'd obviously showered, changed, and drunk enough liquor to dull his brain. He sat down heavily in one of the comfortable chairs.

"I could order coffee, Mr. Bradford."

"No thank you. You didn't tell me what you do, Mr. Ludefance."

"Let's just say I'm retired."

"You're too young for that."

"I keep myself busy with little projects."

"Like this one."

"Yes."

"You have to do better than that, I need to know more about your little project."

"Mr. Bradford, lets level with one another. I'm not here to investigate you or to try and take anything you have. Holler came to Santa Rosaria as a very rich man. I want to know how he made his millions. I'd like to know how he managed to marry his beautiful wife and why she was trying to expose him. All this will cost you nothing but a little time and a little remembering."

I thought he had fallen asleep on me. He stirred and sighed.

"Overseas provides many ways to get rich. We did a lot of flying to Turkey, Indonesia, and India. Holler was there when I started to fly. Like I said, he kept to himself. He was unsociable, but he knew his job well. I made probably two-dozen flights with Holler, working for Outsource Intelligence."

"Did you hear Holler talking about making money?"

"I seem to vaguely remember a few things he said about making money. Holler was very tough, silent and cunning."

"How would it be done? I mean, make money?"

"The most obvious way would be smuggling gold. They could have bought the gold on the black market in Turkey, or India and sold it to the Chinese. The Chinese would pay them in rupees. Basically, buying and selling gold. And, even if they did business in Indian rupees, or Turkish Lira's they could convert it back into dollars."

"According to my source, Holler was making C130 parts from gold and smuggling it into to the US."

"Very possible, but I have no idea how that could have been done."

"It was quite ingenious, Mr. Bradford. They had access to a foundry and machine shop in Adana, Turkey where they converted the gold into parts for the C130. Then, they would change out the aluminum parts with gold parts and when they landed on US soil, they changed the gold parts back to the original."

"So. You knew how he made his money. Why travel all the way out here to ask me?"

"Corroborate what I'd been told. See if you were a part of it and if you knew anything more."

"Holler was a trader alright. He had that instinctive shrewdness and knack of manipulating people. He even sounded me out, but I must have given him the wrong answers."

It was easy to conclude that Mr. Bradford got his ideas about making aluminum from the Chinese. But there was nothing wrong in learning a trade and going into business, and a legitimate one at that.

"Was he close to the other guy?" I took out my notebook and searched his name. "DeAngelo Gonzales?"

"Let's say they were closer than he was with me. They were together quite a long time."

"Then DeAngelo Gonzales is the next man I need to talk to."

"I know where you can find him. I think I have an address for him, if he's still there."

Bradford hesitated. He knew he had something I wanted. He had to stop for a moment and figure out what advantage might be gained. By the look on his face, I imagined this whole line of conversation had taken him back to his younger years and his concerns about the ways of hiding and controlling the fear he felt every day.

He quickly snapped back to the present and into his shrewd businessman persona, cushioned by his money and his authority, and his success as a manufacturer of aluminum products. But, perhaps privately worried about impotence, audits and heart attacks.

"Couple of years back there was an article in Newsweek about me. They used my picture and one of my aluminum foundry. It talked about how I came up with efficient ways to make aluminum for the aircraft industry, which is lighter than steel and several times higher tensile strength than steel. I got letters from people. Gonzales wrote me from Dallas, Texas sounding like a dear old flying buddy, which he wasn't. Wrote it on impressive letterhead stationary 'Gonzales Enterprises.' It was pure bullshit, how well he was doing, and expressing the hope of getting together and talking for old times' sake. I answered with a very cool and brief note, and never heard from him again."

"Obviously he wasn't the type of man you would associate with."

"No. Didn't like either one of them, but it's for nothing I can put my fingers on, other than what I've told you. After all, we weren't working for the US military, but a private company which did contract jobs for military and it was a tough job. Gonzales was ex-military and everything he did was precise and accurate, almost too meticulous. As my copilot, he did everything according to the book, and often would get very sweaty and overly controlled when he made landings. To say the least, he made me nervous. I would say he would have more information on Holler than I would ever have."

"He would have more information on Holler?"

"If he's willing to talk. But, if he was in on something with Holler to make dirty money on the side, why would he talk to anybody about it?"

"I've leveled with you Mr. Bradford, but I might use something else with him."

"And use my name, Ludefance?"

"It occurred to me."

"I would advise against it. I have lawyers without enough to do. They get restless."

"I'll keep that in mind."

"My hat's off to you, Ludefance. I don't often do this much talking for so little reason. You have a nice touch. You are an eager listener like a psychiatrist. You smile in the right places. It eases people's suspicion. And, of course, you haven't leveled with me."

"How can you say such a thing, Mr. Bradford?"

He chuckled and pulled himself up. "End of discussion, Ludefance. Good night and good luck."

As he was opening the door, he turned and said, "I've had you checked out, of course, just for the hell of it. As you might have guessed, I'm a careful and intuitive man."

"Can I give you my address?"

He winked. "Bayside Marina. Slip F-28. *THE LUNA SEA*. Santa Rosaria, Florida."

"I'm impressed."

"Ludefance, if you are in my position and have a company such as mine, you can't remain successful unless you set up your own CIA."

Chapter 12

The next morning, while I waited on my tomato juice and coffee, I booked a flight to Dallas and a rental car through Orbitz. The flight was scheduled to depart LAX 12:45 pm. I didn't bother to book a hotel as I figured I would do that when I arrived in Dallas and had a better idea where Gonzales was located.

After a good breakfast, I went back up to my room, brushed my teeth and went to the bathroom again. Noticing my underwear could use a change, I pulled out the only other pair I'd packed.

"You piece of shit, you need a wife; a woman's touch in your life." But who would marry someone like me? Being a PI isn't exactly the best profession to be in to attract a wife. I've read about too many investigators and policemen who end up divorced and I certainly fall into that category.

As I mentioned earlier, back in New Orleans after my wife and I split, I moved out and bought a townhome to live in while I was refurbishing my floating home. In the eight months I lived there I never once bothered to have the house cleaned. Too busy working on the boat. When THE LUNA SEA was ready for full-time living, I got ready to sell the townhouse. My realtor sent a woman to look at it and she seemed quite interested in buying.

The women told me, "You need a wife, mister."

I replied, "Did you come here looking for a house or a husband?"

Needless to say, she left without making an offer.

I also was overdue for a haircut and it would probably do me good to change my eating habits. Living on the boat, I had put on a few unwanted pounds and my doctor had warned me that my sugar levels were too high.

Hating the thought of daily injections, I was left at the alarming point that it was either take care of myself or else. Okay, time to lose a few pounds. Maybe I might even take up smoking.

Checking out the hotel at 10:45 am, I boarded the shuttle that would take me back down the 405 to LAX. Even in the middle of the morning, traffic was bumper to bumper. And, of course, the security line was long and slow. I barely made my flight and was one of the last to board.

Settling into my aisle seat, 24C, I stopped a flight attendant as she passed by and asked for a Bloody Mary.

"I'm sorry, sir. You're sitting at an economy seat. When we serve snacks, you can buy whatever you want."

I couldn't help but stare as she smiled down at me. She was stunningly beautiful, with blonde hair reaching just to her chin. I had this feeling she liked me. She seemed to have everything a man could possibly want; a perfect face and perfect body. The thought of finding the mother of my children crossed my mind, then my objectionable mind said, 'wait a minute, this is a beautiful woman, surely she is hitched.' I had to remind myself that a girl like this is always taken.

I watched her perfect body as she walked away and stopped to talk to another flight attendant. She turned, smiled in my direction, and then headed back to my seat.

She bent down and whispered in my ear, "Sir, you can move up to seat 11C. That's an Economy Comfort seat and includes free drinks." She stepped out of the way.

Standing up, I started to retrieve my roll-aboard and laptop from the overhead compartment.

She intervened and said, "Just take your new seat and I'll bring you belongings. We're ready for pushback."

As soon as I was settled, she approached with my Bloody Mary, leaving the rest of the mixer. Yeah, I definitely think she was flirting with me. As I sipped my drink, thoughts jetted in and out. How old? Probably mid-30's. But, you know how women are. If she was in her thirties, she would say she was in her early thirties up to when she hit forty. Then she would say she was in her late thirties. Women and their ages are never too close.

After we were airborne, and the first service was completed, she came and kneeled by my seat, her back arched, and a big grin on her beautiful face.

"Dallas is going to be wickedly hot," she said. "I'm going to plunge into the hotel pool as fast as I can and come out every once in a while, just long enough to get a cold Corona beer. Some of the other girls just stay in their rooms, but I think they keep them too cold. I am an outdoor girl. Besides, the cold rooms give me a headache. I have a layover and go out at ten tomorrow. Somehow, Dallas is always a drag, you know?"

Her bright blue eyes watched me, and her mouth smiled. She waited for my move. These are the cryptic talks that attempt to feel you out. I've had hints like this before. If you understand the language at 28-thousand feet high above the earth, nobody leaves a mark on anybody. You meet indirectly, cling for a minute and glance off. She would be that flight attendant in Dallas and I would be that tanned one from Florida with the scar on his face. We would be just two free people rubbing our bodies together and exchanging body fluids, if you know what I mean. Harmless pleasure for harmless plastic people.

But, I've never been in that mindset. Prostitutes and one-night-stands have never been my life-style. Affairs, yes. Plenty. But only once did I have a one-night stand, which inevitably ended my marriage. And, I've never had, needed, or wanted a prostitute.

It is, however rude to refuse the appetizer without at least saying it looks delicious.

"I have some business to take care of in Dallas," was my reply.

The smile didn't change, but eyes became slightly absent.

After we'd landed, I saw her in the terminal walking along with another guy. She was laughing and chattering into the face of a tall, dark handsome young man.

Sitting down in one of the gate-houses, I plugged in my computer to charge up. I Googled Gonzales' address, brought up Orbitz and booked a room at a Motel 6 close by. Picked up my rental car, a Toyota that starts by pushing a button. I kept pushing it, not realizing the engine had already started. Note to self.

After turning on the AC full- blast, I headed out to find Gonzales.

Chapter 13

After checking into the motel, I walked down to room 175, located on the ground floor and the backside of the building. Although not my preference, there was a method to my madness. As soon as I entered, I turned the air conditioning up full blast to get the room cooled down. The flight attendant was spot on, Dallas was uncomfortably hot. After my shower, I called Gonzales.

"Good afternoon. My name is Jacques Ludefance. I'd like to speak to Mr. DeAngelo Gonzales."

"This is Gonzales."

"Mr. Gonzales, is there a possibility I could meet with you to talk about a personal matter?"

He hesitated, and then replied, "What's it about?"

"Mr. Gonzales, this won't take much of your time. I want to talk with you about Jonathan Holler. I just had a meeting with Kevin Bradford, and you are next on my list. I'd appreciate it if we could meet somewhere close by. Your choice. I'm staying at the Motel 6 not far from you."

"Bradford? You say you talked with him? Huh. I'm entertaining some folks here at my house. If you want to come by that would be okay."

"Mr. Gonzales, I don't want intrude on your party. This is a personal matter and I'd prefer not to involve your family."

His voice was wary when he replied, "You from the IRS?"

"No. I can assure you I'm not with the government. This has nothing to do with you, and everything to do with Holler."

"You've got me curious, now. Alright. Let's meet at DG's Bar and Grill. They have great barbecue ribs and it's just down the street from your motel. Let's say about nine?"

"I appreciate that. Nine at DG's."

I was at DG's a half-hour early just to scope out the place. I've always found that in a bar it's easy to start a conversation with a total stranger.

"Sure is hot."

"Sure is," the man sitting at the bar next to me replied. He had just finished his burger and was sipping his beer. "Decent hamburger, tasty fries, and a couple of cold beers always help."

I signaled the bartender. "I'll order whatever this gentleman just had." I turned to face him. "Jacques Ludefance, by the way."

"Matthew McNeals." He held out his hand. "Haven't seen you around. You visiting?"

"Just a day or two. Call me Jack for short."

"Jack. Okay. I own the upholstery shop next door. Cars and trucks."

"Who owns this place?"

"This place? Guy by the name of Gonzales. He's got a few hamburger joints, some real estate, and a trucking business."

McNeals was on his third beer and obviously open to talking.

"Gonzales. Yeah, He lives at large. But they say he has troubles with the IRS. He's married to his third wife, a gal about his oldest daughter's age, and lives in a six-bedroom house."

"You don't say."

"Yup. Quite a character." He chugged down the rest of his beer. "Time to get home to the wife and kids."

"Nice meeting you."

"Likewise."

I had just finished my Samuel Adams and was about to order another one when in walks Gonzales. Recognized him from the picture that Colonel Scott had sent me. In real life he was maybe all of six-foot tall, slim, but starting to have a paunch, and had a prominent mole on his right cheek.

"Over here, Mr. Gonzales."

With a not too subtle look of surprise on his face, he sat down next to me and signaled the bartender. "Jorge, make sure you take good care of my friend here. What did you say your name was?"

"Ludefance, Jacques Ludefance."

He smiled, "Sounds like a French name."

"Cajun French. Born in Louisiana."

"And, you're sure you're not IRS?"

"No."

"What are you?"

"As I mentioned on the phone, all I want is some information on Holler."

"What's it to you?"

I showed him the picture of Lillian's cousin and Holler standing over her.

"Jesus!" He made a quick sign of the cross. "What's this got to do with me?"

"Not a thing. I just want information about Holler."

"I knew a Jonathan Holler once."

"Is that the way you want it?"

"That's the way it has to be."

"What are you scared of Gonzales?"

"Scared? Could be right about that. I want nothing to do with Holler. He knows a lot of bad people."

"This has nothing to do with you. And there's no way he'll find out that we talked."

"Why should I trust you?"

"Holler came to Santa Rosaria a very rich man and he kills people. I want to put him out of business."

"And use me."

"I want to level with you. It's either you cooperate with me, or I turn you over to the IRS. Your choice."

"Hey man. You just said you weren't IRS!"

Pulling out the file Colonel Scott sent me, I quickly flipped through it. I knew nothing, but he didn't know that.

"What's that?"

"This? It came from a Colonel Scott who works at the Pentagon."

"Who's this Colonel Scott and what does the Pentagon have on me?"

"You and Holler both worked for Outsource Intelligence after the Bosnian war. I want to know how he made his money working on salary."

"I wouldn't know a thing about it, friend. Not a stinking thing."

"Because you made it the same way as Holler did and brought it back the same way when you were working with him in Turkey."

"I don't know what you're talking about."

"Because you can't be sure there isn't something official about this. Is that it?"

"Ludefance, I've had a lot of people asking a lot of questions for a long time and they all get told the same thing. It was a good try."

With him thinking he had control of the conversation, I let him talk. He bragged about his successes, and on how smart he thought he was. I kept nodding and listening. I've been told I'm a good listener. Even Bradford said so. It was midnight before he wound down. He smiled and got up to leave; obviously in a good mood because he thought he'd outfoxed me.

I let him walk out the door, then quietly followed him into a nearly empty parking lot. As he unlocked the door of his Toyota Land Cruiser and swung it open, I chopped him under his ear with the edge of my hand, caught him and tumbled him in and over into the passenger seat.

He was nothing more than a cocky, vain man, trying to live the good life. Trying and pretending that he lives in the world of the rich, and running as hard as he can, but always staying in the same place.

I'm sure he thought of himself as a dignified business man. I'd just violated that so-called dignity, which was only a disservice to him. Tonight, he would be used as a puppet by a stranger and would never be able to think of himself in the same way ever again.

Driving around to the back of the motel, I made sure I was not being observed. I carried him into the freezing cold of my motel room, stripped him down to his skivvies, bound his hands behind his back with plastic zip-ties, gagged his mouth and sat him against the wall of the shower stall.

The icy cold water brought him awake and I made sure he was wide awake. He was shivering and looked at me with a malevolence. I sat on a stool just outside the shower stall. I turned the water off.

"Gonzales, do you think any government agency would permit this kind of interrogation? You know, kidnapping is illegal, and I could get rid of you very easily and all would be safe. So, we need to make a deal, or I won't be able to let you go."

I could tell from the look in his eyes he was saying to himself he would never, never give in.

"I'm after Holler's dirty business and I want to put him away for good. I need your help. When you are ready to talk, just nod."

I turned the hot water on full blast. After a little burst, he made a muffled screaming sound into the gag in his mouth. His eyes bulged with rage, but he still refused to nod. I gave him another blast of hot water. When the steam cleared, he was nodding vigorously. I reached down and pulled the gag out.

"Now, Gonzalez, I trust you're going to keep your voice down. All you have to do is talk to me. Tell me all about how you and Holler worked it out. If something doesn't sound exactly right, I'll boil you a little bit more."

"No more hot water! I'll tell you what I can." He took a deep breath. "I worked with Holler in Turkey. We bought gold and brought it back to the US."

"I know all about it how you two bought gold on the black market in Turkey, converted it into structural C130 parts and painted them with liquid aluminum. You were both working together. I know all that. I know that you two trusted each other completely. What I want to know is, did you know him in Bosnia."

"No. I didn't partner with him in Bosnia. He was bad. God as my witness, I didn't want to get involved in that kind of business."

"What kind of business?"

"I heard he and some Serbian guy worked together. The Serbian had connections and they would get passports for young girls and bring them into the US. Once here, they'd hold the passports. They kept the girls in a secluded ranch house somewhere in Texas and made porno movies. As I said, I know nothing about his porno business first hand. I heard about it just like other people heard about it. That's why Holler served five years. I had to testify for the prosecution, but I said I didn't know anything. I haven't heard from him since."

This only served to corroborate the information I'd received from Colonel Scott. Holler was one nasty son-of-a-bitch. Was he doing the same thing with his current import-export business? Exporting parts, importing young girls? Had to be from what I'd seen at his estate.

"Gonzales, you could've told me the truth in the beginning and avoided all this nastiness."

After cutting the plastic zip-ties, I handed him towels to dry off. He was docile as a kitten. After he dressed, I drove him back to DG's to pick up my rental. A nasty night's work, but it had to be done.

Back at the motel, I realized I was starving, but, ignored the hunger pains. I fell into a dead sleep and only woke when housekeeping started banging on the door at eleven. On my way back to the airport, I stopped at a Denny's for a late breakfast, called Katy and left a message that I was on my way home.

Chapter 14

September 14th as I sat in the gate-house in Dallas waiting for my flight to board, a random thought blipped through my mind. Why did I feel paternal toward Katy? Here was this resilient and beautiful nineteen-year-old that guys flipped over; mature for her young years. Did she remind me of myself? Maybe she made me feel that if I had had a daughter, I'd want her to be like Katy?

While I was evaluating this phenomenon, it dawned on me, was I still in love with my wife? Although we were separated several years, and were now legally divorced, I think I secretly kept hoping she'd come back to me.

Remembering was hard. It brought back the pain. I remembered back to New Orleans and the day I saw her in a car with another man stopped at a traffic light. I was driving a Chevrolet pick-up at the time, and in that instant, I seriously thought of deliberately crashing into the car she was riding in.

People did stupid things sometimes. Especially men when they go berserk with jealousy. Thank God, the traffic light turned green and I was prevented from doing something very rash.

And, I remembered the day I got a message from her that she needed to talk with me. My mind went into over-drive hoping that she was ready to come back. Maybe she had forgiven me. I called her back.

"Sarah? You called and left a message?"

"Yes, Jack. We need to get together to talk."

"Let's talk right now."

"I can't. I'm busy at the moment. Maybe we could meet someplace."

I thought about a romantic dinner. "What about driving over to Brennan's for dinner tomorrow night? It's always been your favorite."

"I don't know. I don't think that's such a good idea."

"Why? It's not like it's the first time we're meeting. Let's have a civilized dinner and talk."

There was a pause and I sensed that she was distancing herself. My wishful thinking she'd come back to me was only a pipe dream. Still, I wanted to see her.

"Damn it, Sarah. I miss you! Why can't we have dinner together?"

"Jack, please!"

"Don't give me the please business. Just have dinner with me. I have things to talk about, too!"

In an instant I remembered her leaving me. Walking out on everything we had. I couldn't eat. I couldn't sleep. But, she came back quick enough and claimed the house. I was the one who was forced to move out. One day, I had a wife and a home. The next, I was virtually homeless.

"Jack? Jack? Are you still there?

I heard Sarah's voice.

"Jack, I said I'll have dinner with you. But, I'll meet you there. 7:30 at Brennan's."

The next night, as I was about to leave to meet Sarah, the phone rang. I took the call but shouldn't have. I was late getting to the restaurant. When I walked in, I saw Sarah sitting at our favorite table. Everything went wrong from the start. She stared at the spot on my shirt where I had spilled a drop of red wine, and somehow it hadn't completely washed out. It made me furious that she noticed it, and I couldn't entirely hide my anger. Sarah knew me inside out.

"Late as usual," she remarked, as I sat down across from her.

She had to start off with an insult. Not even a friendly word of affection.

"But, you look just the same. You've got a lovely tan."

"We just got back from a Panama cruise."

"We? Oh, I see. But, Panama was our honeymoon." I know I was pouting, but, I couldn't help it.

"Don't be childish!"

"I mean it."

"Then you are being childish."

"Of course. Yes, I'm childish! What's wrong with that?"

How had our conversation spun out of control so quickly? When a friendly waitress approached our table, it was like being rescued from a deep hole in the ice. After a few glasses of red wine, the mood improved slightly. I kept looking at this woman sitting across from me. This beautiful woman who was still legally my wife. Why, why had I slept with that secretary? Why was I reaping the consequences of it now? I did my best to impress her by calming down, but she knew exactly which buttons to push.

"Come back, Sarah. I'm begging you. Let's start again."

"No, Jack. You have to understand that it's finished. It's over. I've found someone else and I want a divorce. In fact, my lawyer will be sending you the papers to sign."

I felt like my insides were being torn out of me. When dinner arrived, we ate in silence. I couldn't taste a thing and finally pushed the plate aside. I ordered another glass of wine and wondered if I would be too drunk to drive.

"You seem to be doing well," she nodded, firmly.

"I'm having a hell of a time. Otherwise I'm fine."

"What was it you wanted to talk about, Jack?"

I'd forgotten that I was supposed to think of an excuse for our getting together for dinner. Now I had no idea what to say. The truth. Why not the truth?

"I just wanted to see you. I've missed you terribly."

She smiled. "I am glad we could see each other one more time."

My eyes filled of tears. "Did I tell you I've missed you terribly?"

She reached out her hand and put it on my hand but said nothing. In that instant I understood. It was over. The divorce wouldn't change anything, but our lives were irreversibly going in opposite directions. Her silence told me that. When we were about to leave, the final insult came when she insisted that she pay her own share. I let her. I just didn't have the strength to fight her anymore about anything.

"How are you getting home?" She asked.

"I drove my truck."

"Are you sure you're okay to drive?" Did she really care, or was it just the right thing to say?

"Of course. How are you getting home?"

"I'm walking," she replied.

"I'll walk with you."

She shook her head. "It's better to say good bye here. That really would be best."

She kissed me quickly on the cheek and I watched her walk away. When she disappeared around a corner, I followed her. What's the matter with me! Why am I tailing my wife? I stuck my head slowly around the edge of the building and had her in visual. There was a car waiting in front of an Abercrombie and Fitch shop. I could barely see the man in the drivers' seat. She got in the front seat and leaned over to kiss him. As the drove past me, I had a quick glimpse of the man behind the wheel.

Who was he? Did it really matter?

After walking back to my truck, I just sat, not ready to start the engine. I was hurting inside. Not only hurting, but lonely and sad. I felt a tear slide down my cheek. There was also the feeling of being abandoned. That same feeling I'd had when I was a boy. When my father and mother argued, and my mother would leave with my younger sister, Margeaux. I would insist on going with her, but she would say to me, "Sweetheart, you'd better stay with your father. You're a boy."

Being young, I had no idea what that meant, but it would always make my stomach hurt. This was the same feeling. I reached over to the glove compartment and pulled a Celine Dion CD and started playing it. I closed my eyes for a moment, trying to decide what to do, where to go. I didn't want to return to the townhouse. I wanted to escape. Escape the emotions swirling through my head and my body.

Chapter 15

Still stuck in the past, I remember putting the truck in gear and heading toward I-10. I knew I was most probably past the legal limit to drive, but the only thing I could think of was peaceful Santa Rosaria and the quiet little motel on the sound. I don't remember how fast I was going, but I made it to Milltown in record time, and without being pulled over.

It was just past 2 in the morning when I turned south onto 67 South, and knew I was almost there. I kept telling myself I could make it. I was within a couple of miles of Highway 88 when I heard the "blip, blip" and saw the strobing red and blue lights behind me. Pulling over, I turned off the engine, pulled out my wallet, and rolled down the window.

When the deputy leaned down to speak to me, my mouth fell open. Lawson? My old navy buddy was a deputy sheriff?

"Swamp? Is that you? What the hell are you doing in Florida?"

"Hey, Hiker. I could ask you the same thing, but I'm a little drunk and very tired."

Hadn't seen him in several years, but we had automatically reverted back to our navy monikers. Mine had been "Swamp," due to my alligator bite, and Lawson's had been "Hiker," because he was an avid mountain climber.

"Did you know that you changed lanes without signaling?"

"Did I really? Is that all?"

"Where're you headed?"

"That little motel on the sound."

"What? This time of night? Where'd you come from, Swamp?"

"New Orleans. Had dinner with my wife, err, soon to be ex-wife. She wants a divorce. Love her so much, Hiker."

"Good God. You drove all the way from New Orleans? You'd better get out of the truck."

From the glare of their flashlights, I could hardly see the other deputy, but I did what I was told. Lawson turned me around and made me face the truck while he searched for weapons. Luckily, I wasn't carrying. Lawson and the deputy had a brief conversation, none of which I could hear.

"Alright Swamp, you better go with Deputy Tucker."

"Deputy Tucker. Sure. But, where are you taking me?"

"My place, so you can sober up."

While I was trying to process this, Deputy Tucker led me to the patrol car and helped me into the back seat. Lawson got in my truck and headed out with Tucker following. At Lawson's home, Tucker opened the patrol car door and I literally staggered out. Lawson helped me inside and onto his sofa.

"Hiker, why're you doing this? Won't you be in trouble?"

"You let me handle that. Get some sleep. We'll talk in the morning."

When I woke up the next morning, it took me a moment to remember where I was and how I had gotten there. I sat up slowly; my head pounding. Finally, when I felt like I could stand, I went in search of a bathroom. In the hallway I met up with whom I assumed was Lawson's wife.

"Good morning! Ready for a cup of coffee?"
"Yes, thanks. You are...?"
"Linda."

She was dressed in a white uniform and noticed the quizzical look on my face.

"In case you're wondering, I'm a nurse at Baptist over in Pensacola."

She was that all-American girl, about 5-foot-7, green eyes, auburn hair, full lips, full breasts, small waist and healthy hips. Lawson picked a woman who would be both a good wife and a good mother.

"Pleasure to meet you, Linda. I'm Jack."

"I know. Lawson told me about you and your navy years together. Sorry to hear about you and your wife."

"Maybe it's for the best." She didn't know the real reason Sarah left me. Neither did Lawson and I intended to keep it that way.

"My husband tells me that you and he were best buddies in the navy."

"Yeah, we both flunked the Hornet test. Going through a tough situation definitely makes for best buddies."

"I'm sure it does. I'm about to make bacon and scrambled eggs for everyone. There's cereal, too. Oh, and I put some towels in the guest bathroom if you'd like to take a shower."

"Thanks. That would be great. And, thanks for taking me in."

"Please, I hope you feel at home here. We haven't had much time to make many friends since we moved down from Minnesota."

"Thanks again. I'll take a few minutes to clean up."

I went out and got the extra shaving kit I keep in my truck, took a shower and shaved. When I walked into the kitchen, Lawson was reading the Santa Rosaria paper and having his coffee. He introduced me to his son, Forest.

"Forest, say hello to Uncle Jack. He and I served in the navy together."

I extended my hand and Forest shook it with a firm grip.

"Hello there, big guy. How old are you?"

"Hi, Uncle Jack. I'm seven. And, when I grow up, I want to be a navy pilot just like you and Dad."

Looking at Hiker, I couldn't help but smile.

"I'm sure you'll make a very good pilot, Forest."

"Uncle Jack, what kind of plane is a Prowler?"

"The Prowler? It's an electronic warfare plane. Your Dad and I were both trained on the Prowler."

"Does it have bombs on it?"

"Yes, it has weapons. But, it's really designed to jam the enemy's radar system."

"You better tell him the Hornet story, Swamp."

"Ah, yes. The Hornet story. You see, Forest, your Dad and I both wanted to be F/18 fighter pilots, but neither one of us passed the tests. We were permitted to continue on with Prowler training, which both of us passed. We flew quite a bit together. I think you would make a great fighter pilot."

"Yeah, like where we failed, maybe he will succeed." There was a tinge of bitterness in Lawson's voice.

"Yes, I think he will be successful, Hiker. The reason we didn't make it was because we both failed the computer parts of the tests. We were just at the beginning of the computer generation. Unlike us, today's kids do everything digitally. They are the generation that needs to be trained. Besides, by the time Forest graduates from the naval academy, he'll be training on F-35 fighter jets, made just for his generation."

Lawson smiled and nodded. "So, Swamp. What are you doing these days, besides driving over 200 miles in the middle of the night?"

"Got my PI license. But, at the moment, I'm taking some time off and refurbishing a 57-foot Hatteras. Just about have her finished and plan to sell my townhouse and live aboard. How'd you end up here?"

"I was offered the job with the Santa Rosaria Sheriff's Department. They thought that I had the right credentials to be a deputy, and possibly sheriff in the future. We jumped at the chance to get out of the cold Minnesota winters. Haven't regretted the move. Santa Rosaria is as close to perfect as it gets."

"Sheriff, huh? That's impressive, Lawson."

"Hmm. Well, here's something to think about. Now that you're getting a divorce, and you obviously like Santa Rosaria, why not move here and work for the sheriff's department?"

"Move here?" And, the thought suddenly struck me. Why not move here? I had nothing left in New Orleans to stay for. Maybe a fresh start would be the best thing. In that instant, I made the decision.

"Yeah, that's not a bad idea. But, police work isn't for me. I'm sure you wouldn't mind another PI in the area."

"You'd be the only one. And, as long as we stay out of each other's way." He said the last part of it jokingly, but at the same time I understood the implications.

Later that day, before heading back to New Orleans, I drove around the area. Checked out some condos and the marina behind a restaurant called Bayside. It just might work.

Chapter 16

Remembering had taken its toll. I slept most of the flight back to Atlanta in a cramped coach seat. Luckily there were no issues in landing at Hartsfield. As I deplaned at Gate A15 and came out into the concourse, my luck held as I heard an announcement of a gate change for the Pensacola flight. It would be leaving from a gate A18.

That was a life saver. I wouldn't have a long walk to change to a different concourse. I made sure and checked with the gate agent and, yes, I was on that flight. Since my seat was confirmed, I decided not to sit at the gate, and took a short walk down to Starbuck's to get a cup of coffee. It gave me the opportunity to stretch my legs a bit after the two-hour flight from Dallas.

Thirty minutes later, I was sitting in my seat and in another fifty minutes we were landing in Pensacola.

After retrieved my RX7 from the parking deck, I crossed over Pensacola Bay Bridge and into Gulf Bend. That's where luck turned against me. I hit bumper to bumper traffic and it took me an hour and half to arrive back in Santa Rosaria and my floating home.

Stepping on board, I found the salon door unlocked. As I stepped into the room, I noticed the TV was on, but no Katy.

"Katy? Are you here?"

There was no answer. I quickly checked the rest of the boat. Every nook and cranny. Empty. Nothing was disturbed, but there was no Katy. As I walked back up into the salon, the 6 pm news caught my attention. The body of an unidentified young woman had been found floating in the sound near Santa Rosaria Bridge. They didn't show a picture, just a description. Approximately 18-22 years old,

5'2, dark hair, green eyes. Time stopped. A sharp pain hit my gut.

Oh, God. It can't be!

My hand shook as I dialed.

"Santa Rosaria Sheriff's Office."

I recognized the voice. "Charlene, Jack Ludefance. Is Deputy Lawson available? It's important."

She immediately connected me to Lawson. Sometimes it pays to live in a small town and know and be known by the entire sheriff's department.

"What's up, Ludicrous?"

"The body of the unidentified young woman who drowned. Any idea of who she might be?"

"No. No ID on the body."

"I need to take a look at her, Lawson."

"You think you know who she is?"

"God, I hope not. But, I have a bad feeling it might be Katy Ozener."

"Who's Katy Ozener?"

"A girl from Ohio. She's been boat-sitting for me the last couple of days."

"Ludicrous, why are people always dying around you? Alright. Where you now?"

"I'm on my boat."

"Okay. Walk up to Bayside and I'll pick you up in ten minutes."

He was there in five. He peeled the squad car out of the parking lot as we headed to the medical examiner's office in Ft. Williams.

As he drove, he was busy answering other calls. One, in particular, gave us both a momentary chuckle. Dispatch called wanting him to check on a lady who was complaining that two wild pigs had somehow gotten into her backyard and were digging up her garden.

"Charlene! Send Deputy Tucker over there. I'm close, but I've got Ludicrous with me. On our way to check out the body of the girl found in the sound. He thinks he might know who she is."

"That the lady who moved from California?"

"Yup. That's her."

"I thought she called a while back about armadillos."

"She claims she just took pictures of the wild pigs with her cell phone. Guess she can't tell the difference between an armadillo hole and pigs rooting in the dirt."

"Hah. The 'Green Acres' lady."

"Good one, Ludicrous."

At the medical examiner's office, a middle-aged woman at the front desk directed us to take the corridor on the right, and then down a flight of stairs to the basement. In Florida basements are a rarity. This one was all ugly linoleum flooring and walls painted a depressing battleship gray.

We approached a skinny young man with greasy hair. He was sitting with his back to us at a steel desk under an overly bright hanging lamp. As we got closer we noticed him staring at nude pictures on his cell phone. As he heard us approach, he turned his head and looked up with a questioning look. He didn't seem the least embarrassed that we'd caught him.

Lawson, despite the fact he was in uniform, pulled out his ID. "We're here to see latest Jane Doe."

The young man acknowledged Lawson but didn't say a word. He got up and led us to a heavy door, pushed it open, and turned on the inside lights. It was a large, unusually cold room with a high ceiling and suspended lighting.

On one wall was a huge computer screen mounted above a long gray steel desk with a keyboard and several matching gray steel chairs. The screen was dark at the moment, but I assumed was programmed with their filing system for the deceased.

On the opposite wall were three gray steel storage cases, each holding four stacked drawers. Which one of the drawers held Katy?

He took hold of the handle on the middle drawer located in the case on the right, lifted it and slid it back into a slot above the body compartment. He pulled the shelf which held the body outward. Time reverted to slow-motion. Each inch brought cold reality closer.

The shelf rolled easily on its bearings, as if it was riding on air. That had to be the THK railing system. How the mind jumps from one thing to another. I knew of THK, a Japanese manufacturing company, and almost all US machine builders use this system.

As the drawer pulled all the way out, it clicked to a stop and a bright built-in lighting system came on automatically.

All the light was focused on the white cotton sheet covering the body.

"You ready to do this, Jack?"

When Lawson called me Jack, I knew it was serious. Nodding, I held my breath.

I felt cold air against my face as the young man reached out, took the sheet and slowly turned it down. He turned it all the way down to her waist and moved just a little to the side.

I imagine they'd left one of her eyes open to help in identification. I froze. My body was ice cold; my mouth bone dry. I looked at that eye. Katy's green eye.

It was undeniably Katy.

I looked at the young man. He was standing there, staring at her breasts which he had so unnecessarily uncovered, his lower lip hanging away from his teeth, a drool of spit on his chin.

"Hey, you…"

He gave a little start.

"Uh, can you give us an ID?"

I nodded.

Lawson spoke up. "I'm truly sorry to hear that, Jack. Like I said, people expire around you. Let's go up to the office and write that report. You can help fill in the details."

The young man was about to pull the white sheet back up over Katy's face.

"Just give me a moment, Lawson."

"Of course, Jack."

He stepped back, grabbing the arm of the young man, pulling him back as well.

Pulling the course white sheet up to Katy's neck. I touched her face gently and whispered my sorrowful goodbye. I wanted to say how sorry I was but couldn't find the words.

When I was finished, I stepped out of the way.

The young man covered Katy's face. As he started pushing the drawer back in, the bright light clicked off. He pulled the door out of its slot, swung it down, and clicked it into place.

As we headed back out of the cold room filled with death, I said, "What's the matter? Can't get yourself a live one?"

He stopped and looked at me dumbfound. He quickly snapped out of it, turned the room lights out, and pulled the door shut.

As Lawson and I walked back upstairs, my insides tumbled. Sadness, then anger raged inside me. I turned and punched the wall, not even noticing the pain in my knuckles.

I asked Lawson, "How'd she die, Lawson? Did she really drown?"

"No. One chop to the back of her neck. Quick and painless. Then she was dumped in the sound. We haven't released that information to the press. Right now, the public only knows an unidentified young woman drowned."

"Can we keep it that way?"

After we finished the paperwork, we headed back to Santa Rosaria. Halfway there, I yelled at Lawson to pull over. I jumped out of the car and threw up. Then, threw up again.

Lawson handed me some tissues and a bottle of water as I got back in the squad car.

"You alright?"

"No, I'm not."

"You must have some idea about all this."

"Yeah. I think I know who had her murdered."

"Jack, its time you leveled with me. This is God damned serious. Who had her killed?"

My anger turned to sadness and my eyes filled with tears.

"What have I done?"

"Alright. What did you do? This is no time for playing games, Jack."

"I got her a job as a shipping and handling clerk at Holler Enterprises."

"So?"

"So, a couple of weeks ago she called me. She was scared."

"Why?"

"She'd taken pictures of some of the invoices to type up later on. Someone caught her and accused her of spying on the business."

"Why'd she take pictures, Jack?"

"How the hell do I know? Today's digital kids. Their world is a virtual one. I signed a contract not too long ago with a lady. She had me take pictures of the contract rather than giving me a copy."

"So, what're you saying?"

"Like I said. She was scared and wanted to quit. I persuaded her to keep on working and be careful. That if she quit, it would look even more suspicious. Holler's goons must have followed her and got to her."

"Holler's goons? What do you mean, goons? You're making a very serious accusation against a well-respected man."

"It's the only answer that makes sense."

"Somehow, that's not the whole story, is it?"

"No…"

"Jack, you gotta level with me. What's really going on?"

I hesitated. Was it time to let Lawson in?

"Ever since Lillian Holler dropped dead at Bayside, I've been investigating Jonathan Holler. My motive was to put Katy at Holler's company and find out about Holler's business. He's bad, Lawson. Really bad. Served five years at the state penitentiary for human trafficking, and there's more. I intend to put him where he belongs."

"You better give us what you know. We're in the middle of a murder investigation."

"Lawson, that's all I know right now. Do you have any evidence of who killed her?"

"None. Not one concrete thing we can go on. Your speculations only muddy the water. Like I said, you know Holler's a respected business man, and we can't just go barging in accusing him of something we have no proof of."

"He's guilty, Lawson. I know it."

"If you have proof, then bring it to us."

"When I have that proof, I swear I will."

"One last thing, Jack. Do you want us to make the call to Katy's parents, or do you?"

"I'll make the call."

Chapter 17

Katy. Dear Katy. I had told Lawson I'd make the call, but I didn't have any contact information, not even for Katy's mother. I certainly couldn't check with Holler Enterprises, so I decided to check with NAPA Auto Parts where she had worked last year.

The next morning, I drove down to NAPA. Even after briefly explaining the situation, the secretary gave me a menacing scowl and refused to look up Katy's job application forms.

"Sir, we're not allowed to give out our employees' information to anyone, even if they are no longer working for us."

"Miss, can I speak to the manager?"

"He'll tell you the same thing," she insisted in a snotty voice.

"Just get me the manager." I raised my voice.

A middle-aged man approached.

"What seems to be the problem here?"

"My name's Jack Ludefance. I'm trying to contact Katy Ozener's parents. She's the young lady whose body was found floating near Santa Rosaria Bridge two days ago. It would be helpful if I could get her contact information to let her family know."

"Good Lord! Of course, we'll help any way we can. But, shouldn't this be the job of the sheriff's office?"

"I'm taking responsibility for it."

I turned to the secretary and gave her a look. How she interpreted it was her business.

The man returned with files of past employees, checked and found Katy's application.

"Bayleen, check the computer files and find the complete information."

"Of course, sir." The secretary began typing and within a few minutes had found the information.

"Here it is." She turned the computer around for me to see the application forms. Katy had given her mother's name as reference and I copied down the telephone number. I thanked her and left.

Returning to Bayside, I hesitated in making the call. What would I say? I'm responsible for your daughter's death? I don't usually drink in the middle of the day, but I pulled out a Samuel Adams, took a few gulps, and then dialed.

"May I speak with Mrs. Selena Ozener?"

"This is Mrs. Ozener."

"Mrs. Ozener, my name is Jack Ludefance. I met you last year here in Santa Rosaria."

"Yes, I remember. You helped Katy with her disastrous boyfriend. What's happened?"

I could hear her heavy breathing, as if she were expecting the unexpected.

"Mrs. Ozener, I'm afraid I have some very bad news. Your daughter Katy was found drowned in Santa Rosaria Sound two days ago. I've identified her, but, you'll need to come down and claim her body. I'll be glad to pick you up at the airport, help you make arrangements, and whatever else you need."

It sounded so cold, but it was the only way I could get it out. I could hear her sobs as she gulped for air. I could feel her heart break, just as mine was. I barely managed to hold back my grief.

"Why you, Mr. Ludefance? I don't understand any of this."

"I'll explain everything when you arrive, Mrs. Ozener."

"Have the police informed her father?"

"You don't live together?"

"No! We've been divorced over twelve years."

"Do you want me to call Katy's father?"

She hesitated, "No. I'll let him know. Thank you, Mr. Ludefance. I'll call you later today when I know my flight information."

I gave her my cell number. Needing to keep my mind busy, I hunkered down and tried to design a plan what to do next. My assumption was that Katy had gone out for a quick errand. That's why she left the television on and the door unlocked. With Emma on watch duty, she knew it wouldn't be a problem. Somewhere close by, Holler's goons had gotten her.

If Holler had gotten to Katy that easily, he obviously knew about me. But, why Katy? Was it to scare me off? I no longer felt safe in my floating home. Even with Emma. A feeling of paranoia was setting in and I didn't like it one bit.

So, yeah. On the surface, Holler was a respected business man. But, I knew I was dealing with a gangster who had built his fortune on theft, smuggling, human trafficking, blackmail, bribery and murder. Who said, "Behind every great fortune lies a great crime?"

There's also a Japanese saying that business is a form of warfare. I was at war. In reality, this should be a job for the FBI, or, if not FBI, full police involvement. But since they didn't know any of what I knew, I still had the advantage. I could bend the rules, whereas law enforcement couldn't.

After my second Samuel Adams, I started in on more research. Googling different entries for Jonathan Holler, I found further information. Using the time frame of 1990s up until now, I got lucky and found a new article from the Wall Street Journal. After the Pentagon cancelled

Outsource Intelligence's license and stopped doing business with them, several OI employees served prison sentences.

Holler's name was among them, corroborating what I already knew. After Holler served his time, he formed his current company, Holler Enterprises, exporting used machinery to Asian countries. Sometimes you go in circles before you find a way out.

Lillian Holler had paid me twenty-grand, and I was determined to expose him and find out what had happened.

Later that afternoon, my cell phone rang with an 'Unknown Caller' displayed on caller ID.

"Jack Ludefance."

"Mr. Ludefance, this is Selena Ozener, Katy's mother. I'll be arriving tomorrow afternoon on Delta flight 1503." Her voice held the sadness of a bereaved mother trying to accept the unacceptable fact that her only child was gone.

"I'll be there, Mrs. Ozener."

The more I thought about it, the more I knew I couldn't bear the thought of Selena having to go to the morgue, stand in that cold, dank basement and look at her beautiful daughter's face. I called Lawson to let him know Katy's mother was on her way and asked him if there was any way to avoid Selena having to go and claim Katy's body. He assured me it would be taken care of.

The next afternoon, I picked up Selena. We were both silent on the way back from the airport, both locked in our own thoughts and memories. Once onboard, we couldn't escape the fact that plans had to be made.

"Do you intend to take Katy's body back to Ohio?"

"No. There's no one in Ohio. Her father's in California and sadly couldn't be bothered. How can that be? That a father doesn't care that his only child is dead?" Her tears came, and I decided to let her work through them.

"I'd appreciate it if you could help me with funeral arrangements. I've never had to do anything like this before and I just don't know where to start." With that came another round of tears.

While she composed herself, I called a funeral home close by, explained the situation, gave them Lawson's name, and made the arrangements for them to retrieve Katy's body. If it was the last thing I did, Katy was going to have a proper funeral and burial.

Later that afternoon, I took Selena back to the airport to pick up a rental car. She had also booked a room at the motel just down the street. She wanted and needed her space and I respected that.

Chapter 18

Together, Selena and I crafted a brief obituary to run in the local papers:

> *Katy Ozener, 19, of Santa Rosaria, passed away suddenly on September 13. She is survived by her mother, Selena Ozener, of Columbus, Ohio and her father, Baylor Ozener, of Los Angeles, California. A funeral service will be held at Santa Rosaria Funeral Chapel on September 19 at 2 pm with burial at Santa Rosaria Memorial Gardens immediately following. In lieu of flowers, the family requests you consider a donation in Katy's name to be made to your favorite charity.*

In the few days left before the funeral, I was able, in bits and pieces, and in fits and starts, to give Katy's mother an account of what happened that would satisfy her. I couldn't tell her all of it, though. She took it better than I expected, considering my first encounter with her last year. I assumed she must have acquired anti-anxiety medication, which was probably for the best.

The funeral was more than I could have hoped for. In the small chapel a single large bouquet of white roses and calla lilies sat atop Katy's closed casket. The poignant eulogy was given by Lawson's pastor. It was a heartfelt account of a beautiful young girl whose life had ended much too soon. Besides Selena, myself, Lawson and his wife, there were more people than I expected.

As we stood at the grave site and watched Katy's casket being lowered into the ground, for the first time I began having doubts as to whether I could take Holler down. I was but one. He had an army of goons, money and power behind him.

Was Lawson right?

Was it time to turn over what I had to the sheriff's office?

Lawson and his wife were kind to host a gathering at their home after the services for Katy. It was both somber and hushed. People Katy had worked with at the restaurant, at NAPA, and at Macy's all introduced themselves and extended their heartfelt condolences to Katy's mother. Selena graciously accepted the condolences from all of Katy's friends, and I realized just how popular and well-liked she had been.

The only people missing, at least that I could tell, were representatives from Holler Enterprises.

There were the whispered questions. How? Why?

We gave no answers. It was better that way.

The next day I called the hotel where Selena was staying. I had gathered together Katy's meager belongings that she had brought with her when she came to boat-sit and they were piled on the sofa in the salon. Not much for a girl of nineteen. Mostly clothes and makeup, and very few personal papers.

Looking at the items I wondered if this was all that was left of Katy Ozener.

"Hello, Selena? It's Jack. I have Katy's clothes and other things here. Do you want to come by and pick them up? What do you want me to do?"

"Thank you, Jack. But, I don't think I can bear to see her things. I don't know what to do."

"If you want me to give her clothes to charity, I can take care of that. But, don't you want her personal papers?"

"That would be good of you to make the donations. Her personal papers? I doubt there is anything of importance."

"No problem, Selena."

In reality, that is the least I can do. I'm the one who got your daughter killed.

"I'll say my goodbyes now, Jack. And, thank you again for everything you've done."

My goodbye seemed insufficient. I'd had doubts at the funeral, but her parting words gave me resolve to keep going.

"Please, Jack, please get whoever did this to my Katy."

Chapter 19

A few days after Katy's funeral, a Detective Harvey Langi from Santa Rosaria Sheriff's Office called me requesting to set up an interview about Katy's death. I didn't know him but had seen him around. I remembered him as a short guy with a Puerto Rican swagger. Actually, I didn't know either of the two Santa Rosaria detectives, as I dealt primarily with the deputies. Langi wanted me to come up to Milltown and give a statement. I didn't want to go anywhere.

"Detective Langi, could you meet me at my boat at the marina?" I wasn't sure if he would agree and was surprised with his answer.

"I can meet you tomorrow afternoon around three?"

"That would be fine."

"Deputy Lawson will be accompanying me."

"Okay...Deputy Lawson knows where I live."

Why would Lawson be in on the meeting? I decided to tidy up the place and make it presentable. Gathering Katy's belongings, I headed out to take care of some errands and replenish my beer supply.

The next afternoon, at 3:10 pm, Lawson and Detective Harvey Langi arrived. I opened the salon door and invited them in. Langi was short, actually shorter than I remembered. He couldn't have been more than five-foot-six. And stocky. His full body didn't fit his short legs. His hair was short, sideburns beginning to gray, deep, charcoal eyes, frown lines in his forehead and a dark Florida tan.

"Detective Langi, why not check out the rest of the boat, first." Lawson indicated the stairs down to the galley.

I immediately understood that Lawson was playing him.

"Feel free guys."

Lawson indicated to the detective to lead the way. Langi walked down the steps to the galley where Emma was hanging out. As soon as he was down, he hurried back upstairs.

"There's an alligator down there!"

Lawson cracked up.

I tried to keep from laughing at the look on Langi's face. "Detective, you have to be careful with Hiker. He is a joker."

"Are you supposed to keep an alligator?"

"There's no law against it, as long as her proper environment is provided."

"And, what's with the name Hiker?"

"It is his navy moniker. We served together."

"So, you too loonies know each other?"

"Ludicrous, let's get this started. I don't have much time."

"Ludicrous? Is that your navy moniker?"

"No. Hiker gave that name to me when I moved here. Because of my last name and the boat's name *THE LUNA SEA*. My navy moniker was Swamp."

I sat down, and Langi sat opposite me. Lawson, who had no problem with Emma, went down to the galley and I heard him open the refrigerator. I knew he was looking for beer.

"Hiker, bring one up for the detective."

"No! Guys, I am on duty."

Lawson came up and threw a can to Langi. He barely caught it but set it down on the coffee table.

"Actually, I'll have one." Lawson threw one to me. I opened mine and synchronized the opening of cans with Lawson.

Swissshhhh…

"Come on detective enjoy your beer, I won't tell the boss," Lawson was goading him.

Langi shook his head. Straight shooter. That was fine with me.

"Okay! Let's start from the beginning." He pulled out a yellow note pad and a digital recorder. Speaking clearly, he began.

"September 22. This interview is with Mr. Jacques Ludefance concerning the deceased, Katy Ozener. Mr. Ludefance, what was your relationship with the dead girl?"

"Detective, there was no relationship. There was nothing sexual between me and Katy. I was more like a father to her."

He made a face like, *yeah, right*.

"She came to me last year because of boyfriend issues. She was working at the East Bay Inn. All the guys were hitting on her. Her boyfriend was jealous and started beating her. She and her mother came to me for help. In short, I managed to get a restraining order against him. He was arrested shortly after for writing forged checks. He's currently serving time."

"How did she end up living on your boat?"

"She didn't *live* on my boat. Her roommate recently up and left, and she couldn't afford the rent by herself. I was on my way out to California on business and asked her to boat-sit for me for a few days. She was glad to do it until she could find another roommate."

"Then what happened?"

"She showed up and I gave her a short refresher on the boat. I flew out on September 12nd to Los Angeles, spent the night there, and then flew to Dallas on the 13rd and back to Pensacola on the 14$^{th.}$ Didn't get back to the boat until after 6 pm. What I found was an unlocked door and the television on, but no Katy. I thought perhaps she had walked up to the grocery store. Then I caught the local news and the story of an unidentified body of a young woman found near Santa Rosaria Bridge. I immediately called Lawson."

"Did she still work at that restaurant?"

"No." We were getting into the area I wasn't sure I was ready to tread on.

Lawson interjected. "Jack, tell him where she worked."

Langi looked at me as if to say, *please go on*.

"I helped her get a job at Holler Enterprises."

"Holler Enterprises? You know someone there? How did you help her and why?"

"Okay. To answer your questions, no, I didn't know anyone there. I helped her because she had a crappy job over at the mall and there was a want ad in the paper that Holler Enterprises was looking for a shipping and handling clerk. She had worked at NAPA for a little while in shipping-handling, but she didn't have the required experience. So, I helped her with her resume, gave my name as her ex-employer, and that gave her the qualifications for the job. She aced the interview and started work."

"How long did she work there?"

"A little over a month."

"You say you didn't have a sexual relationship, yet you went out of your way to help her. That doesn't make any sense Mr. Ludefance. You still haven't told me why you went to the trouble of helping her get a job at Holler Enterprises."

"I had a motive."

"This is getting interesting, Mr. Ludefance. Care to explain?"

"There's nothing interesting. I've been investigating Holler and his business activities."

"Can you be more specific? Why would you be investigating a well-respected member of the community?"

"You know what detective? I've about had it with this well-respected crap. Okay. Here's what happened. It started the night Lillian Holler died at Bayside. One minute she was sitting next to me asking for my help. The next minute she was dead. I wanted to know why she came to me for help. Since then, I've been investigating Jonathan Holler. When they put that opening on the website about the job, I thought it would be a good idea for Katy to work there and see if she could find out what really goes on. A couple of weeks ago she came to me, scared. She told me that she had taken pictures of some of the invoices to type up later. Someone saw her. They thought she was spying on the company. She wanted to quit, but I convinced her that if she quit they will really get suspicious of her."

"When somebody takes pictures of company invoices, I would be suspicious, too."

"I assure you. That was not her intention. Today's kids take pictures with their cell phones of everything."

"What else?"

"Before they caught her, she managed to text me some of the invoices. They were for C130 spare parts, and bazookas."

"C130 parts? Bazookas? That's military weapons!"

"Yes, indeed. I believe that on the surface Holler is exporting used machinery to Southeast Asia. But among them are spare parts for C130's and military grade weapons. I don't know the legality of it. That's about it. You know all of it."

"If Holler is exporting military equipment, that's for the FBI to investigate. Have you talked with them?"

"Not yet. I haven't put everything together. When I do, I will take it to them. Oh, there is one more thing. At Katy's funeral, there were people from the restaurant, NAPA, and Macy's; all the places she used to work. But, no one from Holler's company that I know of."

"Are you sure?"

"Yes. People introduced themselves, and none of them were Holler's people."

"But it still doesn't prove that someone associated with Holler killed Katy."

Langi turned off the recorder, stood up and handed me his card.

"We may contact you again. And remember, impeding or withholding information in any police investigation is a crime."

"I'll keep that in mind, detective."

Chapter 20

After Lawson and Langi left, I sat down to try and think about how I could find out more about Lillian Holler. I had a lot of evidence on Jonathan Holler, but still didn't know much about her. She was still a big question mark. I knew I couldn't force it, but I was frustrated as hell. I wanted to sit across from Holler and ask him questions. Not a wise idea to reveal myself to this low-life, but I had this feeling that his goons already knew who I was. Obviously, if they knew where Katy was staying, they also knew where I lived.

Paranoia returned. From now on, I decided that every morning and every time I returned to the boat, I would check her from bow to stern, then put on my snorkel mask and check the underside. Holler was a demolitions expert and there were too many places on a boat to hide a bomb. Even with Emma on duty, I no longer felt safe.

Langi had asked about Emma. He, of all people, should have known. Under Florida law, it's legal to keep an alligator as a pet, as long as it has the proper environment. She had free reign inside the boat. Out on the deck, I had made what I termed, 'Emma's alligator door.' From there she could slide into a 10x12 foot cage, much like a shark cage, but partially above water.

Realizing I hadn't fed Emma since before I left for California, I walked up to Publix and picked up a box of chicken pieces and a box of beef slices. Back on *THE LUNA SEA*, I sat on the stern and chucked pieces of meat to Emma, who caught them in mid-air and swallowed them whole. She was happy, and I was ready for a shower. As I stepped under the hot water, I heard my cell phone ring. Turning off the water, I grabbed a towel, and picked up the phone. Another 'Unknown Caller' appeared on the caller ID screen.

"Jack Ludefance."

"Jack? It's Margeaux."

My sister? Why would my sister be calling me? How did she get my number? Crazy questions blipped through my head. I knew she had married and was living in New Orleans, but we rarely spoke and have never been close by any means.

"Margeaux?"

"I'm calling from the police station. Dad was just brought in and I thought I should let you know."

"What! Why was he brought in?"

"Jack, he's been diagnosed with Alzheimer's. He drove himself into New Orleans to Quest Diagnostic for some blood tests and was waiting to be called. Apparently, they took other people back that had come in after him. He got upset and made a scene. The staff tried to explain that those people all had appointments and he didn't. He became so abusive, they called security, but before they even got there, Dad knocked down one of the technicians. That's when they called the police. They came and took him."

"Where is he now?"

"Still at the police station. They haven't booked him yet, just holding him. I told them I needed to call my brother."

"Which police station?"

"The one on Broad Avenue."

"Okay, I'm on my way. Give the police my name and tell them I'll be there in a couple of hours. You go home to your family."

There was a pause. "Margeaux, are you still there?"

"Yes, I'm here. It's just that Chappell and I are separated. I've been staying with Dad."

"What happened?"

"We'll talk when you get here."

"Alright. You go back to Dad's and I'll see as soon as I can."

Forgetting the shower, I quickly dressed, grabbed my backpack with the files containing all the Holler evidence, and threw a change of clothes in my roll-aboard. After locking up, I headed toward I-10 west; regretting now not going back to see my father since I'd move to Florida.

It was just after midnight when I arrived at the police station. I used to know a few guys from my PI days here in New Orleans and hoped one of them would be on duty. As I approached the duty officer at the front desk, he looked up at me.

"Can I help you?"

"My father, Manneville Ludefance, is being held. I'm his son, Jacques Ludefance. Can I speak with the officer who brought my Dad in?"

"He's not here at the moment."

"Can I speak with the captain?"

"Yeah, sure. He's here. Third door on the left."

I walked down the hall to the door marked, "CAPTAIN MURPHY," and knocked on the half-open door.

"Come in," a voice said.

"Captain Murphy? My name's Jacques Ludefance. I don't know if you remember me? I'm here for my father, Manneville."

"Jack Ludefance. I thought I recognized your father's name. Haven't seen you in a while. Your sister said you'd be coming. You know your father made quite a scene. Ended up knocking down one of the techs at Quest."

"Captain, my father's been diagnosed with Alzheimer's. I don't know what's to be done for him."

"Yes, I know. Your sister told me the same thing. We still need to hold him. Depends on if the tech wants to press charges against your father. Other than that, there is nothing more to be done right now. We'll be talking to the Quest people tomorrow."

I thought it was worth a try.

"I know this is a stretch, but can I take my father home just for the night? I'd like to go talk to the people at Quest myself. Maybe if I explained the situation to them."

He hesitated. "You still a PI, Jack?"

"Now and then. Moved to Santa Rosaria, Florida."

He rubbed his chin. "Really shouldn't, but, since his condition is the way it is. I'm trusting you on this one, Jack. You can take him home, but be back here first thing tomorrow morning, after you talk with Quest."

He got up and took me down to my father, who was being held in a small, unlocked room.

"Dad? I came as soon as I heard."

He looked at me as if I was supposed to be there.

"Let's go home Dad."

Thanking the captain, I took Dad's arm and we walked out of the police station into a hot, muggy New Orleans night.

"You still live at the same place, Dad?"

"Where else would I be living?"

"Okay, Dad. I wasn't sure where you and Deloris settled."

"She didn't have a place. She moved in with me."

For the past several years, my father and a widow by the name of Deloris have been together. I met her once, but didn't know her that well, other than she seemed to really care about Dad.

"I'm glad you two are getting along."

"Why wouldn't we?"

I was trying not to antagonize my father, but it didn't sound like I was succeeding. When we arrived shortly after 1 am, the lights were on and Margeaux and Deloris were in the kitchen chatting. Dad didn't acknowledge either one of them but grabbed a beer and headed out of the room.

"Margeaux? Deloris? Should he be drinking?"

"No, Jack. Not with the medication he's taking. We've tried, but you know how stubborn he is." Deloris looked weary-eyed and changed the subject. "Are you hungry? Can I fix you something? I made some soup and there's chicken, if you want."

"That'd be nice, Deloris. I shouldn't eat this late, but what the hell."

"Listen, Jack. It's been a long night and I'm ready for bed. I think Margeaux is, too. I'll fix up the sofa for you to sleep and we'll talk in the morning?"

I hugged my sister and Deloris, said goodnight, and then filled my stomach with homemade soup and bread, and felt a little better. The sofa wasn't the most comfortable bed, but I did manage to get some sleep.

In the morning, the Deloris and Margeaux were up early and made a delicious breakfast. Dad sat at the kitchen table acting as if nothing had happened. I guess I shouldn't have been surprised, but then I didn't know that much about Alzheimer's. As strange as the circumstances were, we managed to enjoy some family time. After the dishes were done, Dad announced he was going out to the garage. For what, I didn't ask. Deloris and I walked outside and Margeaux joined us.

"Deloris, level with me. What's happening with Dad?"

"About a month ago, I came home from grocery shopping and your Dad was still sitting in the same chair. He hadn't moved in over two hours and he was staring off into nowhere. When I asked him if he was okay, he just stared at me as if he didn't understand the question. It wasn't just that, though. Lately, he's been forgetting what day it is, where he puts things, even where he is. Dr. Wiley made the diagnosis and confirmed that your Dad has Alzheimer's decease. He's prescribed medication to slow it down, but there's no cure. He shouldn't have gone to Quest by himself. He shouldn't even be driving, Jack. But, how do I take the keys away? This is all new to me. I want to tell you something, Jack. I care about your father more than you know and I won't leave him. You can trust me on that."

"Deloris, thank you for all your help. You know you can call me anytime. I'll be here. Right now, I'm going to go down to Quest and talk to them and then check in with the police. Margeaux, do you want to come with me?"

"Sure, Jack."

On the drive over to Quest, I wanted to know what was happening with Margeaux.

"What's your story, sis?"

"Jack, it's a long story and I don't want to talk about. Really, I'm fine. I've got a job and I'm staying with Dad and Deloris until I can find my own apartment. My only concern right now is to get Dad squared away."

What could I do but leave it at that? When we arrived at the medical complex where Quest Diagnostic was located, Margeaux wanted to stay in the car. I didn't object. Probably better for me to talk to them myself. I checked the building directory and noticed that Dad's doctor was also in the same building. When I entered the Quest waiting room, the assistant indicated for me to sign in.

"I'm here to talk to your manager." I said.

She looked at me but didn't try to object. She went down the hall and came back with a middle-aged woman.

"I'm Mrs. Brown, the manager. How may I help you?"

"Mrs. Brown, my name is Jacques Ludefance. I would like to speak with you in private regarding my father, Manneville."

She nodded, led me back to her office, and closed the door.

"I'm terribly sorry, Mrs. Brown. I know my father made quite a scene here yesterday. You see, he's been diagnosed with Alzheimer's. The police said that unless Quest presses charges, they won't hold him. I'm prepared to pay for any damages he caused and any medical costs for the tech."

"Alzheimer's." She took a moment to compose herself.

"Well, that certainly explains his behavior. Under the circumstances, I'll call the head office, let them know what the situation is, and that we won't be pressing charges due to his condition. If you'll leave your name and number, we'll let you know the medical charges for our tech. Mr. Ludefance, my mother had Alzheimer's and we lost her several years ago. I know what you're facing. I just hope you do and that you have someone who can care for him."

"Thank you, Mrs. Brown. We do."

The next stop was the police station. I went in to see Captain Murphy and explained to him what Quest had decided. He looked surprised, but assured me that the officer who had brought Dad in would close out the report and that would be the end of it. But, he warned that Dad should not be driving, and, if he was brought in again, he couldn't guarantee the same outcome.

On the way back to Dad's, Margeaux and I really didn't talk much. What was there to say? Back at the house, I found Dad standing in the backyard, staring out at nothing. Not wanting to startle him, I walked around to approach him from the front.

"Dad? Can we go someplace to talk?"

Wherever his mind had been, he snapped out of it.

"I got some bourbon and beer, we can have it here. Don't feel like going anywhere." He seemed, at that moment, quite normal. Not any indication that he had dementia.

Walking back to the house, we decided on the enclosed, air-conditioned back porch. Dad brought out a glass of bourbon for himself and a beer for me.

"Dad? Should you be drinking?"

"That's what they tell me. At my age son, does it matter?"

"I just thought with the medication you're taking."

"Pfff...what do they know. So, Deloris says you're in Florida?"

"Yes, Dad. Don't you remember me moving? I'm less than a three-hour drive from here. A place called Santa Rosaria. I've got a boat I live on and some jobs now and then. Dad, do you ever see mom?"

"Haven't spoken to her in nearly three years. Ever since Deloris. She's close to Margeaux, though. Always has been, you know that. I suppose she's doing fine."

All in all, we had good father-son bonding, catching up with things. Sometimes he forgot I was there.

Where his mind went off to, I don't know. But he'd snap out of it and continue on like nothing had happened. To tell you truth, even with that, I enjoyed being with him. The regret of not coming back over the last year weighed heavy on my mind.

    After a delicious dinner, I said good bye to Dad, Deloris, and Margeaux, with promises to be back soon.

Chapter 21

A few days after returning from New Orleans, it was time for another massage with Sofia. I needed the name of someone close to Lillian, perhaps a girlfriend. As she had instructed me, I called to make an appointment specifically with her.

"Sofia, this Jack. I'd like to make an appointment for a massage."

"Long time no see…"

"I had a few things to do. Sofia, do you know anybody who was very close to Lillian? A girlfriend, perhaps?"

"You come this afternoon. 3 o'clock. I write down name for you."

"So, you know someone then?"

"Yes."

"Thank you, sweetheart."

"Me no sweetheart."

"Okay, Sofia. No sweetheart. See you in a while."

That seemed too easy. And something in her voice had changed; more distant, on edge.

When I arrived, Sofia had another girl attend the front desk while she took me back. After washing my back and front, she dried me off and gave me the towel to wrap around. I went into the massage room and laid on my back on the table.

"We can talk. Nobody here."

I was relieved that we wouldn't have to revert to writing notes or whispering. But I was also suspicious as to why there was no one else around. She started in on my feet, then my legs, moving up and down with her experienced hands, and I waited for her to begin talking. And, boy did she. Something was definitely off. Sofia nervously jabbered on. Halfway through my hour, I turned over onto my stomach and her jabbering continued.

Toward the end of my massage, she did something she hadn't done before. She stepped up on the massage table, grabbed on to the bars suspended from the ceiling to balance herself, and began walking up and down my back.

"You like?"

"Sofia, this is good, but you're killing me."

As I was leaving, she handed me a piece of paper with a name and telephone number on it. Another hundred-dollar tip was in order.

I was debating whether to call the girl whose name Sofia had given me. Ly Hie Minh Ha, but her American name was Lila. Instead, I decided to text her.

Miss Lila, my name is Jack. Sofia gave me your number. I would like to meet with you and talk about a very important matter. Call me.

As soon as I put the phone down, it rang.

"Hello, Lila."

"How do you know it's me?"

"Because I just texted you and it's the same number."

"So, what do you want to talk to me about?"

"I thought that Sofia told you about Lilian Holler."

"She did."

"I'd like to meet you somewhere and talk in private. I don't want to talk on the phone."

"Are you anywhere near Starbucks in Gulf Bend?"

"Not far."

"Meet me there at two tomorrow."

The next afternoon when I entered Starbucks, there was a beautiful Asian girl, maybe early 30's, sitting at a corner table. As I walked toward her, she stood up and smiled. She was about 5-foot-6 inches tall, a little on the thin side, but still a beautiful figure. Why is it that Asian girls always seem so much thinner than western girls? She had raven black hair, flawless skin, deep, dark charcoal eyes, a round nose, perfect white teeth set off by deep red lipstick, and long fingers with perfectly manicured nails. She was wearing a navy-blue blouse tied above her pierced belly button, and tight white pants which revealed the outline of her triangle. Two perfectly matched white diamonds adorned her ears.

"You must be Jack. I'm Lila."

"Lila. Thank you for your time. I'm going to order some coffee. What would you like?"

"Cay tea with honey would be fine."

I ordered an 'Americano with room' and cay tea with honey, waited for the order and came back to sit with her.

"How did you know Lillian Holler?"

She had that faraway look. "Our fathers were both in the Vietnamese army. Her father was a colonel. We were both educated in Hanoi and went to an American university. After she married Jonathan, I envied her. She had everything I wanted. Most of all, I wanted to live in America, so she helped me come here. Actually, Jonathan helped me get a visa and here I am. I manage one of his spas."

Her English was very good. She didn't have the problem most Asian people have with the R and L.

"How did Lillian meet Jonathan?"

"Lillian and I were in Malaysia. We both worked at a modeling agency in Kuala Lumpur. And, we also worked in this place where if a rich man needed a date or to take a lady to entertain other business clients, they would hire us. They would pay our time for dinners and whatever else they wanted. He was one of our clients. He took to Lillian the first time he saw her and didn't want anyone else."

"Why was she unhappy?"

"I didn't know that she was unhappy."

"The night she died, she came to the restaurant where I was, sat down beside me, and asked for my help."

"Maybe she wanted you to call 911."

"Yes, it's possible that's what she meant. But, I think she was afraid of something or someone."

I wasn't sure how much to tell her about the envelope or its contents, but took a chance.

"She handed me an envelope."

"I see. What was in the envelope?"

I looked her straight in the eyes. Curiosity?

"I'm afraid I can't tell you that. You know, client confidentiality is crucial."

"Are you a lawyer?"

"Private investigator."

Glancing up quickly, I saw a completely different expression in her eyes. There was absolute coldness along with total indifference. In that moment of time I saw a whore's look and a whore's secret; and that colossal unconcern which insulated her. It was gone the instant she knew I'd seen it.

My initial impression of her had been totally wrong. The impression that she was this sweet and stunningly beautiful Vietnamese girl who had survived a difficult time in her life, and was, perhaps, still vulnerable. But, now it was different. She was nothing but a paid whore. It took me a moment to analyze it. Totally against my character, but I realized, if only for a fleeting instant. I wanted to take this whore to bed, even though there would be no spice of pursuit, and it would generate no particular tension between us.

"If there's nothing more, I'd like to get back to work."

"I'd like to see you again. If that's okay."

Her whore look come back. "Mr. Ludefance. I run a business. I don't waste time on romantic excursions. But, I do entertain gentlemen for a fee, of course."

"Of course…"

She was a whore before coming to the US. An escort girl who went out with clients for money. I had this sudden thought that she was Holler's whore and she was deep in bed with the Holler organization. I put my thoughts aside.

Curious, I asked her, "So, if I'm to hire one of your girls what would it cost?"

"A thousand dollars a night. That includes nude modeling."

"What if I want to hire you?"

"That's perfectly alright. My price is two-thousand dollars a night."

I tried not to blink.

"You're hired."

"Not now. As I said, I need to get back to work. We can make it tomorrow night."

"Where do I pick you up?"

"Come by my spa."

She handed me her card. The address was familiar. It fronted Highway 88 not too far down from Starbuck's and was part of the group of smaller business next to Holler Enterprises.

"Where are we going?"

"I thought you might enjoy Club 12."

"Club 12. Pretty fancy place."

"Did you know that Mr. Holler owns that club?"

"No. But, I'm not surprised. So, you'll feel right at home."

"Tomorrow night at nine?"

She stood up. Her sweet, innocent persona returned, along with a big smile showing off her perfect white teeth and red lips. As she walked out, she did so with a sexy, captivating walk. The perfect model. I watched her get into her car and put her handbag in the passenger seat; all the while taking her time. When she slowly drove off, I noticed a black Lincoln sedan pull out and follow her. So, she was being tailed and she knew it. I couldn't see who was in the car through the tinted car windows, but I wouldn't be surprised that whoever it was got a good look at me.

Getting up, I ordered another Americano and a blueberry scone, and then sat for a while longer, thinking of more questions to ask Lila tomorrow night.

Chapter 22

It was late afternoon when I returned to the marina. Emma was in the water, hanging out in her Emma cage, ignoring me. After checking the boat over, including the underside, I decided a long walk was in order. Changing into shorts and flip flops, and taking only my driver's license and cell phone, I drove over Santa Rosaria Bridge. My habit is to park in the last public lot and walk down to the tower in Ft. Williams Beach, an hour and a half one way. My chronometer indicated a total of five and a half miles. During my walk, I contemplated the possible danger I might face, but I was determined to keep my 'date' with Lila.

It was dark by the time I drove back over the bridge. Seeing the lights of Santa Rosaria reminded me of a wonderland and why I was glad I'd moved here. After rechecking the boat inside and out, I grabbed my water-tight flashlight, and my mask, and did a quick check underneath. Nothing suspicious.

After a quick shower, I took a ribeye steak out of the fridge that I had cooked earlier, nuked it, made a quick tomato and sweet onion salad and grabbed a Samuel Adams. I made sure to write on my calendar, September 30, my date with Lila, meeting her at the spa and then Club 12.

I spent the next day keeping busy with small projects. When you own a boat, there is always something that needs doing. A little before eight, I took my shower, shaved, and splashed on some aftershave. I put on a pair of dark brown slacks, beige shirt and my suede sports jacket, slipping the envelope with Lila's two grand in the one of the inside pockets, my cell phone in another, along with enough cash to pay for drinks at the club.

My only identification would be my driver's license; no wallet, no credit cards. After taking all the keys off my key ring, I hid them, and left just the key to my car. I decided to conceal carry my 9-millimeter in my shoulder holster and wrapped a small army knife around my ankle. I also slipped a very tiny, thin burn phone programmed with Lawson's number into a hidden pocket in my slacks. My other handgun was locked in the glove compartment in my car.

Time to see what else I could learn from Lila.

At the spa, there were no cars left but Lila' car, and no black Lincoln sedan waiting nearby. Probably because she was taking me to Holler's club and his goons would be part of the backdrop. As we drove up the circular driveway to the club and stopped, a valet attendant opened the car doors, helping Lila out. I closed mine, waved off the attendant and parked the car myself away from the front of the club, hiding the key under the left front tire.

We entered Club 12 jammed with classy people. The lighting was the kind which makes women look mysterious, and men appear to overly attentive.

It surprised me to see people smoking, as most places have gone smoke-free. Thankfully, some huge suction gizmo yanked the cigarette smoke up and out. Soft acoustical music blurred and merged with all the shoulder to shoulder yakking. As Lila led the way to our table, she stopped and whispered something to a guy sitting with several others. It figured she probably knew all the personnel here.

"Nice club."

"Of course, it is." Despite her beauty, her voice and face took on a look of haughtiness.

She had parted her raven hair in the middle and pulled it all to one side, wrapping a strand of her hair around it, then let the rest cascade down to her waist. Her brows were darker than her hair and arched lightly in an expression of smugness. Her upper eyelashes were so thick, they partially hid her dark, charcoal eyes. Tonight, she wore a slightly orange shade of lipstick setting off her skin, the texture of which was as fine as a baby's. She was dressed in a body-hugging sheath dress in a shade of orange almost identical to her lipstick.

A waitress approached to take our drink order.

"White wine for me," she replied.

"I'll have a bourbon with ice."

Tonight, she had no whore look or whore manner that I could detect. But there was a definite inadequacy about our conversation. We both knew there was an envelope of money in one of my pockets and it would end up in her purse. What she didn't know was that I had no intention of sleeping with her. I was after information. Whatever I could get.

For her, though, she was at work. She obviously knew her part, and she believed everything was preordained. She looked as if she had the capacity for passion, but one would never know whether her responses would be genuine or faked.

My guess was she had begun judging and appraising me from the moment I'd picked her up at the spa, and she would continue, trying to react in all ways which would please me tonight. She was trained to give full value in return for her payment. I had no doubt this expensive whore had lost track of the number of bald heads, fat, smelly bodies, CEOs, and all those others that had come before me. She was in her prime with her career of handling executives, and no doubt couldn't recount how many times she had skillfully drained their body fluids.

"It's a bit crowded in here, Lila."

"Don't you want to stay here for a while, Jack?" she hesitated slightly.

Had I thrown her off? I decided to throw her another curve ball.

"You must have been doing this for a very long time."

She responded immediately with her prepared line.

"Dear, don't bother yourself on such silliness. It will only make us both unhappy. I worked all day. I like to go out and, if only for tonight, I'm your date."

"Just trying make a small talk, Lila."

"Dear, I'm only trying to make you feel as though I really am your date. Let me keep pretending."

"What you're saying is, you're trained to please."

"Don't you want me to please you, darling?"

She was skilled alright. As standard practice, it would inflate a man's ego. She was trained to make every man believe he was special. Every customer was unique.

"Perhaps, but I want to talk about it."

She pouted in a rather pretty way and said, "What you're really asking is, 'How did a nice girl like me get into something like this?' Isn't that a very trite question Jack? Besides, I've already told you. Aren't you and I better at having a more seductive conversation than that?"

"I do know the old joke, and what the lovely girl answers." I continued to play with her.

"Of course you do. But, darling, it really is very boring to talk about morality, don't you think? Just accept me as this innocent girl, all clean and fresh and sweet, just for you."

She looked down at her hands, her long fingers, and checked out her well-manicured nails. Under all that tasty trimming, the coarseness was beginning to show. And yes, I already knew how she'd gotten into the business.

"Perhaps, if you can wait here for an hour, someone will come along who might suit you taste better."

"I wasn't trying to offend you, Lila."

She smiled. "My dear Jack. It would stagger the imagination to think of any way you could possibly offend me. I was merely thinking of making things more agreeable for you."

"You are agreeable, Lila."

"Don't worry, Jack. I *will* suit you very, very well. You're a rough but an exciting man. We've come this far, I don't want to give you up now. So, can we forget all this boring talk? I just want to be your dream date. I'm still a very proper girl for what I do, but I can be reckless, too."

She reached into her purse, looking for something. She pulled out her lipstick, opened the case and freshened her lips. After closing the lid, she ever so carelessly dropped the lipstick case.

"See? You're actually making me a little nervous, darling."

Being the perfect gentleman that I am, I sat on my heels beside our small booth and peered under the table for the lipstick. I saw the glint of it back against the wall. Ducking my head under the table, I reached for it, picked it up, sat back in the booth, and handed it to her.

"Thank you, dear," she said with her splendid imitation of fondness.

We finished our drinks and ordered another round. I felt incomparably shrewd. I would take her to the new

Marriott Hotel on the island. All I wanted from her was a little conversation about Holler.

Lila excused herself, went to the lady's room, and seemed to be gone for a long time.

Reality is a curious thing. It is the special norm for each of us. Based upon the evidences of our own senses, we have each established our own sense of reality.

Now, mine began shifting, ever so slightly.

While I waited for Lila to return from the restroom, I remembered a summer night long ago in San Diego, and another reality. On furlough from the navy, I was staying with my then current girlfriend in another friend's condo. In the middle of the night, I happened to be sitting in the bathroom.

Suddenly, the condo began to sway, swinging one way, and then back the other way. I heard my girlfriend scream, then saw her jump out of bed and head for the stairs. I shouted for her to come back. The swinging started to lessen, and finally stopped.

An earthquake is so powerful that you have no time to adjust your senses, your reality totally misleads you, and you don't know what to do.

That night gave me a primitive terror like I'd never felt before. And, for some reason, that same primitive terror was taking hold of me right here and now. I could no longer depend upon my evidence of reality. Lila was leaning toward me, speaking as if she was a million miles away.

"Darling," she said. "Darling, darling, Jack..." she repeated.

It had an echo chamber quality. I felt dizzy and the room began turning. I grabbed the edge of the table thinking I needed to hold on something. It felt like I was being thrown out of a swing. Then, everything went black.

Chapter 23

When I slowly opened my eyes, I found myself sitting in a chair, in some kind of a very large industrial warehouse space. I tried to adjust my eyes to the light that was shining directly into my face. I could see the halo of two very large men standing on each side of me, and another heavy-set man standing directly in front of me, a few feet away. What surprised me was that my wrists were not tied.

"Jack Ludefance. We finally meet."

Instinctively, I knew who it was.

"Mr. Holler."

"What do you want with me?"

"Your wife came to me, asking for my help."

"Yeah. So?"

"I've been investigating you. Found out a lot of interesting things. How you and your buddy, DeAngelo Gonzales, converted gold and smuggled it back into the US."

"You talked to Gonzales?"

"And Kevin Bradford."

"You could've come to me. I'd have told you everything. Including my serving time. You know about that, too, I suppose. It's all public knowledge."

"What about Bosnia and human trafficking, your porno business?"

"Too bad. You're a smart man. You could've worked for me."

"I don't work for mercenary killers. Isn't what that they call you and your army buddies?"

"Better be careful, Ludefance. You'll end up like that girl you put in my business to spy on me. You know what I mean?"

"You won't get away with her murder and you can't get away with mine. Sheriff's department knows I was with your whore. Sooner or later they'll come after you and your enterprise."

"My enterprise? I only own, ah, not even half of the entire Florida operation. You have no clue who you're dealing with."

"So, you're just a puppet?"

He looked at the other two men.

"Make sure you rough him up real good. But, don't kill him. Not yet."

Holler turned and walked away. I tried to stand up and took one to my face from one of his goons. My head turned heavy; my face was burning like somebody was holding a welding torch to it. I don't remember much after that, except curling up into a ball of pain.

Next thing I remember was waking up on swampy ground and it was beginning to spit rain. I had no clue where I was, but I was hurting like hell. It was hard to take a breath; probably a broken rib or two? I felt around. My gun and knife were gone, along with my shoes and jacket with my cell phone, driver's license, and the two-thousand in cash.

But, they hadn't found my burn phone in the hidden pocket of my pants. It was small and thin enough that they had missed it. I struggled to sit up, pain coursing through my body, but couldn't manage it, and I laid back down.

All around me I could hear the sounds of frogs. I could only hope there were no alligators. I struggled to pull the burn phone out. My right eye was swollen shut, and my left wasn't much better, but I could make out the illuminated numbers. I had Lawson on speed dial and punched the number.

"Lawson."

"Lawson, can you come and get me…"

"Who is this? Speak up! I can't hear you!"

I tried to raise my voice. "Lawson, it's Swamp."

"Swamp? Is that you?'

"Lawson, tobacco-tasty."

Old habits never die. Tobacco-tasty had been our distress call.

"Where are you?"

"Don't know. Can't move. Somewhere swampy."

"Alright, Swamp. I'll find you. Don't hang up. Just keep talking."

"Okay, I'll keep talking. But, don't bring anybody with you but Tucker."

"Can't promise that, Jack, but I'll try."

All around me, I heard movements of night creatures. *God, don't let me be eaten by the alligators.* The irony was not lost. I kept talking nonsense and waited for what seemed like an eternity, struggling not to pass out. I could only hope there was enough battery power until someone found me. Finally, I heard a woman's voice.

"Jack, it's Charlene from the sheriff's office. We've located where you are and Lawson and Tucker are on their way."

"Where am I?" I barked into the phone with a coarse voice.

"You're in that thin strip of the National Park close to Gulf Bend. Just off 88."

"Are there alligators here? I hear noises."

"I don't know, Jack. Lawson will be there very soon. You sit tight."

"I think I see lights coming towards me."

"That must Lawson. You keep the phone open."

Lawson and Tucker finally reached me.

"What the hell happened to you, Swamp?"

"Lawson, just get me out of here."

"Okay, buddy. Just keep still. Tucker's going to call for an ambulance."

"Lawson. No ambulance. No hospital. Just take me to my boat."

Lawson paused a moment. "Tucker! No ambulance!"

Both men helped me stand. Hurt like hell. I struggled to put the burn phone back into my pocket. With Lawson on one side and Tucker on the other, they led me to Lawson's car, and gently eased me into the back seat.

"Appreciate if neither of you said anything to anyone."

"Alright, Swamp. Don't worry. You don't have to talk."

Chapter 24

The next thing I knew, Lawson was opening the car door and he and Tucker were helping me into Lawson's house. Linda directed them to take me into the guest bedroom and sat me on the bed, where she did a quick evaluation of my bruised and aching body. A few moments later, she returned with medical tape, several pills and a glass of water.

"Jack, I'm going to tape your ribs. I don't think they're broken, just badly bruised. This might hurt. You really should get an x-ray."

"I'll be fine."

She shook her head, handed me two pills and the glass of water. I was barely able to swallow them, but they took immediate effect. I looked over at the clock on the nightstand. 4 am. My eyes closed and that was the last thing I remember.

With the pain killers Linda had given me, I slept over ten hours. I woke to find it was mid-afternoon on Sunday, and every inch of my body was stiff and aching. I heard a knock on the door, and Linda peeked her head into the room.

"How do you feel, Jack?"

"Very sore. Very hungry."

"When you're ready, come on into the kitchen and I'll fix you something."

Lawson was sitting at the kitchen table with a scowl on his face, obviously not happy with my latest antics.

"We need to talk, Jack."

"I know, I know. But, not now. Need to get my car back."

"Where is it?"

"Club 12 parking lot on the outer edge."

"What happened to the key?"

"I hid it under the left front tire."

"But, Club 12? Good, God, man. What were you doing there?"

"It's a long story. Just, please, Lawson. Can you go get my car?"

Lawson called Tucker and they headed over to Club 12. While they were gone, Linda fixed a big bowl of hot soup. Nothing better when you're hurting. After eating, I went back to bed, my ploy to try and avoid talking to Lawson. When he returned, I heard Lawson open the door to the guest room. I closed my eyes, pretending to be asleep. He called my name, but when I gave no response, he set my car key on the nightstand and left the room.

On Monday morning, I woke to find the house empty. I assumed both Lawson and Linda were at work and Forest was at school. After fixing myself a bagel and some coffee, I left a note for Lawson, and headed home.

Driving was excruciating. Bruised ribs and an RX7 don't make for a good combination. Neither does driving without shoes. And with no license, I had to be doubly cautious.

I managed to make it back to the marina and on to my floating home without incident. Retrieving my hidden keys, I crashed on the sofa in the salon. No way could I do a security check. I laid there and thought about all of it. Lila must have poured some kind of drug into my drink when I bent down to retrieve her lipstick. I'd let my guard down and let it happen. Lila obviously was not just a whore, but, as I'd thought, part of Holler's enterprise and did some of his dirty work.

For some reason, Holler's goons hadn't taken my car. Why? They could've found the key. They'd taken everything else. Why not my car, too?

I remembered Holler's words, *"Make sure you rough him up real good. But, don't kill him. Not yet."* They'd beaten me up badly and left me in a swampy area, but close to the highway. Still, I had no idea where I was. I had no shoes. If I'd not had the burn phone, how would I have ever walked, if I could have walked, out of there on my own? Had they found it and left it in my pocket so I could call for help?

My jacket and shoes were gone. My gun and knife were gone. The two grand was gone. My cell phone was gone, but I hadn't left much information on it. My driver's license would be replaced. I could live with those losses.

One thing Holler's goons didn't get from me was the envelope Lillian Holler had given me. It was locked securely in my safe on the boat. That was the last thing I wanted Holler to get his hands on. My only option was to get a safety deposit box at Wells Fargo to keep it, along with the photos Katy had taken, and the photos I had taken of Holler's dirty business, safe until I was ready to turn everything over to Lawson and the FBI.

Even with the beating I had taken, something that Holler said clicked in and coincided with something Bradford had said. Holler had made the remark, *"My enterprise? I only own, ah, not even half of the entire Florida operation. You have no clue who you're dealing with."* Bradford had said to me, *"I didn't have that impression of him. Quite simply, he was a nasty man and a loner. Didn't talk much. Thought he'd make a bodyguard of some executive. I just can't picture him a business man."*

This opened a completely new direction. Holler was nothing more than a puppet. But for whom? And the most crucial question, was I in over my head?

The undeniable silent answer came back, "Ya think?"

I stayed hunkered down. Reported my cell phone stolen and ordered a new one, which arrived several days later. First thing I did was call Lawson and give him my new number. Linda stopped by, re-taped my ribs, and gave me a few extra pain pills. They helped get me past the worst of the pain. I managed to get to the county annex and replace my license. Lawson kept badgering me for information. I kept on evading his questions. On the one hand, even though we often had our differences, it made me realize how close he and I were. Simply put, he cared. On the other hand, I still wasn't ready to turn over what I had.

It was now a personal thing for me to continue this investigation. Not just because Lillian Holler had hired me, but because I knew definitively they'd killed Katy, and now they were targeting me.

After a couple of weeks, though, cabin fever, or, in my case, boat fever set in. I still couldn't do too much of anything. My ribs still hurt and my face looked like I'd been in a fight and got the bad end of it, but for some reason I wanted to go see Dad.

What is it about being ill and wanting to go home? This time, there was no Katy to boat sit, so I left Emma out on the deck where she had access to her Emma cage. I closed up as best I could and decided to do a 'hold mail' as I wasn't sure how long I'd be gone.

I took my time on the drive over to New Orleans, stopping and stretching whenever I started feeling stiff. In Mobile, I took time for lunch at a local shrimp restaurant.

It was so good that I ordered three extra portions and a six-pack of Samuel Adams.

I wondered how Dad would be. It had been over a month since I'd seen him. There were things I wanted to talk to him about while we still could. How quickly did Alzheimer's progress even with medication?

Chapter 25

It was late afternoon when I arrived at Dad's house. Deloris answered my knock on the door.

"Jack! What a nice surprise to see you here!"

She stepped aside for me to go in, staring at my bruised face. I handed the shrimp dinners and Samuel Adams to her.

"Deloris, you're looking good. I thought I'd pay you and Dad a visit."

"Of course, Jack. You know you're welcome anytime. Your Dad's out back in his garden. I'll go out and let him know you're here."

"Actually, can you wait on that? I'd like to talk with you for a bit, if you don't mind."

"Let's sit in the living room, then. I made a fresh pot of coffee. Would you like some?"

"Yes, thanks."

She went into the kitchen and brought back a tray with the coffee pot, two coffee cups, and some freshly baked chocolate chip cookies. Setting the tray on the coffee table, she poured us each a cup, then came over to the sofa and sat next to me.

"Deloris, how's Dad doing? Is his condition getting any better, or worse, or what?"

"Before we get into that...Jack? What happened to your face? Are you okay?"

"I had an unfortunate encounter and I'd like to leave it at that for the time being. So, about Dad?"

She looked down at her hands holding her coffee cup.

"He's been having some bad days, Jack. Sometimes he sits in one place for a long time, not moving, not saying anything. But, that's what his doctor said would happen. Alzheimer's patients don't know where they are sometimes. Other times he is just fine and functioning with no difficulties. But, overall, I don't think he's changed that much since you were here last. Margeaux has found her own apartment and moved out, but she visits whenever she can. She went with your Dad and me to his last appointment with Dr. Wiley. He spoke to us and gave us a list of things to be prepared for next."

"Such as what?"

She took a deep breath and tried to hold back her tears.

"For example, if we're out in public and your Dad has an episode and behaves badly, I need to try and explain to people that he has Alzheimer's. I also need to be prepared for him to act out and yell at me. Things of that nature."

"Why would Dad yell at you?"

"He's scared, Jack. Alzheimer's patients know something is happening to them. They get scared and lash out to those around them, particularly those closest to them."

"Deloris, does Dad know that he has Alzheimer's?"

"Dr. Wiley asked if we wanted him to talk to your father about what's happening, and we agreed it would be for the best. I don't know if he actually realizes the implications of the disease, but, yes, he knows."

"Deloris, I'm so sorry you have to go through this. You don't know how much I appreciate your being with Dad. Is there anything I can do?"

"It's okay, Jack. On the practical side, I have no place of my own and with my pension, there's no way I could make it by myself. On the emotional side, I love your Dad. I couldn't imagine not being with him. We'll be fine.

Thanks for asking, but nothing for you to do at this point, but visit him whenever you have the time."

We both looked up to see Dad standing in the doorway, a look of confusion on his face.

"Hi, Dad. I came to visit you and Deloris."

I got up and walked towards him. He extended his hand and we shook hands.

"How's Sarah doing?" He asked.

"Dad, we're divorced. I haven't seen her for quite a while."

He's already forgotten that Sarah and I are divorced?

Deloris stood up and came over to Dad and me and led him back to the sofa.

"Why don't you two sit and talk for a while, I'll bring you some more coffee and then I have some things to do in the kitchen."

I settled on the sofa next to Dad and waited for him to continue. He didn't look at me, but rather stared straight ahead. The strange think was that his eyes were not focused on anything in particular.

"I was cutting the flowers in the garden. They're getting too bushy."

"Dad, you've always been a good gardener."

"Where do you live now?"

"I live in a boat, Dad. I'd love to show it to you sometime. When I bought it wasn't in very good condition. I worked over eight months to restore it and now it's my home. I rent dock space in a marina over in Santa Rosaria, in Florida."

"So, what do you do? You still work at the air products company?"

"No, Dad. I left that company a couple of years ago. They paid me well for some investigating I did for them, and with that money I bought the boat."

"You're unemployed?"

"No, dad. I'm a private investigator. I have job, but it's not like a nine-to-five job. If a job comes along, I investigate for a fee. That's is how it works."

"You have a job now?'

"Yes. I'm working on a job that's very complicated."

"How're you feeling?"

"I'm fine Dad. Why don't you show me what you have been doing in the garden?"

Once outside, Dad showed me what he had been working on. He'd taken one of his old apple trees and grafted a portion of a plum tree to it. He'd always been a genius with plants, but I wasn't sure if this was actually going to work. Or was it because of the Alzheimer's? It really didn't matter, though.

"Dad, do you still talk to your plants?"

"All the time. Trees and plants are living and breathing just as humans are, son."

I took a chance with my next comment. Did he know any of what was happening to him?

"Dad, you seem to be going very well right now. I don't see any indication of dementia."

"Dementia? Oh. You mean, Alzheimer's? Dr. Wiley explained it all to me. Sometimes, it's scary. I forget where I am. Or, I pretend I know what I'm doing, but really have no clue what I'm doing. Sometimes I can remember something that happened a long time ago, but can't remember anything that happened say, yesterday."

"I know that, Dad. I'm glad Dr. Wiley talked to you about it. And he also talked to Deloris and Margeaux about what to expect going forward. I'm going to stay close, Dad. Deloris will always be with you. And Margeaux will visit often, too. Thank God, it's not mom who stays with you. If need be, and when the time comes, we'll hire a nurse. I want to you to know that we'll be here for you. We'll take one thing at a time."

Dad seemed suddenly lost and confused. Had I tried to tell him too much? I still had one more thing to ask him.

"Dad, I need to talk to you about something that's been bothering me for a long time. Remember when you and mom used to have fights and she would leave? I wanted her to stay and when I knew she wasn't, I wanted to go with her. But, she would say, *'stay with your father, you're a boy.'* It's a feeling of abandonment that I've never been able to shake. I had the same feeling when Sarah left me."

I waited for an answer, didn't really expect one, and was surprised with the depth of his response.

"What can I say, son? I loved your mother. But, sometimes two people love one another, while at the same time they bring out the very worst in each other. As your father, I always tried to do everything in my power to be a good father. I never abandoned you. But, I can't help the fact that your mother betrayed you. No family is perfect. We can only try and do the best for our kids."

"Thank you, Dad. I love you."

I turned and hugged him, and it felt good for him to hug me back.

"Dad? Where are the gardenias? They're gone."

"No, son. I cut them down, but they'll grow again."

I put my arm around his shoulder as we walked back towards the house. Back in the kitchen Deloris was setting out the shrimp dinners I had brought.

"Margeaux will be here in a while. She called and said she'd just left work."

"Deloris? Why don't you save the shrimp for another time? I'd like to take you all out for dinner. We haven't done that in a long time."

I called and reserved a table at Brennan's. Since my RX7 wouldn't hold all of us, we took Dad's car to drive into New Orleans. And, for that one night, we were a typical happy, laughing French family, enjoying our meal, without a care in the world.

I stayed on for a few days, not wanting to leave. Not wanting to get back into the filth that surrounded Holler. But, I knew I had to get back to it. Get my hands dirty. Finish it up. Whatever it took to bring Holler down. Holler and whoever else was involved in it all.

I said my goodbyes and headed back to Santa Rosaria and whatever was waiting there for me. After Milltown, I headed south on 67 and remembered the night I got stopped by the sheriff's department. Thank God it had been Lawson and I didn't get my driver's license suspended. Thank God for Lawson for rescuing me from the swamp.

I wondered, *would I ever be able to repay him?*

Chapter 26

Returning from Dad's, I stopped by the post office to get my mail, and then Publix to get a few groceries. Arriving back at the marina, I completed my usual checklist, sans snorkel gear, and fed Emma. It astounded me how much junk mail there was after only a few days. Amongst all of it were a few bills and an official looking letter from an attorney over in Pensacola.

Scanning it quickly, I wasn't sure what it was about. *October 19. Pensacola Court House. Judge Hendrix chambers. Witness for Mrs. Irene Lawrence.* When I read the rest of the letter, I realized it was one of my previous cases. I'd been hired by a woman to find out it her husband was cheating on her. He was indeed. In fact, I caught him in a compromising situation with 'the other woman.' My client had filed divorce papers and the final hearing would be next week.

Judge Hendrix. Wow. I'd been in her courtroom before on another case in June. She's both an impressive judge and a beautiful woman. At least five-foot-nine or so, late thirties, long blonde hair and blue eyes. She reminded me of Tish Reugan on Fox. She had that very serious look about her, which said, 'you don't want to mess with me.' Of course, I noticed she wore a wedding ring. Too bad for me.

The day of the hearing, after my testimony, I decided to stick around and have a bite of lunch in the courthouse cafeteria. As I walked around looking for a place to sit, who should I see? Judge Hendrix. I was surprised that a judge would be in the cafeteria, but there she was. I tried to be oh so casual as I passed by her table with my tray of cold beef salad, fries and coffee.

"Your Honor," I acknowledged her and kept walking.

"There is seat here," she called out after me.

Turning back, I was a bit hesitant to sit with her.

"Oh, please. Come sit and enjoy your lunch."

"Thank you, your Honor."

"The name is Debra Hendrix. Today isn't the first time you've been in my courtroom, Mr. Ludefance. So, you're a private investigator?"

"It's Jack. And, yes, I do what I can to help my clients."

"Indeed! Especially women with unfaithful husbands. Anything to do with the bruises on your face?"

"Kinda hard not to notice, I guess. No, not from any unfaithful husband. I do handle other cases, as well. Right now, I'm heavily involved in a case that I shouldn't really be tackling with. But, that's the business. If something gets my attention, I can't seem to separate myself from it."

"Interesting! Care to explain?"

"Not really! You're a judge because you want to see justice being served. I help people who can't help themselves."

"I see."

"You haven't been here for long, have you?"

"I'm still sitting in temporarily for another judge. But, I think I might be here for a while. Judge Tarkan had his gall bladder removed, and, unfortunately, there have been complications in his recovery. I don't think he'll be returning to his duties any time soon."

"Do you have family?"

"My husband and two boys live over in Apalachicola. Sometimes they come visit me and sometimes I take Fridays and go home. Right now, I'm renting a house over in Gulf Bend."

"Have you checked out the area?"

"No, not really!"

"I'd like to show you around, if I may."

"What's there to see?"

"I think we have some great restaurants and some of the most beautiful beaches in Florida."

"Of course."

"It would be pleasure to show you around. Have you been to Bayside Restaurant? People come all the way from New Orleans to eat their famous barbecued ribs. In fact, why don't you join me this Saturday night? Unless your family is coming…"

"I was thinking about what to do with myself this weekend. Thank you. I'd like that."

"Okay, then. It's a date. Oh, God! That didn't come out right. My apologies. I mean, I'll see you Saturday night. Did you want to meet me there, or can I pick you up?"

I felt my face turn hot with embarrassment. Must have looked great with the bruises. Debra just smiled, pulled out a piece of paper, wrote something on it, and handed it to me.

"You can pick me up."

"Shall we say seven?"

"Look forward to it, Jack. But, right now, I need to get back to my courtroom."

I smiled to myself. Wow, what a woman.

Busying myself with mundane chores for the next several days, I kept wondering just what was I expecting to happen? I had to keep reminding myself she was a married woman, and a respected judge. But, I was a man and still human, wasn't I?

Dinner at Bayside was as good as it gets. I ordered my usual ribs, Debra had a thick rib-eye steak, and we shared a bottle of Sauvignon. She talked about her schooling and I talked about my navy years. I felt comfortable enough to tell her about failing my Hornet training. She complimented me for being truthful.

"Most men wouldn't allow the truth to be told."

"Why? Because I told you about my failure at flight school?"

"All my life men have tried to impress me. Yet, you seem to not be afraid to tell the truth about your failure. I like that in a man."

We enjoyed our coffee and when the bill came, she insisted on going Dutch. I didn't protest, if that made her feel more comfortable about our 'non-date.' It was tempting to ask her back to my floating home, but I hesitated. She suspected that I was withholding something.

"I think you were about to say something and then changed your mind?"

"Am I that transparent?"

"Don't forget. I'm a judge. It's my job to see that people tell the truth. Sometimes people go around and around trying to say something. I'm good at discerning when someone is dancing around the truth."

"You got me. I was about to say that my floating home is here at the marina and I thought about showing it to you. But I also thought how inappropriate that would be for a smart judge."

She laughed. I could tell she was amused.

"The answer is no. Maybe some other time."

On the drive back to her place, it crossed my mind to kiss her, but I controlled myself. Not the right time, or place.

Chapter 27

Why does recovery from injuries take longer the older you get? My ribs still ached, and even though my face was at that fading purple-blue in the healing process, I still looked like I'd been in a fight that I'd been on the losing side of. Which of course I had been.

My next move? Still not sure. I'd returned from Dad's all set to dig in again, but also knew I needed more time.

I kept busy campaigning for Lawson's bid for sheriff. The last several weeks leading up to the election were hectic with Lawson meeting and speaking with as many local groups as he could to get his message out. My job was to canvas local neighborhoods, place as many yard signs as possible, and keep ahead of any trouble Holler might cause. The last thing Holler wanted was for Lawson to be elected sheriff.

About two weeks before the election, a friend of mine who works at the NW Florida Daily News clued me in to a story Holler was paying to have run. It was going to be a splashy hit piece on how corrupt Lawson 'supposedly' was. Holler even went so far as to have pictures photo-shopped of Lawson and one of Holler's whores.

Using some of my persuasive talents, I managed to get the story squelched.

Election Day, November 7. Lawson won handily and was sworn in as sheriff of Santa Rosaria.

I also invested in a new computer, a MacBook Air. All my files and info had been transferred over, but I was having difficulties getting used to a completely different operating system; particularly with using Pages vs Microsoft Word.

Thinking about attending a computer class, I found one being offered at Pensacola State College on Saturdays. I wanted my knowledge to be more than just getting by. In my business it was crucial I be efficient and computer savvy. Wouldn't you know, who do I run into but Judge Hendrix?

"Your Honor? What are you doing here?"

"Jack! Hello! And, it's Debra. We're on a first name basis, remember? And, I could ask the same about you."

"Just bought this Apple, and I'm trying to learn about Pages. Thinking now maybe I shouldn't have changed over from Microsoft. Should have stuck with what I know best."

"It seems we both have similar agendas."

As we walked into class, she continued, "Since my family isn't here, I seem to have some time on my hands and thought I should learn a few things about this Apple. Quite a system, isn't it?"

I nodded and went to sit at one of the tables near the front, feeling like a schoolboy wanting to be close to her, but also not wanting to intrude on her space.

The class instructor knew her stuff and conveyed it in such a way as to make it easy to understand. In two hours' time, she covered how to lay out Pages, how to use editing and spell-check, and how to save Pages to iCloud. It certainly helped me have a much better understanding of what I needed to know.

After class I walked over to Debra. "What do you say we go to the Starbucks, have a cup of coffee, and catch up with the news?"

"That would be nice, Jack, but I've got to get going. I'm expecting a call from a friend, and I'd rather take the call at home. Why don't we try another restaurant, say, tomorrow night? That is, if you're available. I really enjoyed our last dinner together and our conversation."

"Sounds good. It's a date."

This time I meant it and I wanted to see how she would react.

"Alright then."

I was pleased that she didn't make any fuss about my using the word 'date.'

"Shall I pick you up at your place?"

"That would be very gentlemanly of you, Jack. Thank you. Here's my number, in case you need it."

"I'll pick you up around six?"

"Um. No. Let's make it seven."

"See you then."

Returning home, I realized just how comfortable I felt with Debra. A crazy blip through my mind's eye saw her divorcing her husband and the two of us becoming a couple, perhaps even marrying.

Why was I dreaming the impossible dream?

But, my internal dialog kept going. A future of happiness with Debra.

What was wrong with me? Why was I was having romantic fantasies about a married woman?

I wondered, if, in reality, was I taking advantage of Debra? My mind went back and forth. She's alone and away from her family. But, this time, she suggested dinner. I'd noticed the way she looked at me. Definitely interested. She's an adult, and a very smart woman. Probably much smarter than I am.

Thinking from that angle made me feel a little better. But, what was really happening was that I felt good just being around her. I felt good for the first time since my divorce.

Chapter 28

The next morning, I called my occasional cleaning lady, Yolanda, and asked if she was available to come clean my boat that afternoon. I thought about it being Sunday, but Yolanda is a workaholic, and doesn't turn down business. She agreed to come by at one that afternoon.

Yolanda is from Guatemala and cleans like nobody's business. Spit polish clean. So clean, I could eat off the kitchen floor. She arrived promptly at one, shook her head at the mess and dug right in. Three hours later, everything was like new and I knew this would probably last me a couple of months.

Later that afternoon, I got out my brown striped suit. Perfect occasion to wear it. Before taking my shower and shaving, I cleaned out the inside of my RX7.

At a quarter to seven, I called Debra to let her know I was on my way.

When I arrived at her home, she was standing by the front door. Pulling into the driveway, I stopped and got out to open the door for her.

"Jack, you don't have to do everything for me."

"Sorry, Debra. I'm still an old-school guy. Can't help it. Would you like to try an Italian restaurant this time?"

"Actually, yes."

The Vineyard happens to be one of the best Italian restaurants around. Cozy atmosphere, traditional red-checked tablecloths and authentic home-cooked food. I ordered a plate of antipasto and a bottle of Pinot Grigio to start. Sipping our wine, we settled on Caesar salad, shrimp Alfredo and a large basket of garlic rolls. We finished the bottle of wine before the main course arrived, so I ordered another one. One additional caveat with the Vineyard is that there is never a feeling of being rushed through a meal.

"So, what are the latest cases you're handling?"

"It's disturbing that I've had two sex-offender cases in the last week. Both men are in their fifties. Why it is they all seem to be middle-aged men, I'll never understand."

"Now I'm beginning to get uncomfortable about my gender, especially as I'm approaching that age."

"I can't imagine a man like you would have any issues with women. You're both handsome and quite a character. Perhaps a bit rough around the edges, but that lends to the attractiveness. Women like those types."

Encouraged, I added, "You mean you find those qualities attractive?"

"You got me Jack…"

Perhaps it was the second bottle of wine combined with the relaxed atmosphere, but I found her more open and enjoying our conversation.

"It is nice to be able to have an open and honest talk with the opposite sex."

"Yes, I agree." I raised my glass. "To honesty, Debra."

"Jack, tonight, I want to be a woman. It's very hard to be who we truly are. People always put up a pretense, a mask if you like, and try to be politically correct. I'm not a politician, but I do admire President Trump for his being so blunt."

"I agree. But I thought it was the women who are the ones who make everything an issue about being politically correct."

"Not all women, Jack. It's the feminist groups and the liberals. Times are changing. The progressives argue that we must change. Change is sometimes unpleasant, but they have a point."

"You mean all the gay rights and gender issues, globalism, open borders?"

"I would say yes. Think about it. Two-hundred years ago, slavery was thought to be normal."

"I wouldn't say normal, Debra. There were some good people who thought it was wrong but couldn't do anything about it."

"I would argue that today we are having the same difficulties accepting gender and same sex marriage. And, a hundred years from now perhaps people will see that our mass production of poultry, or meat was wrong."

Our steaming hot dinners arrived, and we settled in to enjoying them.

"You know, I could live on shrimp and pasta," she smiled as she finished her last bite.

"Italians are the best when it comes to pasta variety."

After dinner, the waitress came and cleared away our plates and crumbed the table. She returned to ask if there was anything else we wanted.

"Would you like desert?" I looked over at Debra.

"Do you have some sherry?" She looked up at the waitress.

The waitress started to list the after-dinner drinks, including port wine.

"I'll have glass of Sherry Manzanilla and a cup of coffee."

"I'd like some Irish Coffee."

Debra gave me a quizzical look.

"Yes, I know. I'm from French ancestry, and I'm supposed to know about fine wines and exotic drinks. But,

I'm just a simple Cajun boy with no knowledge of wine culture."

"My parents sent me to a private boarding school. There, among everything else, we learned proper etiquette, and fine dining including dinner drinks and after-dinner sherry."

"Your parents must be very well-educated people."

"Mmm, my father was a judge, and my mother was a professor of political science."

"My folks were country people. My mother divorced my father when I was a teenager." As soon as it was out of my mouth, I regretted saying it.

After finishing our coffees, the waitress brought our bill, and Debra insisted on going Dutch. I didn't object. But, I did open the car door for her. While holding it, I commented, "Yes, I know. I don't have to be chivalrous."

As we pulled into her driveway, she commented, "I feel refreshed. Why don't you come in and I'll make some Irish coffee?"

At that moment, I was, indeed, a very happy man.

Chapter 29

"Make yourself at home, Jack. I'm going to change into something more comfortable and make us that Irish coffee."

She came back wearing a silky, dare I say it, sexy Kaftan and carrying a tray with two Irish coffees. She set the tray on the coffee table, handed me my cup, and then carrying hers, sat on the sofa across from me, pulling her legs up under her. At that moment, she was, to me, the most beautiful woman in the world. The admiration must have been evident.

"Do you have any idea how you look?" She asked with a laugh.

Even though I felt my face begin to flush, I decided not to acknowledge my predicament.

"What's the story with the scar?"

"Alligator bite."

"Really! Did you know your scar can be eliminated with the surgery?"

"I know, but I don't want to."

She went into the kitchen and brought the bourbon bottle back with two glasses. I didn't object when she poured them full. Intoxication had taken over. I wasn't sure where the conversation was headed but thought it best to completely change the subject.

"The police bring criminals to trial and judges let them go. Don't you think this so-called justice is defeating the purpose?"

I regretted saying it the moment I opened my mouth. I really didn't want to talk about any heavy stuff, but nothing else came to mind, except the fact that I wanted her. Wanted her badly. Could she tell?

"Yes! Sometimes, as frustrating as it is, we must let the criminal go due to insufficient evidence, or a poorly investigated case. But, the laws apply to everyone."

"That's crazy! I'm involved in an investigation in which I'm certain the individual is operating under the law, and I know he's a criminal. On the surface, he seems like law abiding citizen. You know the type. Big contributions to the right causes, but underneath his entire operation is involved in criminal activity."

"What can I say, Jack? We are still a Constitutional Republic."

"The republic worked fine at one time. But I don't believe it does anymore. Laws no longer protect the innocent. I mean, look around, there's drugs everywhere. Sometimes I drive around and wonder how many homes have illegal drugs labs in their kitchens?"

"How long have you lived in the area?"

"Little over a year. But, it's it is the same in New Orleans and everywhere, for that matter. Sometimes I don't blame people for taking the law in their own hands."

"You sound like my father. I told you he's a retired judge. A true, old fashioned, reactionary civil servant. So, you probably understand how some misguided individuals can fatally shoot innocent people."

"Yes and no! The insecurity in this country is enormous. People are afraid, especially in small towns like this. People are coming in come from all over the world, and we don't know who's who. Politicians are welcoming these illegals just to gain more votes and to be reelected."

"We have a policy in this country as far as people who come here illegally."

"Oh, come on, Debra. What about sanctuary cities? And now, California is a sanctuary state? When was the last time the government passed sensible immigration reform? It seems no administration wants to tackle the issue head on. Refugees and others come in and overstay their visas. Our southern borders are so porous that people are pouring in, most of them criminals. The INS is paralyzed. There are plenty of unsupervised airfields where dope and illegal immigrants are unloaded every night. People who belong to fascist secret police in other countries come here seeking asylum. In many public places you can hear Russian and Serbian language spoken. They're not here to make a good life in America, but rather, they've escaped their crimes in the countries that they left."

In that moment, I became aware that I was losing my cool.

"The principle has to apply equally."

"Does it really? Always? Even if it's wrong?"

She got up from the sofa and refilled our drinks.

I realized then just how different we were. Depression overwhelmed me. I was angry with her views, but, at the same time, aroused. How long has it been since I'd been with a woman? More than a year? I groaned at the thought of sex.

"Are you in pain?" she asked.

I nodded. Really I wasn't, but yielded to my desire for sympathy.

"Maybe it would be best if you went home."

That was the last thing I wanted to do. I didn't feel that I had a home since Sarah left me. Taking another gulp of my drink, I finished the last of it and held out my glass for another refill. I was so intoxicated that I was starting to shed my inhibitions.

"One more please."

"Then you have to go."

Her voice turned serious, but I didn't let it bother me. When she brought my glass, I grabbed her and pull her down on the sofa.

"Sit here by me." It came out as a command.

Before I knew it, my hand was on her thigh. She pulled herself free and slapped me on the cheek with her left hand.

"Go home now!"

I saw the fury in her eyes. I set my glass on the table and stumbled as I stood up. Suddenly, I realized what I had done. That realization had an instant sobering effect.

"Forgive me. I'm exhausted."

"We'll forget all about this. But, right now you have to go home."

"I don't know what came over me."

I put out of my hand. She took it.

"We'll just forget it. Good night."

I tried to say something more, but nothing came to mind. There was that sudden realization that I'd done something both unforgivable and dangerous, and I felt as bad as when Sarah and I had had our last meeting. Walking out the door, I heard it slam behind me. I had to stop this heavy drinking. I couldn't handle it.

Before getting into my car, I sucked the cool night air into my lungs. How the hell could I be so stupid?

Early Monday morning, I stopped by the local flower shop and bought fifteen yellow roses, then drove all the way over to the Pensacola Court House to deliver them in person.

Approaching her secretary I asked, "Could you deliver these flowers to Judge Hendrix?"

"She's in court all day, but, I'll put them in her office. Did you want to leave a note?"

I wrote a brief note, not much of an excuse, but it was all I could think of.

I'm so sorry. Please forgive me. I'm really quite shy by nature.

As I wrote it, I knew the first part was true, the other part about being shy wasn't. But, I thought she might forgive me, and maybe give me another chance. Or, she could never speak to me again.

"Can you do me a favor? This is very important to me. When Judge Hendrix sees the flowers, can you call me? I want to know how she reacts."

I handed her a twenty-dollar bill and my cell phone number.

"Please, have lunch on me. It's the least I can do for the favor."

Chapter 30

As the weeks passed after returning from my father's, I realized I was accomplishing virtually nothing on the case. Instead, I'd behaved brutishly toward Debra and angered her to the point that I wasn't sure she would ever want to see me again. She did accept my apology flowers, but that didn't mean she'd forgiven me.

Before I knew it, it was late November. In a few days December would arrive. I was restless. Everything was bothering me. The case, Debra, my life. I'd recovered from the worst of my injuries Holler's goons had inflicted on me. I was angry at times and felt I had to do something. A sweet revenge would be nice, but I didn't want to be pulled into another trap.

I'd never imagined I could be fooled and drugged at the hands of an Asian whore. I was an idiot and had let my guard down. Sofia had given me Lila's name. There was no doubt in my mind she had been coerced. It also explained Sofia's strange behavior during my last massage. She had been distant and worried. Nothing like the previous times. It had been too well planned. Lila was nothing more than a very clever set-up.

I wanted revenge.

An idea began percolating in my mind and I decided to let it come slowly into full view of its own accord.

For the next several nights I drove over and parked in the vacant lot of an old gas station across from the Holler complex which had a good view of Lila's spa. I'd noticed other cars parked there before, so I knew my car wouldn't draw attention. The pattern was always the same. Every night after eight, her employees left for the day. Lila was always the last to leave and close up.

Not once did I see the black Lincoln sedan. Probably figured since Holler's goons beat me up, I was no longer a threat. Little did they know.

Patterns are a good thing. They always make my job easier.

The completed idea finally emerged. The question was, how to do what I wanted to do?

How many times had I passed by Blue Water River on my travels to and from New Orleans? It was a vast inland area, halfway between the Gulf Coast and Milltown, with back-waters, marshes and, most of all, very secluded.

Google brought up several secluded cabins located on the river that were for rent. I decided on a two-story built entirely of logs and with V shaped roofing. It fronted on a small lake with access to the river and included a small dock. After contacting the owner, he e-mailed me a map with detailed driving directions, and I drove up to check out the property.

The only way into the cabin was on a dirt road barely noticeable from a side road off 67 North. If I hadn't paid close attention to the map, I never would have found the place. It was definitely designed for maximum privacy and with very little chance of anyone accidentally discovering the location.

As I approached the property, I knew I had found exactly what my plan called for. The cabin was built from water treated wood, sturdy and solid, with the floor elevated on thick pilings at least eight-feet above ground, and wide stairs leading up to the entrance. Along with driving instructions, the owner had also e-mailed instructions on where to find a hidden key. I opened the heavy, portico covered door and entered a large open living room with a high stone fireplace.

The floors were expensive-grade oak, covered with thick Oriental rugs. The ceilings were high and vaulted, and there was both air-conditioning and heat. Off to the right was the kitchen. To the left was the master bedroom with a four-poster king-size bed, and another thick large Oriental rug. It included an on-suite, oversized bathroom with both a large Jacuzzi tub, and a separate large marble-tiled shower, complete with plenty of thick Turkish towels and two bathrobes. The large master bedroom window had to be more than twelve feet above the ground the door had a lock with a key. I found two additional bedrooms and baths upstairs.

Returning to the living room area, I opened another large door opposite to the door I had entered through, and discovered a wide, covered porch which ran the length of the cabin. It included several comfortable rocking chairs and faced the small lake. Sturdy stairs led down to a small dock with two Adirondack chairs.

According to the Google map, the river did lead all the way into Milltown. After checking out the cabin, I walked the property which was well over two acres of heavily wooded land including Florida live oaks, pine, sea grape, mahogany, bald cypress, southern red cedar, and southern magnolia.

I quickly pushed the fantasy of a romantic weekend with Debra out of my mind. *Not in the plans, Jack.*

Google had listed the property in several high-end tourist magazines as well as locally, and it was obviously geared to wealthy customers. This time of the year, late November, there weren't many tourists, so I thought I could bargain for a reasonable price. Not that it really mattered; I would have taken it at any cost, but old habits die hard.

I called the owner, we haggled, and I ended up renting it for $700 for the coming week. $700.00 dollars of well-spent money. He asked what groceries I wanted delivered, and I gave him a long list off the top of my head.

After taking care of business, I drove my car into Milltown, parked in a paid city lot and rented a small outboard. It took me over a half-hour to get back to the property, but it was much easier to find the cabin by way of water than on land. I hid the boat on the bank near the dock and covered it with branches. It would be safe and not easily detected when the owner stopped by with the groceries.

The last item on my list was to call a taxi to take me to the airport to pick up a rental car. Funny guy. He kept complaining the whole way about how hard it had been to find the cabin. Couldn't blame him though. I tipped him an extra twenty for his trouble.

Using one of my fake ID's, I requested an unobtrusive, beige Toyota. I didn't want anything easily recognizable, and certainly didn't want the rental traced back to me. Back at the cabin, I muddied up the license plate just a bit, so in the event of that "what if," it would be difficult to read the numbers.

Chapter 31

On the first Sunday night of December, I assumed my spot in the empty parking lot across from Lila's spa and waited in my rented beige Toyota. I'd retrieved the brown envelope from my safety deposit box and had put it into my backpack along with several burn phones, my gun and knife, my backpack, my Mac laptop, a new digital recorder, and several other necessary items, including tape and plenty of plastic zip-ties. I was ready to get this done.

Just after 8:30, I moved and parked right next to Lila's car on the driver's side. There were a few cars parked farther down, but the front of the spa was empty. At 8:50, she came out, never even glanced at my car, and put her key in the door lock of her car. I snuck up behind, hit the side of her neck with the side of my palm, and she slumped against the side of her car.

The whore never knew what hit her. I took her handbag off her shoulder and then grabbed her under the arms before she slipped to the ground. It was easy to open the back-passenger side door of my car, shove her inside and lay her on the back seat. I quickly taped her mouth and tied her wrists with plastic zip-ties.

Security cameras? Never once considered they would be an issue. If Holler did discover Lila missing, soon enough, he would know it was me who'd taken her.

So far, so good. Traffic was unusually light, and a half hour later I pulled into the driveway of the rented cabin. During the drive, Lila had regained consciousness and she stared at me with daggers as I opened that back door to the car. I pulled her out of the backseat and put my arm around her waist. We slowly maneuvered the stairs, and I managed to get the door unlocked. I brought her into the master bedroom and laid her on the side of the king-size bed closest to the bathroom.

I did a quick return to the car and retrieved her handbag and all my gear. When I returned to the bedroom, I took her handbag and emptied it onto the bed. What do you know? The first visible items were her passport, a cheap nine-millimeter Chinese-made pistol, and pepper spray. Other items tumbled out including her makeup, an old-fashioned address book, and her wallet with her driver's license and credit cards. I took her purse and its contents over the bureau and put them in the top drawer. She watched every move I made, trying to make sounds.

"Ahh...Darling, did you say something? I can't understand you."

"Ihhhmmmm mahhhh ihnmm."

"Sweetheart, didn't you know? You and I are going to have sort of honeymoon for the next couple of days. And then I'll give you back to your owners. But first, we need to establish a way to communicate. Okay? Now darling, for the time being, you will shake your head side to side, that means NO. When you nod your head up and down, that means YES. Are we clear?"

She nodded vigorously.

"Now we're getting someplace. You must realize, Lila, that here with me, the tables have turned. You're no longer in control. And, it's so nice to see your conceited attitude is gone. Remember all the very naughty things that were done to me? Because of you, I'm out not only $2000 grand, but my gun, my knife, and my cell phone. Did you know that my ribs have just recently healed? Now darling, listen carefully. I don't want any screaming. Not that anyone would hear you if you did. But, for that I have a perfected method that I plan to use on you. First, I am going to strip you naked and put you under the shower. And, it's going to be a very nice shower."

She started to shake her head.

"My dear Lila. I don't think you are in any position to refuse."

I cut the zip-ties off her wrists, pulled her top off over her head, undid her bra, and then put on new zip-ties. Next, came her slacks, which I quickly pulled down and off her. Then her dainty, sexy, barely-there underwear. She started to struggle and I reverted to zip-ties on her ankles, as well. What a little fighter she was.

Fully exposed and naked, I lifted her and carried her into the bathroom, setting her down in the shower enclosure resting up against the cold marble tiles. Let's see what happens when the water hits her. If this had worked with Gonzalez, it certainly would work with Lila.

Turning the water on, I adjusted it first to lukewarm water, and turned the shower-head on her. I could see the terror on her face. What had happened to that confident, ego-driven woman who had told me, "You couldn't possibly offend me?"

Her face now had the expression of a terrorized pussycat. I turned on the cold water until she started shivering. Then, I turned on the hot water. She stopped protesting and started mumbling, so, I turned on the cold water again. That's when she started crying. Can't stand to see a woman cry.

"Lila? Lila, stop crying and pay attention to me. I'm going to take the tape off your mouth. And, if you scream, sweetheart, I'll either put very hot, or very cold water on you. Depends on my mood. Now, nod your head if you understand."

She started nodding her head. I reached down and ripped the tape off her mouth in one jerk of a motion. She opened her mouth and was about to scream.

"Uh, uh, darling."

She closed her mouth, then spat out, "You're cruel!"

But then, she started blabbering about how grateful she was that I hadn't killed her. That had never been on my mind, but it was okay for her to think it. This scenario had quickly become a sort of dependency relationship, something like patients who get emotionally hooked on their psychiatrist. I touched her shoulder, gently caressed it, and told her if she was very good, everything was going to work out fine for the both of us.

This type of interrogation doesn't inflict any physical damage, but rather another kind of damage which is the worst kind. It lasts longer. I stopped for a minute, because it really started to bother me. It crossed my mind that perhaps I was no different than Holler himself. On the one hand, I thought about how she was nothing more than a very cold, cocky whore who had drugged me, and who'd enjoyed the power she had had over me. But, then again, what if she had been coerced into doing it?

My mind did battle with itself.

I reasoned that, through this experience, if I accomplished making her less confident, less self-assured, less faithful to Holler, she would be a better person from here on out. Perhaps her mask would start to slip, and her tone of voice wouldn't be exactly the same when she said, "Darling, you couldn't possibly offend me." The shrewd whore would again become the naive Vietnamese girl. Then again, if I hadn't gotten careless and been beaten up by Holler's goons, none of this would be happening.

We are all killers. All that has to happen is have the right buttons pushed.

Chapter 32

"You haven't seen anything yet, Lila. I want you to tell me everything I need to know. If you give me wrong answers, or answers that don't help me, it will either be very cold, or very hot water."

I went back into the bedroom, retrieved the brown envelope and my digital recorder. Coming back into the shower enclosure, I knelt down and pulled out the photo of the girl with the slashed throat and put it in front of Lila's face. I turned on the recorder.

"Lillian's cousin, Duyen. Why did Holler kill her?"

Lila stared at the photo and cleared her throat.

"How did you get that?"

"Doesn't matter. You didn't answer my question."

I reached up to turn on the cold water and she quickly answered.

"She threatened to go to the police about the other dead girls."

"The ones who were drugged for the porno movies?"

"Yes."

"Explain to me what kind of drugs, and where did Holler get them."

"The drugs come from Malaysia."

"Did you ever take the drug yourself?"

"Yes, but just once. Holler forbade me to take it when I started working for the company."

"So, you are one of the officers of Holler Enterprises?"

"Yes."

"Are you Holler's whore?'

"Yes."

"So, while Holler was married to Lillian, you were sleeping with him?"

"Holler would come to the spa and always wanted me to give him a massage."

"Did he ask for other girls?"

"For massages? No, not that I know of. He only slept with me. He and Lillian were having problems."

She started to shiver. I turned the recorder off and put the shower head on her with warm water.

"Please. Can you get me out of the shower, please?"

"I could. But, I don't trust you, yet. You'll have to manage until I'm satisfied with your answers."

I turned the recorder back on.

"Lillian died of bleeding ulcers she didn't know she had."

In that instant, a wild thought came to me. I went out on a limb.

"Or, maybe, just maybe, her death was arranged?"

Lila hung her head. Was I on to something?

"Lila?"

"They have a drug for that, too. When a person takes it, they don't know that they're bleeding. Their blood count gets low very quickly and they die."

"And, it's not detectable in an autopsy?"

"No."

"So, someone gave her that drug?"

"Yes…"

"Sorry, Lilia. I didn't hear you."

Lila looked up at me as I reached up to turn on the shower faucet.

"Yes. Someone gave her the drug."

"Who? Who gave her the drug, Lila?"

She hung her head again.

I raised my voice. "Who?"

"I don't know."

"I don't believe you. You seem to know just about everything that goes on in both the business and on the estate. Did you give that drug to her?"

Lila didn't respond.

"You did, didn't you?"

"Yes!"

"Where are Lillian's two boys?"

"They're away at boarding school in New England."

"Okay! Who shoots the porno movies?"

"They come from outside. Sometimes they bring unknown actors and actresses. Or when they find a good-looking teenager, they promise them acting careers. For some of the girls, they were promised modeling jobs. That's how they lure them in. When they bring them in, they lock them in until the film has been completed. There have been times when they realize what's going on and they don't want to do it. But, it's too bad."

"What they do with the porno movies?"

"They sell them in Asia."

"How about here?"

"I only know they market them in Malaysia, but I don't know about here."

"Who entices these teenagers into this?"

Silence. Again my hand reached up to turn to the shower faucet.

"Me and some of the other girls. That was part of our job."

"So, you would talk to an innocent high school girl and pursue her."

"Sometimes. But that's not the way I approached it. If I saw a beautiful girl at the mall, I'd walk up to her and say something like, 'Excuse me, are your parents here? I'd like to talk to them. I think you're gorgeous and I'd like to talk to them about the possibility of having you come to our studio for a shoot.' If she said her parents were there, I'd talk to them, but never really pursued it. If she was alone, that was all the better."

"So, these American girls, are they enticed to become escort girls?"

"Yes, sometimes."

"Okay. What about the girls that come from Asia?"

"Holler has people in Malaysia. They target the girls who work in the streets, approach them, and promise them modeling and acting jobs in the US. They obtain passports for the girls who don't have them. Sometimes the Vietnamese girls already have passports. Once they get their passports, his men keep them. The girls come over on cargo ships, and they stay on the Holler estate. Some girls make porno movies, and others work in the massage salons, like mine. They send the girls all over the country, New York, Los Angeles, Seattle, Miami, all the big cities wherever there are massage salons. These girls always live above the massage salons; they're not permitted to out on their own. Some of the girls work as escorts."

"So, they bring the girls to Holler's first. Huh…what a treacherous estate."

She looked up at me with acknowledgement.

"Yes, I guess you could say it is."

"What else?"

"They send them to the places where they're needed. Sometimes the girls get sick while coming over here. And if they die, their bodies are thrown overboard. Only two girls have died on the Holler's estate and they're buried there."

"Only two...how comforting. So, it's an ongoing business."

"They even hire girls who are from here. I mean, Asian-American girls are valued and are given managerial positions, because they speak English."

"Valued. That's a crock. What else goes on there at the estate?"

"There's a horse barn and track. They bring in racehorses from outside, and I've heard that they are very expensive...some costing over $2 million. Several American girls work in the barns, grooming the horses and exercising them. They have jockeys who ride the horses, and sometimes they take the horses out in a trailer, but I don't know where they take them. Holler even has a veterinarian on call at all times."

"Anything else?"

"Sometimes Holler invites his military friends and they target practice."

"How big is the house?"

"It has six bedrooms, and sometimes Holler's friends come and stay."

"How many people total work at the estate?"

"It varies, depending on the time of year. Holler has a dedicated housekeeper, and two cooks. The one you talked to, and another cook. Then there's two gardeners, and two chauffeurs. Holler has several cars, all black, with black-tinted glass. The two girls for taking care of the horses, and a man who tends to the alligators."

"How many bodyguards?"

"Six at last count."

"Who killed Katy?"

"Katy? I don't know anything about that."

"Think harder."

"You think Holler tells me everything he does?"

"You're Holler's whore."

"I heard that she was a spy taking pictures of the invoices. That's all I know."

"Does Holler bring cocaine and heroin from Asia?"

"I wouldn't know about that."

"But you hear everything."

"I know about the other drugs, but not about heroin or cocaine."

"Has Holler ever sent you to another city and you carried his luggage?"

"He sent me to Seattle once. I had my luggage and another suitcase of Holler's. At the airport I was met by a chauffeur who took the luggage."

"And you didn't know what was in the luggage?"

"NO!"

"Has Holler had you travel anywhere by car?"

"Yes. To Philadelphia. Again, I don't know what was in the luggage."

"Just a few more questions, Lila. Anything else on the estate I should know about?"

"There's also a helicopter pad."

"Holler owns a helicopter?"

"No. The helicopter brings military people in and out. Sometimes Holler goes with them."

"One last question. Holler told me he's just a small part of a larger organization. Do you know who he's connected to?"

"All I know is, their military."

Bingo. It had been staring me in the face from the very beginning!

Turning off the recorder, I cut the plastic zip-ties from around her wrists and ankles. I gave her a towel to dry herself off, and one of the thick Turkish bathrobes to put on. When she came out of the bathroom, she curled up on one side of the big bed. Settling on the other side, I had just a few more questions, but none I wanted to record.

"What did they do with my cell phone after they beat me up?"

"After the bodyguards took it, I don't know what they did with it."

"Fair enough."

"Jack...I'm hungry. Is there anything to eat here?"

Chapter 33

"Why, how inhospitable of me not to offer you anything to eat. Sure, I can whip up something. But, while I do, I think I'll tie you up again. Just in case."

"Jack, please, I promise I won't do anything. Please."

"Lila, with our history, you expect me to trust you?"

After retying her wrists and ankles with the plastic zip-ties, I fastened her to the headboard of the four-poster. I didn't bother with taping her mouth. Even if she did scream, there was no one around to hear her.

In the kitchen, as I started to pull out items from the refrigerator, I realized that I was starving as well. Bad deeds do have a tendency to make me hungry. I put together sandwiches, filled with meat, cheese, tomatoes and onion on thick Italian bread, added some dilled pickles and chips, and topped it off with two beers. Why not? And, from all Lila had already spilled, I thought she deserved a drink.

I returned to the bedroom with a large tray, set it on the bed and cut the zip-ties off her wrists, but not her ankles. The sandwiches literally disappeared in the blink of an eye, washed down by a bottle of Samuel Adams. What strange bedfellows we were.

"Do you mind if I take a shower?"

"You haven't had enough water for one evening?"

She shook her head. Strategy?

"Can I have my handbag with my makeup, Jack?"

I retrieved her handbag and its belongings from the bureau drawer, putting her gun and the pepper spray into my backpack. After removing the plastic zip-ties from her ankles, I gave the handbag to her. She grabbed her clothing and disappeared into the bathroom. The water ran for an unusually long time and I was about to go in and check on her, when she demurely walked out, hair brushed, mouth made up, and not wearing a stitch of clothing, except her barely-there bikini underwear. I noticed that first of course, but then noticed the bruise on her neck where I had hit her.

"Don't be shy sweetheart, it isn't like I haven't seen a naked body."

She came into the room, scuttled for the bed in a knock-kneed half run, slightly hunched over. She crawled in under the covers. The demure attitude threw me off. Where had that suddenly come from? My senses went instantly on alert.

"I wish it were under different circumstances then it is now, Jack."

"Stop fussing, darling. This is our new relationship. Only this time, I'm your captor. Tomorrow you and I are going to call your boss, and I want you to be good little whore. You are mine for now. Not in any intimate way, but just that I now have control over you."

"Maybe I want to change that. I'm willing to forget what you put me through. Let's say it's all forgotten."

As she was talking, she pushed back the covers, inched close to me, and was going quite directly and efficiently to work on me. Working with the quickness of a little kissing, and an arching and presentation of all her sexy curves. Along with that, there was a whole lot of cleverness in her hands, the convincing steaminess of her breath, and her fake growing excitement. Within moments she was working her way astride my lap.

She started to unbutton my shirt and I was curious to see how far she willing to go. All the while, she tried to be that sweet, innocent little girl that she'd probably used on many a gullible man.

This was the commensurate whore at work. The work she knew best operating from her lifelong knowledge of the male animal. Quite convinced apparently, that a good, quick, solid bang would make everything okay, and make the man go away, much too happy to care about being sent away.

Already she was working her way out of those skimpy, oh so sexy panties, and simultaneously beginning the right amount of pressure that was beginning to topple me over onto my back.

I got my left arm in between us and my palm flat against her wishbone. Then abruptly, I straightened my arm, sending her catapulting back onto the floor, sitting hard on the carpet.

"I don't sleep with whores, baby. So, don't try to sweeten me up. It wouldn't mean a damn thing to you, and it would mean just a little less than that to me. You are my merchandise that has cash value for your owners, and, until I receive my cash, you sit tight and be a good little whore."

Chapter 34

I left her sitting on the floor with a shocked expression on her face and told her she could sleep in there, but if there was any funny business, I'd come back in and tie her hands to the bed. I grabbed my backpack from the bureau. After locking the master-bedroom door, I checked it to make sure she couldn't escape. I didn't think she would attempt crawling out the bedroom window. At over twelve feet above the ground, it wouldn't have been a wise idea.

Not comfortable with sleeping in either of the two bedrooms upstairs, I grabbed some extra pillows and a blanket and made myself as comfortable as I could on the long, wide, plush sofa in the living room. At least here I could hear her if she tried anything.

After a few hours of restless sleep, I opened my eyes, and checked my watch. 7 am and I was hungry again. In the kitchen I made a pot of coffee, cooked some bacon, scrambled up a half-dozen eggs, and toasted several slices of sourdough bread. I left my portion in the kitchen, plated Lila's breakfast and headed back to the master bedroom. Unlocking the door, I saw her pretending to be sleeping in the big bed.

Setting the plate down on the night table, I went closer to the bed and threw the covers off, not at all surprised to see her naked body. She looked up at me with her sexy, come hither, whore smile, and began showing off her perfectly proportioned body. My eyes settled first on her perfectly round breasts, and her nipples, erect with arousal. The areola was at least an inch in diameter, with pale skin beyond. My eyes then traveled down to her flat belly and tiny waist, then down to her long legs.

I had to give her credit. She was going to give it one more try. She turned over slowly, displaying her shapely, oh so sexy, ass. I knew one thing. Any whore that attractive always has dozens of little automatic tricks, a way of looking at a man, speaking to him, holding herself. Not so much flirtatiousness as awareness of the weapons she has always owned, and how to use them at all times.

I thought of other categories of women I have run into; women who can turn the whole arsenal on and off at will; well-trained actresses, ballet dancers, and, of course, whores.

All the while, she was quite aware that I was beginning to be aroused. She turned herself over onto her back again, displaying the triangular shade of her crotch and breathing heavily. It was an invitation to, 'come take me, if you're man enough.' There was no doubt she knew every trick in the book.

Using all the willpower I could muster up, I barked at her.

"Baby, I told you I don't sleep with whores. So, you can stop inviting."

"I like sex better than breakfast."

"Darling, you can save your sexy energy for your next client. I'm not interested. Put your clothes on and come to the kitchen."

With a pout, she got up off the bed, grabbed her clothes and went into the bathroom.

While she was getting dressed, I took her plate and went back into the kitchen, setting both plates on the table. When she walked in, fully dressed, there was no indication of what had just transpired. We sat across each other and began eating in silence.

The morning light was brilliant against her face as she sat opposite me. Her dark hair, brushed to a gloss, hung free like two dark curved parentheses framing the oval of her face. After a few minutes, she got up and went to the refrigerator, found the orange juice, and poured herself a glass. She put the juice on the table, and finished her eggs and toast with jam, but made a snarky comment about how terrible the bacon was.

After a while, she seemed to relax, and we had what amounted to a "heart to heart" conversation about her childhood.

"I cooked breakfast, now you can wash the dishes."

"What if I don't?"

She was definitely testing the grounds of this odd relationship.

"I'll spank your very white ass until it's red, and then I'll tie you to the bed."

After the cleanup, I was ready for her to call Holler. I grabbed my backpack, entwined my hand in hers, locked the door of the cabin, and helped her into the passenger seat of the rental car.

"Jack, I need my purse!"

"No, you don't. Not for this little excursion."

After getting in on the driver's side, I locked all the doors of the car, using the child-proof safety lock. We left the cabin and the dirt road behind, and headed west on the small, narrow, two-lane side road. I drove quite a way from the cabin before I stopped at an empty gas station that was closed for renovations.

There seemed to be quite a few of those around. Hurricanes have a tendency to take their toll.

Taking out one of the burn phones, I had her dial the number, then took it back from her, and heard his voice.

"Jonathan Holler."

"Listen very carefully, Holler. This is the unlucky guy your whore drugged, and your goons beat up. Got the picture? I have here a piece of merchandise that belongs to you. I am willing to exchange her for a certain amount of cash."

I handed the phone back to Lila, "Say hello to your owner."

"Jonathan, he kidnapped me!"

"That's enough." I took the phone back from her.

"You see, Holler, your people have caused me quite a lot of collateral and bodily damage. It's time for you to pay up."

"Kidnapping is a federal crime, Jack."

"Ahh, that's where you're wrong. I intend to turn her over to the Feds, unless you pay for the damage you've caused me."

He didn't answer.

"I don't have much patience, Holler. If you say no to me, she *will* become the property of the Feds. They'll put her into a witness protection program, and she'll sing like a bird about all your dirty businesses; the offshore bank accounts in the Caymans, your illegal business of selling weapons to terrorists, your porno business, human trafficking, the girls that you had killed. Shall I go on?"

"How much do you want?"

"I want a hundred-grand in cash. I'll give you the exchange details later."

"That is totally out of the question. You really think you can get away with this?"

"I think I will. And you annoy me any further, the price goes up. In fact, let's make that two-hundred grand. I'll call you later, Holler."

After hanging up the phone, I waited another thirty minutes, then took another burn phone and dialed Holler's number.

"Holler!"

"Decision time, Holler. Two-hundred grand. Any excuses and it goes up to three. I'll call you at 12:30 and give you instructions and directions to where the exchange will take place. You will come alone. There will be no bodyguards, and no funny business."

"How do you expect me to get that much cash in such a short time?

"That's your problem. I have no doubt for you, it's probably chump change you keep around on your estate. You have almost four hours to complete your chores. If not, the Feds get her."

Chapter 35

Back at the cabin, Lila was in a pouty, disagreeable mood as I steered her toward the master bedroom.

"I want to stay in the living room."

"Sorry, but no, Lila. I'm going to be busy, and since I don't trust you, you'll stay in the master bedroom and the door will be locked."

"I want my phone."

"No."

After powering up my computer, I checked e-mails, the weather forecast and the local news. The weather was going to be cooler than usual and windy for the next several days, but no rain. And, there wasn't a thing about Lila being kidnapped. I emptied Lila's gun, and put it and the bullets back in my backpack.

Next, I took out and familiarized myself with a new gadget I'd purchased. It never ceases to amaze me all the new technologies that are being developed. This one was perfect for what I had planned.

What I'd purchased was an advanced type of headphone that has no earpiece. The headphone is attached to the lower jawbone, and the vibration through the bone connects the conversation to the brain. It's as if you hear the voice in your head. It's made so that when you answer back, your voice is observed into the system and, although you are conversing, other devices are not able to pick up the conversation. This makes it so that if the other person has an extra device, it will be of no use in talking to a third party.

My thinking was, while talking to me, Holler wouldn't be able to talk to his goons and instruct them to follow. Holler's ex-military. He figures that with all the gadgets and manpower he has, he will have no problem killing me and perhaps his whore as well. He'll do what I say, but he'll have his own plan to deal with me. He thinks he has the muscle and resources, but I'm determined to outsmart him. Thank God, I'd done my research. Nothing substitutes for that.

Knowing what I now know about him, I also figured he would have to answer to his bosses. Holler Enterprises was only a subsidiary of another larger entity, which I knew now was in the private military business.

Through Lila's interrogation, it had all come together. Since the Pentagon stopped issuing contracts to Outsourcing Intelligence, they had formed other companies, both in the US as well as foreign countries, and partnered with the local ex-military people. They had free reign to do whatever they fancied. And, it was obvious, Holler still worked for them.

I could turn Lila over to the Feds right now and Holler would be in a much worse position than simply coming up with the money to pay me. But at this point, turning Lila over was no longer an option. I wanted revenge. I also knew it was my nature to live on the edge. It's my character flaw, ever since I was a kid and wrestled with that alligator.

I was as ready as I could be. Calling for a taxi, I gave them the address of Lila's spa, and instructed them to be there at 1 pm to pick up a party of one. I gave Lila her options. Either cooperate with me or I would turn her over to the Feds. She agreed to cooperate.

At 11 am, we left the cabin with my backpack with all my gear, including her gun and mine, her purse, warm jackets, two baseball caps, and sunglasses. I drove to the gas station across from the Holler complex, left one of the new gadget headphones in one of the garbage cans, and then parked down the road where I could see the gas station, but not be observed.

    At 12:30, I called Holler. It rang three times before he picked up.

    "Holler."

    "Listen carefully, Holler. Go to the empty gas station on Highway 88 across from Lila's spa. Be there by 12:45 pm. There will be a headphone in the garbage can at pump three. Don't forget, I'm watching you, so don't try any funny business."

    At 12:50 pm, I watched as a black Lincoln sedan drove slowly into the parking lot and stopped. Holler exited the passenger side with his briefcase in hand, and the sedan drove off. He looked around and walked over the garbage can at pump three, picked up the headphone and put it on. Mine was in place. I called, and I could see how puzzled he was.

    "Holler, you can talk, and I'll hear you. If you're wired to communicate with your goons, you can forget it. They won't be able to talk to you or hear you. The only voice you're going to hear is mine."

    "Okay. You guys get that?"

    I had to laugh. Obviously, he didn't believe me.

    "Holler, your men can't hear you. If you try to take off the headphone and talk to your men, I'll know it's been detached. So, let's stop wasting time."

    I watched him as he reached inside his jacket, take out something and throw it on the ground.

    Good move, Holler.

    "Good. Now, look across the street. There's a cab parked in front of Lila's spa. Have the cab take you to the north side of Santa Rosaria Bridge, drop you off, and give instructions to wait for you. I want you to take the pedestrian walkway, walk to the highest point on the bridge, and wait there."

Santa Rosaria Bridge is the only access to the island and the National Seashore for many miles. It has two lanes for car traffic and a pedestrian walkway on both sides built several feet below the level of the roadway. It's used often in the summertime by walkers, joggers and bicyclists. But today being a Monday and with the cold wind, I doubted there would be anyone but us on the bridge.

Waiting until the taxi pulled out onto Highway 88, I then followed at a discreet distance. At the turn to the bridge, I saw Holler get out of the taxi with his briefcase and start walking.

Continuing on over the bridge, I found a place to turn around and parked the rental car on the side of the road facing back towards the direction of Highway 88. When we got out of the car, we put on the jackets, baseball caps, and the sunglasses I'd brought. I made sure that Lila saw me putting her gun into my left side jacket pocket.

With Lila on my left, and holding her hand, we began our track up the pedestrian walkway to the top of the bridge. My gun was in my right hand at my side, Lila's empty gun was in my pocket, and my knife was taped to my ankle.

Halfway up, I saw the silhouette of the figure of Holler, already at the top. I let Lila's hand go and smiled to myself, as she took the bait. I pretended I was not aware of her stealthily reaching into my pocket and removing her gun. So far, so good. What she didn't know was her gun was empty.

When we reached the top, we stopped a few feet from Holler. I showed my gun, kept it low to my side, and kept it pointed at him. He was holding his briefcase in one hand, while his other hand was in his jacket pocket. The wind was picking up and I had to raise my voice, so Holler could hear me.

"Very slowly take your hand out of your pocket, Holler."

He complied and dropped his hand by his side.

"Okay, Holler. Here's your merchandise."

I shoved Lila at Holler and as he grabbed her with one hand, he threw the briefcase at me. I caught it, quickly opened it, saw the stacks of money, and closed it again. I looked up to see Lila pointing her gun at me.

"Give me back the briefcase, Jack," Lila demanded.

"Why don't you shoot me, Lila? Wouldn't that be the easiest thing to do?"

Her gun went click, click. Nothing more. The 'victim' had just turned deadly. My gun was still pointed at Holler.

"So, Holler, are you planning on marrying her, so she can't testify against you?"

In rapid succession, I saw Holler pull his gun out of his pocket, and the flash as he fired it at Lila. From such a close range his aim was completely off, and the bullet ended up barely grazing Lila's hand. I fired at Holler's gun, knocking it out of his hand. As he bent down to try and retrieve it, I kicked it over side and it slid into the water. He straightened up and I kept my gun on him. With that, Lila came back over to me.

"Why don't you go with your owner?"

"So he can kill me, too? I'm sorry about pointing the gun at you. I really thought he would marry me. Obviously, I was very wrong. Please, I want to come with you."

In the flash of a moment, the guilt I had for Katy's death flooded through me. I didn't want to be responsible for the death of another, whore or not. Perhaps she should go back to her home country of Vietnam and be the girl she was, if she could. At that moment, I didn't know.

"Holler, I think your taxi's still waiting."

"This isn't over. Not by a long shot."

He turned and started back down the bridge.

In the space of less than five minutes it was over, and Lila and I headed back to the rental car. I put the briefcase in the trunk and we headed back over the bridge towards Santa Rosaria. By the time we got to Highway 88, Holler and the taxi had disappeared.

"Here's how it's going to go, Lila. You have two choices. Either go back to Vietnam, or I deliver you to the Feds and they'll put you into witness protection. Your choice."

"I don't know what to do."

"My suggestion is you go back to Vietnam. If you stay here, even if the Feds put you into witness protection, you know his goons will still find you and kill you."

"That doesn't leave me with much of a choice, does it? I've got my passport. Take me to the airport."

Chapter 36

"Airport it is."

As we passed the Holler complex and Lila's spa, I noticed another black Lincoln sedan with tinted windows pulling out of the parking lot. Less than a mile down the road, the sedan was directly behind us. I put petal to the metal and began haphazardly weaving in and out of lanes, leaving the sedan stuck behind a slow-moving van. He was stuck only because another car was in the left lane keeping pace and there was no room for the sedan to get ahead of either vehicle. When I felt it safe, I made a quick right turn and hid behind a Dollar General, watching for the sedan to pass by.

We crossed over Pensacola Bay Bridge, took the shortcut under Graffiti Bridge, and another right on 9th which would take us to Airport Boulevard. We were about to reach the departure concourse, when Lila uttered a scream.

"Ohh, shit!"

"What?"

"One of Holler's cars."

"Where?"

"Just up there in front of Delta."

"I can't turn around, Lila. It's one way. Slump down in the seat so they don't see you."

Lila lowered herself out of sight and I drove by as quickly as I could. If I sped, I knew I'd get a ticket. But, I also knew, as slow as I was going, the sedan was sure to spot us and give pursuit. Looking in the rearview mirror, sure enough, I saw the black sedan coming after us. We were now back to Airport Boulevard. If I turned left, it would take us back towards Pensacola Bay Bridge. I made a quick decision and turned right.

I knew this part of the city, and increased my speed, aware there was a sharp bend up ahead. The black sedan kept right on our tail. It was only a matter of minutes before we heard the blaring of the Pensacola police sirens.

As we approached the sharp bend, I applied the brakes and maneuvered slightly left. We braced for impact from behind, but the sedan shot past us, plowed into a strip mall, and came to rest just inside a T-Mobile. Several police cars screeched to a halt. They'd made the decision to stop and investigate the black sedan.

I pulled out, kept going, and took the first on ramp to I-10 East. There was no way of knowing if they'd radioed ahead with the car make and model. If they had, I could only hope they'd not gotten the license plate number.

The exit for Garcon Bridge loomed ahead and I took it.

"Lila, reach in my back pocket for my wallet! We need three to get through the toll!"

As I lifted my butt, I felt her hand reach in my back pocket and pull my wallet out. She handed me three ones. Traffic slowed as we reached the toll-booth, and I handed the three dollars to the attendant. The barrier raised agonizingly slowly, but soon we were back in Gulf Bend and headed east on Highway 88.

When I spotted a Santa Rosaria deputy's car parked on the side of the road, I slowed down and drove as normally as possible. My heart sunk when he pulled out and began following several cars behind us. Luck was back on our side as we approached the turn for 67 North. We had a green light, just turning to amber, and I blew through the intersection, leaving the deputy still stuck behind several cars, as the light turned red.

Despite turning his siren on, there was nowhere for him to go with two lanes of cars ahead of him boxing him in, which gave us time to put some distance between us. Hopefully enough distance that he'd not be able to catch up. My only fear was he'd radioed ahead for another deputy to intercept us. Traffic on 67 North was always heavy at this time of day and we took advantage of it. My heart sunk when I heard sirens not far behind. There were now two deputy cars in chase.

At the point where 67 North became two-lanes, I settled in front of an 18-wheeler. There was heavy oncoming traffic, making it impossible for either deputy to pass the massive truck. And, I hoped it would be enough cover for what I had planned.

As we reached the side road turn off to the cabin, I took a chance and made a quick right turn. Pulling off the road behind some thick trees, we waited. My heart was pounding. It wasn't long before the 18-wheeler passed us, followed by two deputy cars, sirens still blaring. Pulling back out on to the side road, we made it to the dirt road and the cabin, and I hid the car in the woods to the side.

We went in and locked the door. First order of business was attending to Lila's hand. As I had thought, it was a very minor graze, but I applied peroxide, antiseptic ointment and a small bandage. No use in attracting attention when she boarded her plane.

We waited it out for over forty minutes. There was only the sound of the wind through the trees. Even if the deputy had gotten a look at the license plate number, which I didn't think he had, it wouldn't do them any good. With the fake ID I'd used, there was no way it could ever be traced back to me.

On the other end, how much trouble could I be in? I didn't even want to contemplate that. Kidnapping, speeding and reckless driving, fleeing a police officer and a sheriff's deputy, and probably minor offenses, as well. The only priority right now was getting Lila on a plane and out of the country. I had the recording of everything she had told me and that would soon be in the hands of the Feds. I hoped that would be enough to cancel out my transgressions.

I took a few minutes, powered up my Mac laptop and Googled flights from Atlanta to Ho Chi Minh City, Vietnam. There were several airlines that flew the route, but only United had availability for a Tuesday morning departure.

I locked the doors, hid the key, and we headed down to the dock. After retrieving the small speed boat, we headed for Milltown. We'd gone about a mile, when I remembered the briefcase in the trunk of the rental car and I made a quick turnaround. How careless could I get?

"Why are we turning back?"

"I forgot something."

I approached the cabin, turned off the engine, and quickly tied up the boat. I listened for anything unusual. All clear. I retrieved the briefcase, set it on the car trunk, opened it, and counted the money. One-hundred grand. Ha! So, Holler had stiffed me. But, it was more than I had before.

I went back in the cabin and rifled through cabinets until I found a large trash bag. Back at the car, after taking a stack of hundred-dollar bills out and slipping them in my back pocket, I closed the briefcase, put it in the trash bag and tied it tightly closed. I locked up again and slid the key back in its hiding place.

At Milltown, I turned the boat in and retrieved my car. Before heading up to Atlanta, we went shopping and bought some clothes and other essentials for Lila, along with a suitcase to pack them in. I made sure to observe all the speed signs through Alabama; there are just too many speed traps to take a chance. We reached Montgomery just after 9 pm, stopped for a bite to eat, and then we were back on the road.

We arrived at Atlanta Hartsfield Airport just after 1 am. I couldn't bear to spend another night with Lila. I parked my car in the parking lot C, and we proceeded to the United Airlines ticket counter. I paid $2400 dollars cash for a one-way ticket to Ho Chi Minh City, (SGN) Vietnam, leaving at 6:45am via Toronto and Hong Kong. Even though her passport and papers were all in order, there were lots of questions why. Especially a one way and paying cash. But Lila was an expert on lying.

"My mother very ill. Must get home before she die."

I must admit the crocodile tears and poor grammar helped. I waited with her until her flight was called and walked her to security, where she wrapped her arms around me and kissed me on the cheek. I stood outside security and watched her pass through with no issues. As she got inside the security gate, she sent me a kiss and mouthed, 'I love you.' She should. I just saved her life.

Mine, on the other hand, was definitely in question.

Chapter 37

Walking back through the terminal, I spotted a cozy café. I decided to sit and have a cup of coffee. Even though I was completely exhausted, I wasn't yet ready to head back to Santa Rosaria and face the music, whatever that might entail. Perhaps some reflection was in order.

Who was Lila, really? Back in the cabin, during breakfast, we'd had the time to talk about her youth, and how it was when she was growing up. This time, she gave me what I believed was the truth. She'd had a hard life. The kind no one wants to hear or talk about. The kind that is repeated thousands of times the world over.

Her father abandoned her and her mother when she was ten. They had very little money to live on, and she was on the streets by herself very soon after. To earn a living, she started selling energy drinks, selling anything she could. Soon she was selling herself. Her life as a prostitute started when she was only 12 years old. This was a girl had seen the very worst of the ugly side of street life. But, had her earlier life on the track coarsened her beyond any hope of salvage?

Though it might be ironic to sentimentalize or romanticize a whore, I could respect the certain toughness of spirit Lila possessed. She hadn't howled after I kidnapped her. She hadn't dwelled on her situation as I put her through the water test. I really believed she thought those situations were a part of the design of her life. She picked herself up be tougher and carry on.

I couldn't think of any woman I had ever known who could have taken such punishment. At that moment, I realized that in a way I felt proud of her. This reaction was so irrational, it startled me. Then I tracked it down to its obvious source. I once had a brief meeting with a gentleman from Turkey. It was one of those chance encounters in which things are revealed to a stranger, thing that might not otherwise be disclosed.

He'd inherited a great deal of wealth from his parents at an early age. He told me he tried everything that was exciting for a young man to do. From race car driver, to sky diving, to rock climbing. When he was about 45-years-old, an incident happened to him in which he ultimately found both satisfaction and pleasure. He was walking down a city street late at night when a young woman rushed up to him, demanding if he had any money. Just for the sake of it, he replied that he did. She offered him sex for money, but the way she said it was half-hearted, "Okay, give me your money and I'll give you sex in return."

He didn't know why the scenario intrigued him, but it did, and he went along with the woman's request. She demanded that they go to her place, explaining that she had a baby that needed attending to. Again, he complied. When they arrived at the prostitute's hovel, she immediately went to her baby and fed him. Then, she demanded that they do it in her bedroom. He told her that there was no hurry, to which she replied that she couldn't take the whole night with him.

The man happened to be carrying a box of special tea that he purchased earlier. He gave her the box of tea bags and asked if they could have some tea before sex. She was perplexed but did as he asked. They talked through the night about her life and how she got into prostitution. She was from Ukraine and had come to Turkey to find work, but her plans didn't work out and she ended up selling herself.

The next morning, the man took her to his mansion, gave her a room for herself and her baby, and arranged work for her. In the end, she was able to turn her life around; later becoming one of the employees of a foundation which rescued girls from prostitution, provided them with a safe place to live, and honest work. Soon the home became a very well-known place. The Turkish gentleman was able to get government subsidies to sweep the streets for young girls and help turn their lives into something much better.

"They become your people," he told me. "Your kids. You want good things for all of them, and for them to use life well. When they crap around, wasting what you gave them, you feel forlorn. When they use it well, you feel wonderful. Maybe because it's some kind of a ledger account, and they have to make up for what those others would have done, those ones you lost for no damn good reason."

I knew that the risk I'd taken had been for the sake of trying to redeem a whore. But, I had to believe she had enough essential spirit and toughness to be able to make it some other way and would. Or maybe I felt so guilty about Katy that I was simply trying to find atonement.

Chapter 38

Enough ruminating for one morning. Leaving the terminal, I collected my car, and paid the $26.00 parking ticket. Heading south on I-85, I realized I couldn't go any farther. In the small town of Monroe, I pulled into a motel, paid cash for a room and crashed. It was after three in the afternoon when I finally woke up.

I was starving, and my car was low on gas. Chevron came first for the car. Thought of buying some sandwiches, but decided against it, as my craving for McDonald's quarter pounder with cheese and large fries was overwhelming. After satisfying my hunger, I drove all the way to Santa Rosaria with no incident.

Thinking that I had outsmarted Jonathan Holler, at least for the time being, was a good feeling. I knew for sure Holler had plans for getting rid of me, and he wouldn't stop until he had. Was I prepared for his next attempt to kill me?

There was no question, I had to be. I didn't think my kidnapping Lila would get out in the open and I didn't believe he was going to report anything to the sheriff's department. I took that chance, although I didn't want Lawson to know about the kidnapping.

Arriving back at the marina after 8:30 that night, I completed my security checks. Everything on my floating home was just as I'd left it, including Emma. I made a mental note to go to Wells Fargo in the morning and put the money into my safe-deposit box, but I did keep out another bundle of hundred-dollar bills.

As I was about to hit the shower my phone rang.
"Jack? It's Margeaux."
"Margeaux? What's up?"
"I'm sorry to call you this late, but I had to."

"First of all, it's not late, and second, you know you can call my anytime. How's Dad doing?"

"That's why I'm calling. Dad's illness is getting worse. His medication isn't working any more. He got lost again, and the police brought him back to the house. He said he didn't know where he was. I'm so upset, and afraid not only for him, but for me, too. I don't want to be like that when I am old."

"That's not something you should worry about right now."

"How can I not worry? We're both descended from his genes, and if Dad's gotten Alzheimer's, then what's to say you or I won't?"

"Look, little sister. Don't go ahead of yourself. If we go get it, we'll worry about it then. Don't forget, we also have mom's genes, and I'm sure she's doing just fine. Besides, our generation is different; we're healthier, and more active. Where's Dad now?"

"Dad's still at the house with Deloris. But, she thinks that it's time to place him. He needs constant looking after, and she's afraid that he'll put himself in danger when she's not around."

"Okay, sis. I'll leave in the morning. I have some errands to do fist, but I'll see you around lunch. We'll talk about what's best to do."

"Thanks. I can't decide this by myself, Jack."

"Nor, should you. Margeaux, I know you and Dad are close, but you don't need to worry. We'll all decide together what's best to do."

"Thanks, Jack."

"Good night. I'll see you all tomorrow."

I stayed up to check the local late newscast. Nothing about Lila. But, there was a segment on the car chase in Pensacola and back through Santa Rosaria.

Pensacola police and Santa Rosaria sheriff's deputies were still trying to piece together and make sense of the events, and the fact that the driver of the car that escaped still hadn't been found.

In the morning, several items were on my list. I called the owner of the cabin and extended the rental for another week. Ditto with the rental car, giving them the excuse that my car was in the shop for extended repairs. I was relieved that neither rentals would be a problem. I didn't have the time or energy to deal with them right now.

Before heading down to Wells Fargo, I gathered up my passport, deed for the boat, several other important items, including Lillian's brown envelope, the recording I had made of Lila, and the money, stuffing everything into my backpack.

I usually deal with Robert, a newlywed, whose wife is military. Robert is also in the Coast Guard Reserves. We've talked a lot about our families; his parents are from Mexico, my ancestors are Cajun. We have a lot in common in a cultural sense.

I'm a fairly familiar face in the bank and as soon as I walked in, one of the assistants, a huge woman with a constant smile on her face, walked up to me.

"Good morning, Mr. Ludefance. How may we help you today?"

"Is Robert in?"

"Robert's at another branch today, but he'll be back tomorrow. I'll be happy to help you."

"I have some items that I'd like to put into my safety deposit box."

"Let me get the paper for you to sign and the key."

She walked away. After a few moments she returned, and I followed her to the vault. Opening the large, heavy door with her key, I signed the paperwork, she put her code into my box and left me to myself. I punched in my code and opened my box, adding all the items from my backpack. It was tight, but everything fit. I closed my box, came out, and the perky assistant relocked the door.

"Tell Robert I stopped by."

"Thank you for your business, and yes, I will tell him."

On the way back to the marina, I stopped at the post office for another mail hold, and then at Publix to pick up food for Emma. After feeding her, I packed my overnight bag with a change of clothes, grabbed my Mac laptop, my backpack, and locked up my floating home. I filled up my car just after turning north on 67, and then it was on to I-10 West. This was becoming all too familiar. 211 miles of four-lane highway, passing through Mobile, past Pascagoula, Biloxi, Gulfport, Pass Christian, Bay St. Louis, then turning south at Slidell and across Lake Pontchartrain into New Orleans proper. I probably could have driven it in my sleep.

Just before reaching my father's house, my cell phone rang.

"Ludicrous? Where are you?"

As soon as it was safe, I pulled off the road. With Hiker, I never knew how long the conversation would be.

"What's up Lawson?"

"I want you to come see me."

"Why? What's wrong?"

"Nothing's wrong. I just need to know where you were Monday afternoon."

"Monday afternoon? Let's see. I think I was driving around the outskirts of Atlanta."

"Atlanta? What the hell were you doing in Atlanta?"

"Hiker, why the hell do you need to know my whereabouts?"

"Deputy Tucker has filed a report about a car he was chasing east on Highway 88 and then north on 67. Said the driver looked like you and there was a woman passenger."

"Tucker was chasing me and a woman in my car?"

"Not your car. A beige Toyota."

"Well, sorry to disappoint. He's mistaken. Besides, I don't own a beige Toyota. You know I own a blue RX7. And, I was driving through Atlanta."

"I'll ask you again. What were you doing in Atlanta?" His voice had turned low, concerned, but not angry.

"A friend of mine was flying back to Vietnam and she asked me to give her a ride to Atlanta."

"Huh. You just happen to have a friend who was flying back to Vietnam and she hit you up for a ride to the airport in Atlanta. Somehow, I'm not convinced Swamp."

"I don't know what more to tell you. I'll give you her name and you can check with United Airlines. She bought a ticket to Ho Chi Mon City, Vietnam. Oh, yeah. I did loan her the money. $2400 to be exact."

"$2400? Who is she?"

"You keep repeating yourself, Lawson. She's a friend. That's all you have to know."

"I need proof pal. This is a serious charge against you."

"What's this about, Lawson?"

"There was a car chase in Pensacola Monday afternoon. One of the cars landed inside the T-Mobile near the airport. Thankfully, no one was injured. Then it picked up again in Santa Rosaria. Two deputies lost contact with the car on 67 North."

"And?"

"Do you know whose car landed inside the T-Mobile?"

"If I wasn't there, how could I possibly know?"

"Jonathan Holler's. And, you're trying to tell me you had nothing to do with that?"

"Look, Lawson. I'm in New Orleans right now. My Dad's in bad shape. When I get back to Santa Rosaria, I'll show you my parking ticket from Atlanta Hartsfield. I'll show you the mileage on my car. I'll show you the receipt for the $2400-dollar airline ticket. I'll even show you the hotel receipt from where I stopped to sleep on the way back. Does that satisfy you?"

"What's wrong with your Dad?"

"I told you he has Alzheimer's. He's bad off. My sister called me to come home. We're going to decide on a facility to place him. Look, I'm almost there. I'll come see you when I get back. That's all I can do."

"I'll count on that. Sorry to hear about your Dad."

Chapter 39

Twenty minutes later, I pulled into Dad's driveway. Deloris came out and greeted me.

"Margeaux called about Dad."

"I know, Jack. I'm just glad you're here. Your Dad's inside and Margeaux is on her way."

I walked into the living room, not sure what to expect.

"Hi, Dad. How're you doing?"

He stared at me. Just stared. He didn't recognize me. My own father didn't have any clue who I was. Thankfully Deloris walked in.

"Jacques has come to visit you, dear."

"Who's Jacques?"

"Dad, it's me. Your son, Jacques."

"I know who you are. What are you doing here?"

Did he know, or was he pretending he knew me? I sat down next to him and took his hand in mine.

"Dad, I heard you got lost the other day, I came to see if you're doing all right!"

"I'm fine. But, sometimes I'm afraid that I don't know where I am. How's Sarah doing?"

"Dad, Sarah and I are divorced." I come close and hugged him.

"Dad, you're going to be okay. We're going to take good care of you and you don't have to be afraid. I came home to arrange a place for you where you will be with other nice people. Someplace where someone will be with you all the time. Someplace where you can play cards. Margeaux and I and Deloris will come visit you."

He withdrew from my hug and didn't say anything. Had I said too much? I heard a car in the driveway and then Margeaux's voice.

"Hi, Jack. Hi, Dad."

She walked over, bent down, hugged and kissed Dad. He seemed to recognize her.

"Thanks for coming Jack. Why don't you and I go into the kitchen and talk?"

After settling at the kitchen table with fresh cups of coffee, I started.

"The first thing we need to do is go see Dad's doctor. See what stage Dad's in."

"We've already done that. Dr. Wiley told me that Dad is at the point that he needs full time care and professional help. Neither Deloris nor I can take care of him like that. He needs to be in a secure place, where there are people who know how to deal with this."

"I figured as much. One of those assisted living places. But, first we have to get a power of attorney so that you'll be able to handle his financial affairs. Since I'm not here, you're going to have to be the one. I'm sorry that's the way it has to be."

"I know. It's okay. I've started checking into a few places. Some are okay, some are not. I had no idea there'd be such a range. I do like one over on Brandon called, "Captain's Quarters." It's a beautiful place; modern, clean, with skilled attendants, and it's owned by a father and son rather than by some large conglomerate. But, it's $3200 a month. There are other places that are cheaper, but I don't like them. It's kind of a first impression thing."

"Dad's Social Security won't be enough."

"Not even close. But, don't forget his pension and investments. Added to his Social Security, I think it could work."

"First thing we should take care of is that power of attorney. I assume Dad has a living will somewhere? And, let me do some checking into facilities as well, before we commit to anything."

"Agreed."

We both walked back into the living room where Dad and Deloris were watching reruns of "Mash." Something familiar. For the moment, he looked content. But, I couldn't forget the look on his face from earlier. He understood enough to know we were arranging a place for him, and he was not happy with that. I realized I made a mistake to tell Dad that we are going to accommodate him elsewhere, and knew that going forward, I had to be very cautious in how much I told him.

I also realized it would be a task to remove Dad from this home he had lived in for so many years. The home where Margeaux and I grew up. The home he now shared with Deloris. I had to come up with something without alarming Dad more than he already was.

I spent the rest of the afternoon on my Mac laptop checking out all the places Margeaux had looked into. When I started my research into "Captain's Quarters," I dug deep. Deep enough to find it was surprising that they were still in business. Nice spit and polish on the outside, but, way back, over ten years ago, the father had been found guilty on some minor charges of elderly abuse. They may have been 'minor,' but there was no way I would put my Dad into that facility. I turned and looked over at Margeaux and Deloris talking in law voices.

"Margeaux, I'm going to disappoint you, but the place you liked? 'Captain's Quarters?' There's some very bad history."

She came over to me. I turned the Mac laptop for her to see the news article. I felt bad to disappoint her, but there had to be a better place. Another few hours of research and I found what I felt was a facility suited to

Dad with a perfectly clean history. I called and made an appointment for Margeaux and me to visit the next afternoon.

The next morning, before Margeaux and I visited the assisted living facility, I called Dad's lawyer and explained that Dad's Alzheimer's had progressed to the stage that it was necessary for Margeaux to have power of attorney to handle Dad's affairs. The lawyer said that we both needed to be present to sign the papers and was kind enough to fit us in later in the morning.

After we finished at the lawyers' office, we drove over to the assisted living center. It was a small facility, dedicated solely to Alzheimer's, with only a dozen rooms, and one spot left for Dad. It turned out to be one of those two-way interviews; they were checking us out as much as we were checking them out. We met with each member of the dedicated staff and were introduced to the residents, each one at various stages of this God-awful disease.

We signed all the necessary papers, paid a prorated fee for the coming two months, and agreed that Dad could move in the next day. It came at a cost of $3800 per month. With Dad's total monthly income of just over $4600, there was enough to take care of not only his assisted living, but also utilities at the house. Of course, Deloris would continue living there and, I hoped would be able take care of any additional expenses with her small income. If not, I intended to cover whatever she needed.

Our last stop was the bank, to present the power of attorney and have Margeaux sign papers so that she was cleared to manage Dad's finances. It was a long, exhausting, but productive day.

We both knew the hardest part was yet to come. Moving Dad.

The facilitator at the facility suggested using the "hurricane" excuse and explained what to tell Dad.

When we arrived home, thankfully dad was taking a nap. Perfect timing to explain our strategy to Deloris. Would it work? It was early December and we were officially out of hurricane season. Did Dad even know what month it was?

During dinner, we brought up the subject.

"Dad, we're going to have to evacuate. There's a bad hurricane brewing out in the Gulf, and we need to have you and Deloris move to a safer place."

"What hurricane?"

"Dad, remember Katrina? That kind of hurricane. We need to leave first thing in the morning."

He did not answer, just stared off into space. This was absolutely killing me. What I had to do to my Dad. Did he know what was really happening? If he did, would he forgive me?

Chapter 40

On Friday, after getting Dad settled, I said goodbye, hugged him tight, and told him I would be back to see him again very soon. But, I wondered if he would remember me the next time I came to visit. I couldn't think about that now. It was just too hard.

On my drive back to Santa Rosaria, I kept trying to think of ways to convince Lawson that I had been in Atlanta, and not a part of a car chase. Yes, I could show the receipts that I had been to Atlanta, but if he looked hard and saw the time stamp on the airport parking ticket, he'd know it was a ruse. I decided I would just present the ticket and hotel receipt and hope for the best.

It was after dark before I returned to my floating home. I left my roll-aboard, backpack and Mac laptop in my trunk, thinking I'd do my security check before bringing everything in. As I opened the salon door and turned on the lights, the first thing I noticed was that one of the throw pillows on the couch was now sitting on the floor. I knew I was messy, but that's not how I'd left it. I froze. What was happening?

I made myself move. On the rug was piece of green wire, not more than a quarter of an inch. As I bent down to pick it up, I saw another piece of yellow wire, even tinier. My heart stopped, then started to beat heavily. What else had been moved, or left, and why?

I walked down the stairs to the galley. Nothing was amiss. I checked both staterooms and heads, then double-checked every nook and cranny of my home. Everything was just as I had left it. I came back to the galley and opened the refrigerator to get a Samuel Adams. I always keep an extra rib-eye steak on the top shelf. Now, that steak was sitting on the second shelf.

No joke, genius. Someone has been in here.

I went back outside, turned on the flood light and saw that Emma was happily floating in her "Emma cage." It took a moment to register in my mind, but her 'alligator door' had been wedged shut.

Think, Jack, think!

I called Lawson's cell phone.

"Ludicrous, are you back?"

My words came out in gulps.

"Lawson. I just got back. I'm on my boat. Someone's been in here. Can you come down to the marina?"

"What the hell are you talking about Swamp?"

"Better yet, meet me up at Burger King. I'll tell you when I see you. I'm out of here."

"I'll be there in a few minutes."

I was taking the first sip of my coffee when Lawson showed up. He strode in and sat sown across from me. I showed him the two wires.

"Someone's been on my boat, Lawson."

"How can we be sure of that?"

"Where'd the wires come from? And, Lawson, I keep my steak on the top shelf of the refrigerator. It's now on the second shelf."

"Did you look around? Find anything else besides two little wires and your steak was moved? And, are you sure you didn't move it and just forget? Was there anything missing?"

"Yes, I looked around. And, no. Nothing was missing. Besides that, Emma's alligator door was wedged shut."

"Jack, I can't do something just because you think that someone might have been on your boat."

My mind did the leap.

"Lawson, I think someone may have planted a bomb in my boat."

"Okay. Let's start from the beginning. You walked in and you found two pieces of wire."

"No. I walked in and noticed one of the throw pillows on the floor. Then I saw the two pieces of wire. You tell me these are not the kind of wires that are used in C4 bombs? Then my steak had been moved. And, yeah, that's not a big deal, but still it was moved. I know how I arrange the inside of my refrigerator. And I certainly wouldn't wedge Emma's door shut."

"So, you're absolutely convinced that someone placed a bomb in your boat?"

"I'm rattled Lawson. I've got that same feeling I had when I did my first solo flight."

"A guy who wrestles with wild animals is now terrified."

"Hiker, this is not the time for sarcasm. And, yes, I'm terrified. I'm terrified because I know Holler's background is bomb making. Expert bomb making. He could well have placed a bomb in my boat."

"I hate it when you put ideas in my head, Swamp. What do you want me to do?"

"How the hell should I know? You're the sheriff now! Call the bomb squad or whoever you need to call. Just do something!"

"Jack, the entire northwest part of Florida only has one bomb squad unit and they're located in Bay County."

He looked at me again, pulled out his cell phone, and then changed his mind.

"I'd better call from the car."

He stood up and went out to his squad car. I noticed he was talking to someone, then hung up and made another call. He quickly walked back in.

"They'll be here in less than an hour, coming in by helicopter. I've instructed them to land on at the west end of the marina parking lot. Should be enough room. We need to get back. I've got to get that parking lot cleared out."

With that I followed Lawson back to the marina and parked my car in the parking lot at Bayside Restaurant, which, typically for a Saturday night, was crowded. I walked over to where Lawson was setting up his impromptu command post, coordinating the operation. Deputy Tucker gave me a look as I approached.

"We should inform the other boat owners." Tucker pulled out his cell phone and was ready to make some calls.

"Let's not alarm the people," Lawson barked. "I've called in our detectives and Pensacola detectives, just in case."

Very soon, several civilian cars screeched into the parking lot and what I presumed were detectives from Pensacola and Santa Rosaria got out. Lawson was giving everyone something to do. When the traffic on Highway 88 started to slow down, Lawson assigned deputies to position squad cars, lights blinking, to direct traffic in both directions. 11 pm and it looked like New Year's Eve.

I bit the bullet and approached Deputy Tucker.

"Look, Tucker. I know that you filed a report saying you saw me on Monday afternoon. I can assure you, it wasn't me. I was in Atlanta, and I have the receipts to give to Lawson."

"I saw what I saw."

"Tucker, would I lie to you? I know we've had issues in the past. I want to be friends not adversaries. It wasn't me you saw."

"Maybe, maybe not."

I walked away from him, all the while hoping that he wouldn't pursue this any further. I stopped in my tracks as I heard bombs go off in the distance. I quickly recovered, realizing it was one of the nearby military bases conducting their nighttime bombing practices. In this part of Florida, with three military bases close by and it's a normal occurrence. But, still, it made me think of my boat. Would I still have one come morning?

I recognized several of the other boat owners coming in and parking their cars in the parking lot, all with the intent of getting to their boats. I was the only permanent resident at the marina, but there were at least a half-dozen other boats moored there.

Who'd called them? Didn't matter. It's still a small town and news travels fast. They started arguing with Lawson when they found out he wouldn't let anyone down to the docks. He stationed a deputy to make sure no one got past.

Lawson walked over to me.

"Bomb squad's coming in."

Chapter 41

I heard the roar of the helicopter approaching, looked up and saw it circling above us, lights flashing. Whether it was military or a coast-guard aircraft, I couldn't distinguish. Finally, the bomb squad was here. Now we would know for sure.

The noise was deafening. Everyone was shouting over each other trying to communicate, while the crowd was increasing by the minute. Lawson waved the craft in and soon the helicopter was lowering down and finally sat in the parking lot. While the rotors were running, four individuals vacated the copter, two of the men had their diving suits on and carried their gear, including masks and fins. The other two men came out trying to unload their bomb detection gear. Lawson approached them, and they were all shouting at top of their lungs.

I literally ran up to Lawson. "I'll go down with them!"

"Stay back, Swamp. I'll take them down."

Lawson grabbed something that belonged to the squad and waved them on to follow him.

We all watched as the five men walked down the pier and stopped at my boat. While the two bomb detectors geared up, the divers disappeared into the water. They came back up very quickly, their heads bobbing above the water.

"Swamp! Come down here!"

I barely heard Lawson shouting above all the noise, but knew as quickly as the divers had come back up that they'd seen the cage and Emma.

As I neared my boat, one of the bomb squad members shouted, "You do know there's an alligator down there?"

"Yes, I know. I keep an alligator! Her name's Emma."

"Emma? Okay. We have an alligator named Emma. Is there any way to remove her?"

"I don't know. That would take at least two people. Probably animal control could do it, but it would take time to call them. To tell you the truth, at this particular moment, I'm not worried about Emma. Whatever happens, happens."

It sounded harsh to my own ears, but, at the moment, that's how I felt.

He shouted back to the divers, "There's nothing we can do to rescue the alligator. It's in a cage, so you're safe to go back down!"

With that, the two men dove back down again to inspect for any bombs attached to the underside of the boat. I timed it. Twenty long minutes before they came out and confirmed that everything was clear.

While all this going on, the other two men geared up with their armor, and began trudging along towards the boat. Lawson and I helped them to climb onboard.

"Okay! You guys step back to a safe distance!" One of the bomb experts shouted.

Lawson and I walked back up to the parking lot and were quickly absorbed by the crowd. The scene was not only chaotic, but in a strange, bizarre way, exciting. While the sheriff's deputies worked to keep the onlookers from getting on the pier, the squad cars were still parked on both sides of Highway 88, with their flashing lights on. The stroboscope lights flashed red, and blue, and the colors mixed together in the pitch-black background of the night, making it look like we were on top of an aircraft carrier with its night takeoff and landing lights, all at the same time.

We waited another good forty minutes. The only people near the boat were the two divers, and when the other two bomb squad members come out of the boat, the four men consulted each other. We couldn't hear anything they were saying, but one of the men signaled us to come down. Lawson and I started to walk towards them as the four men walked most of the way up to meet us.

"We've searched pretty much everywhere, and we haven't found anything. Except, there is one place left that we haven't yet checked, which we are going to do right now."

"Which place?" Lawson asked.

"The boat's gas tanks."

"I keep extra-large container with extra fuel."

"Okay. Good to know. Just in case, you guys move back out of the way."

Two men started back down to the boat, one to check the extra tank, the other to check the boat's gas tanks. But, before they could reach the boat, there was a deafening roar, and everything turned to daylight. The blast was so intense the two bomb squad men were thrown into the water. We saw pieces of debris reigning down everywhere.

The detonation made huge waves which shook the other boats up and down. A fire started in several of the boats and they were quickly consumed in white hot flames. Water waves come splashing into the Bayside Restaurant outside deck. There was debris, both big and small.

The entire marina area was covered with splintered boards; there were pieces of wood floating in the water, and most of all, there was the overpowering smell of sulfur and gasoline. Parts of the pier were missing, and what was left was now completely distorted, with one side slanted down, the other slanted side up.

The most obvious thing was, my boat, my home was no longer there.

I had no idea where Emma was. Probably she had become little pieces of food for the fish. Poor Emma. Another momentary pang of guilt. I watched as the two divers helped the other bomb squad guys out of water. I experienced a sense of relief, of sadness, and of anger all at the same time. Relieved because my instincts had been correct. This hadn't been a false alarm. If it had been, I could imagine the jokes Lawson would have been throwing at me.

I also felt relief because Holler had now tried twice, but hadn't yet been able to kill me. I believed now that he wouldn't succeed, because before he could, I would have him put behind bars.

Overwhelming sadness mixed with anger began to descend as I realized I was now homeless and Emma was gone.

When Lawson pulled out his phone and called both ATF and the FBI to the scene, I decided it was time to leave. I wasn't yet ready to talk to them.

"Hiker, I'm going to find a place to crash. You and everyone else can interview me tomorrow."

"Where are you going? You can't just leave the scene! Besides, you don't have any place to go. Come back to my house. You can sleep there."

"No. Absolutely not, Lawson. I'll find a hotel."

As I walked away, I heard Lawson yelling after me.

"Ludicrous! Come back! You'll stay with me!"

I turned back to him.

"Lawson, stop the interrogation. I'm not going to disappear. I'll see you tomorrow."

I left without turning back. Lawson didn't know it, but I did have some place to go.

Chapter 42

As I drove north on 67, the cabin was the only thing on my mind. In the blink of an eye, it had become my temporary home, my sanctuary. For now, I had no intention of letting Lawson know anything about it. I kept driving through the pitch-black night, not paying attention; yet, not wanting to think about anything. It dawned on me that the cabin turn-off shouldn't have been this far. I'd somehow missed the turn. This late at night there was little traffic, so I maneuvered a quick U-turn, heading back south towards Highway 88.

Once again, I missed the turn. I kept driving until I was nearly back to Highway 88. Pulling off the road, I realized my hands were shaking. Taking a deep breath, I tried to calm myself. Delayed reaction? No doubt. Turning around, I willed myself to keep to the speed limit and pay attention to the landmarks.

This time I noticed the outline of the tall pine tree and right after, the oddly shaped oak tree that indicated the turn off to the side road that would lead to the dirt road and the cabin. I turned on the bright headlights. It seemed both weird and spooky driving through the dark forested land. Everything seemed enlarged and grotesquely out of shape.

Finally, the cabin appeared in my headlights and I breathed a sigh of relief as I drove around to the front of the cabin facing the lake and parked my car. I turned off the engine but kept the headlights on. My first priority was to check on the rental car. Yes, it was still there. Returning to my car, I turned off the headlights, locked the door and walked up the stairs to the door. Now, I couldn't find the key to get in. Where was it? I searched my pockets, but nothing. I thought I'd brought it with me. Was I really that rattled?

I made myself stop and think. Had I taken it with me? Or had I left it in a secure hiding place. After some searching, I found it, and remembered I'd put it there myself. Opening the front door, I switched on the lights, illuminating the large open living space. Being a creature of habit, I checked every inch of the cabin. Nothing suspicious, so I went back out to my car and retrieved my backpack, Mac laptop, and roll-aboard, dropping them on the sofa. I walked into the kitchen to get a cold beer. Opening the refrigerator, I pulled a bottle of Samuel Adams out, then put it back.

Sleep. I needed some sleep and to try and forget. Forget everything. Crashing on the bed, I didn't even take the time to pull off my shoes. A restless sleep and strange dreams quickly ensued. Dreams of being on the bridge with Holler...grabbing for his gun before he tried to shoot me...Lila lying dead on the concrete...Lawson making jokes about me and how all the young girls die around me...Holler grabbing my feet and pulling me, preventing me from reaching his gun...being inside Holler's estate and the dogs grabbing my feet and pulling me down, their teeth barred.

I woke up with a start and found that my right foot had fallen asleep. Pressing the button on my cell phone, I read the illuminated numerals - 4:36 am. I pulled off my shoes, stripped naked, and crawled under the covers. More dreams of the bomb exploding and the dark sky lighting up like day...Emma floating among the debris... her skin taking on the same color as the splintered wood and which wasn't visible to anyone but me...only I could distinguish between Emma's skin and the wood pieces...shouting that she was still alive...Lawson arguing that there was no Emma...telling me that I was hallucinating...that what I was seeing was the armor of the bomb squad men and one was dead...I had killed him because of my sloppiness.

The next time I woke, it was 7:23 am. Rushing to the bathroom, I emptied my bladder, than washed my hands and face. With those priorities out of the way, my next mission was to fill my growling stomach. Still naked, I walked into the kitchen to find something to eat. Looking inside the refrigerator, my mind did a Deja vu to the boat, and my steak being rearranged. But, everything was just as I'd left it. I willed my mind to accept the fact that I was here in the cabin. For the moment I was safe.

While the coffee was brewing, I toasted sourdough bread, fried a half-dozen slices of bacon, and cooked three eggs in the bacon juice. As I literally gobbled down my breakfast, I tried to analyze my jumbled dreams. Arm chair psychology 101 – dreaming Lila was dead meant she was out of my reach, as well as Holler's. Dreaming that both Holler and his dogs were pulling on my feet meant that he was still going to try and kill me.

After a hot shower, I put on one of the thick Turkish bathrobes and sat down with another cup of coffee. What do I do next?

My cell phone rang, indicating an unknown number. I debated whether to answer or let it go to voice. Curiosity got the better of me.

"Jack Ludefance."

"This is special agent Johnson with the FBI. I'd like to meet with you and go over the preliminaries of what happened last night."

"Excuse me?"

"You are Jacques Ludefance, right?"

"Yes, I am. How'd you get my number?"

"Come on, now. I'm and FBI agent. You think that's difficult for us? For your curiosity Sheriff Lawson gave me your number."

"I don't know. I don't want to talk to you until I see my lawyer."

"That's fine. But this is how it works. First, we need to briefly go over the preliminaries at the scene. Then, yes, you'll need to consult with a lawyer and come in to make a formal statement and be interviewed under oath. Sheriff Lawson informed us you're investigating Jonathan Holler. This adds to the complexity of the situation."

"It certainly does."

"So, as I said, we'd like to set up a meeting at the marina."

"There's nothing left to see."

"Come on, Ludefance. You're a PI. You know there's plenty to see."

"When do you want to meet?"

"How about this morning at 11?"

"11? This morning?"

"11 this morning, Mr. Ludefance."

"I'd like to have Sheriff Lawson there as well."

"I'll call him and make sure he is."

I immediately called Lawson.

"Ludicrous? How are you? And, where the hell are you?"

How many times have I heard that?

"I've got a place to stay, Lawson. I'm okay for the moment. I just got a call from the FBI. An Agent Johnson wants to meet with me this morning at the marina for preliminaries. I asked him if you could be there, too. Hope you don't mind."

"That's a stupid question. Of course, I'll be there. I may be the sheriff, but, I'm also your friend, remember?"

"I don't want them to trick me into something I don't want to admit."

"I told them last night about your investigating Holler. You can't avoid it much longer. Maybe not today, but in an official interview, things are gonna come up."

"I know. Johnson told me."

"You need to get a lawyer, Jack."

"Yeah, I'm well aware of that fact. I'll add it to my list."

Pulling into the marina just before 11 am, I noticed everything had been cordoned off with yellow crime scene tape, and Lawson was standing in the parking lot talking with who I presumed to be agent Johnson.

As I approached he held out his hand and shook mine.

"Agent Johnson, Mr. Ludefance."

I did a quick appraisal, beginning with the vice-like grip of his handshake. He was tall and skinny, dressed in a pin-stripe suit. His face was rough and pitted with acne scars. His nose was long and aquiline in shape, with the usual prominent bridge, giving the appearance of being slightly bent. When he smiled his insincere smile at me, his nose drooped down and met his lips which barely covered a full set of teeth. He'd combed his hair straight back, revealing a small, nasty scar over his sunken right eye. As he spoke, he articulated his words with clear enunciation.

"Okay, Mr. Ludefance. I'll reiterate, this is just a preliminary meeting regarding the bombing of your boat. Since we can't walk down the docks, we'll do our best from here. Now, your boat was in which spot?"

It was a stupid question. It was obvious where my boat had been. All the other boats around it were either splintered or had fire damage.

"The large empty spot."

"Start from the beginning as you walked onboard."

"I walked into the salon and first noticed one of the sofa pillows laying on the floor. That's not how I'd left it. Then I saw a tiny fragment of green wire on the carpet. As I bent down to pick it up, I noticed another even smaller fragment of yellow wire. I picked that one up, too. I then checked every inch of the boat, but didn't find anything else amiss, until I opened my refrigerator door. I usually keep my steak on the top shelf, but it had been moved to the second shelf. Obviously, someone had been on my boat. Because of the case I've been working on, my mind went into overdrive and I suspected someone had planted a bomb in my boat. I called Sheriff Lawson."

"You called Sheriff Lawson."

Already frustrated with his demeanor, I couldn't help myself.

"Yes. I. Called. Sheriff. Lawson. Who else would I have called?"

"But, you called the sheriff on his personal phone, rather than calling the sheriff's department? Why?"

"Sheriff Lawson and I go way back. We served in the navy together. We had each other's backs then, and we still operate under that same scenario."

"Fair enough. Then what happened?"

"Lawson met me up at Burger King. I explained what I'd found, and what I suspected. He called the bomb squad. You know the rest."

"Sheriff Lawson has informed me that you've been investigating Jonathan Holler and that you suspect him of planting the bomb. Correct?"

"Spot on."

"One last question. Where were you prior to the bomb explosion?"

"I'd been in New Orleans, visiting with my father."

"I see. Father's address?"

I gave him what he needed, and knew, just from this short exchange, that the formal interview was going to be a real bitch. He ceremoniously excused me with the admonition to not talk to the press, and that he would get back to me with the date and time of my 'formal interview.

Chapter 43

Returning to the cabin, I did a walk around outside for a stretch and some fresh air. It was gloomy and overcast, but not yet raining. Walking down to the dock, I stood staring out. Anything to avoid what was to come.

Back inside, I checked e-mails, and turned on the local news. The explosion at the marina was the lead story. I cringed when the newscaster mentioned my name. He went on to report that I was an ex-navy pilot living aboard when my boat was bombed. Both the ATF and FBI have been called in. Believing that the bomb was a professional job, they were concentrating on ex-military people and my enemies. He ended the segment with the fact that I had kept a live alligator on board and locals referred to me as Alligator man.

Good God. Now the entire world knows. My cell phone rang. The display read, 'Debra Hendrix.' I wasn't prepared to talk to her but decided to pick up.

"Jack? It's Debra Hendrix. I heard the terrible news that your boat exploded. Are you okay?"

"Thanks, Debra. Can't say that I really am okay. I was just lucky to escape. Got suspicious and called Sheriff Lawson. My suspicion paid off. I'm alive, but my boat is gone."

"My God, Jack. Judges do live under threats, too. But, a bomb would scare the hell out of me if it ever happened. I don't know if I'd have the intuition to call the police. I'm just glad you're alive and well."

"Alive, but shaken, and, not looking forward to an interview with the FBI."

"FBI? Yes, why of course they'd want to speak with you. I'm sure it's nothing more than a formality. Do you have a lawyer? I can suggest someone if you'd like."

"Thanks. I'll let you know if I need a name. So, Debra, you're not mad at me anymore?"

"No. I'm not mad at you. It was just as much my fault to lead you on. Besides, in my book, a man who thinks of sending nice flowers has to be a romantic at heart. And, I did enjoy the flowers Jack."

"You're welcome."

"We'll get together sometime after all these unpleasant things settle down."

"Thank you."

"You take care. And if there's anything I can be of help with, don't hesitate ask."

"Thanks for the offer, but I'll be fine."

Fine? I wondered if I would ever be 'fine' again. I was homeless and still being hunted. Both were daunting circumstances to contemplate.

I thought about taking a long bath in the Jacuzzi. I needed to relax and to contemplate. To try and put the pieces together and to stay alive. Holler was a professional, and I needed to be extra, extra careful.

I turned the water and the jets on full blast, making waterfall sounds, and added some liquid soap. I needed to relax and think. Getting my gun and a can of Samuel Adams, I placed both beside me and laid back in the hot, soapy water.

The water felt good, but deep down inside I was still shaking. I slowly went through my mind and played back the video as to how things had unfolded during the last a few days. I thought about the exchange on the bridge with Holler. He could have killed me right then and there. Perhaps he didn't want to attract the police. A dead body on the Santa Rosaria Bridge would certainly have that effect. Besides, with his big belly, he was totally out of shape to handle any kind of a fight.

I'd been lucky to hit his hand and separate him and his gun. I still didn't have any idea whether he wanted to kill Lila, or was it simply his sloppiness that saved her life? It was obvious that Lila was convinced that Holler was going to kill her. Once again, her street-smart instincts had saved her life. I felt good giving her the money to go back to Vietnam.

I came full circle back to me and Holler, knowing he wasn't going to stop until he killed me. I'm sure he had all kinds of plans for me. It might be him personally, or it could be one of his goons, or totally someone outside of his immediate circle. People like Holler have unlimited funds and friends who are willing to do anything for that money.

For me, giving all the information to the FBI was a good start. But, was it enough to bust Holler and shut down his operation? For me, the sooner Holler got taken out, the better. Preferably before he took out a contract on my life.

My eyes began to close, and I must have fallen asleep. I woke with a start, fear filling me again. I had to be alert at all times. What a life to have to stay constantly looking over my shoulder. But, for the moment, Holler had no idea where I was. I briefly thought of calling Lawson back and telling him where I was but decided against it.

An hour later, I drained the Jacuzzi, dried off and made a fresh pot of coffee. I didn't bother to dress. The cabin was warm, and I was by my lonesome. After a bagel filled with pastrami and cheese, some chips and pickles, I opened my Mac laptop to look for an attorney.

I thought about Debra's offer, but decided against it. I'd rather find someone on my own. I picked one name but couldn't make out what nationality he was. Not that it mattered. I just needed a sharp lawyer. Curious, I dug deeper into the background of Andronikashvili

Dolaberitze. Turned out to be Georgian. I didn't like the name but didn't really care where he came from.

The important thing was that he had good, solid reviews. I read some articles covering the several famous cases he'd had over the years. His office was over in Pensacola and he also worked alone, which was good. He couldn't pass me off to some other junior lawyer.

I also assumed he wouldn't come cheap. I still had most of the hundred-grand from Holler and the twenty-grand from Lillian. What I needed was strong representation in my interview with the Feds. And, God forbid, anything that might follow. At this point, money didn't matter. So, **Andronikashvili Dolaberitze it was.** I made a mental note to call him first thing Monday morning.

The gloomy late afternoon light turned into a dark, overcast night. After watching the local news at 10 pm, and not hearing anything new on the case, I threw on a pair of jeans and sweatshirt, grabbed my flashlight, and went outside to check on the cars. It seemed strange to say I felt safe here in the middle of the forest. The rain had stopped, and all around me I breathed in that rich, earthy smell.

Walking down to the dock, I sat and listened to the sounds of the wilderness around me. From behind, I could hear the wings of the insects. Attracted to the light from the cabin, they made a faint plunking sound as they hit the windows. The frogs began their chorus of croaking, and there were noises I didn't recognize.

I listened, and just for a while, I forget about Holler. Forgot about everything. Refreshed, I walked back up to the cabin, and shut and locked the doors.

After tossing and turning for over an hour, I gave in and took three Melatonin. It helped take the edge off and the next thing I knew it was 6 am. Completing my morning ritual of a shower, shave and breakfast, I settled in with another cup of coffee.

    I had one day before I called to make an appointment with Dolaberitze. After powering up my Mac, I opened Pages. Might as well put my new-found knowledge from the computer class to work. Even though I knew I had every detail memorized, I began an outline, starting from the beginning of my encounter with Lillian Holler at Bayside Restaurant.

Chapter 44

Monday morning I waited until just after 9 to make the call.

"Good morning. Andronikashvili Dolaberitze's office."

In just those few words, I could both hear and feel the haughtiness oozing from the woman's voice.

"Good morning. My name is Jacques Ludefance. I'd like to make an appointment to see Mr. Dolaberitze as soon as possible."

"Are you an existing client?"

"No."

"Mr. Dolaberitze isn't currently taking any new clients."

"He'll take me."

"Excuse me? And, why would that be?"

"You heard about a boat being blown up in Santa Rosaria?"

"Yes, of course."

"It was my boat."

The silence was deafening. I could just imagine the wheels turning in her head. She cleared her throat.

"I'll check with Mr. Dolaberitze."

I heard the click as she put me on hold. Soft classical music filled the space. I timed it. Ten minutes later she came back on the line. She tried to soften the smugness but didn't do a very good job.

"Mr. Ludefance, I'll connect you to Mr. Dolaberitze now."

"Thank you."

The phone clicked, there was a momentary pause, and then I heard Dolaberitze's booming voice.

"Mr. Ludefance. I hear you have a bit of a problem. How is it that I can assist you?"

"I'm going to be interviewed by the FBI regarding the circumstances surrounding the bombing of my boat. I need a competent attorney to advise me."

"I see. Thank you for having confidence in me, but you don't need a firm like mine to represent you. Besides, my fees are rather on the high side."

"I'm sure they are. But, I need a good lawyer. This is a complicated situation."

"Any time the FBI is involved, it's a complicated situation, Mr. Ludefance. My fees are $500 per hour."

"That's fine."

There was a moment's hesitation.

"Very well. This call will not be counted, but any office consultation will be. Are we clear?'

"Perfectly."

"Give me a quick background."

"I'm a PI and I've been investigating a case involving a high profile, local businessman and his operation. I have quite a bit of information and evidence including photographs, paperwork and tape recordings, which I plan on turning over to the FBI. It's my conclusion that my boat was blown up in retaliation for my investigation."

"Who's the subject of your investigation?"

"Jonathan Holler."

He could barely hide the surprise in his voice.

"*The* Jonathan Holler?"

"Yes."

"Let me speak with my secretary and see what we can arrange."

There was another long wait and more classical music. I could only imagine what they were discussing.

The phone clicked back in, and the woman came back on the line, her voice not quite as haughty.

"Mr. Ludefance. Thank you for waiting. Would this afternoon at 4:30 be convenient for you?"

"That would be fine."

Mission accomplished.

My next stop was the bank. I needed money to cover the lawyer's expenses for this afternoon's meeting. I intended to be a 'pay as you go' client. I was relieved that Robert was in and assisted me with my safety-deposit box. I took out all the papers and photos, as well as the tapes I'd made of Lila. I counted out $5000 and separated it into smaller wads.

Thankfully, Robert was understanding and didn't ask any questions about my boat. He wished me luck as I finished up, but, I knew I was going to need more than 'luck' to come out of this in one piece.

Chapter 45

Dolaberitze's office was located in a well-kept high-rise in downtown Pensacola. After parking my car in the covered parking structure belonging to the building, I retrieved my backpack and my Mac laptop, found the elevators, and pushed the button for the 10th floor.

The elevator door opened directly into Dolaberitze's offices. I was immediately impressed, both with the subdued elegance of the space, and with the receptionist who greeted me. She reminded me of Lila. Late 20's, Asian, with the same flawless skin, large eyes, and a round nose that suited her beautiful face. Her full lips and colorless gloss lipstick only enhanced her sexiness. Perfect white diamond earrings adorned both ears. She swung her hair to one side of her neck as she looked up at me.

"Good afternoon, sir. May I help you?"

"My name is Jacques Ludefance and I have a 4:30 appointment with Mr. Dolaberitze."

"If you'll just sign the check-in sheet, and have a seat, I'll call his secretary."

Her voice was polished and not in the least bit haughty. This definitely wasn't the woman I'd talked to on the phone when I'd called to make an appointment. Her practiced smile showed off her perfect white teeth. But, behind it was something more, perhaps a bit of a welcoming invitation?

I signed my name, took a seat, and wondered how long Mr. Dolaberitze would keep me waiting. I was more than surprised when not long after, an older woman came down the hallway and approached me. I recognized the haughty voice from my previous call.

"Mr. Ludefance? I'm Dina, Mr. Dolaberitze's secretary. We spoke on the phone when you called to make an appointment. If you'll follow me?"

Gathering up my Mac laptop and backpack, I followed her down to the end of the long hallway and into a formal interview room, complete with a highly polished mahogany table, and several ornate chairs upholstered in fine leather. On one wall was a large mahogany buffet, compete with both a coffee and tea service in polished silver, expensive china cups, along with a silver carafe of ice-water and crystal tumblers. On the opposite wall stood a large bookcase, filled with leather-bound law books, framed diplomas, and a framed photograph of Dolaberitze in a courtroom arguing in front of an imposing judge.

Mr. Dolaberitze, who was sitting at the head of the table, stood as I entered the room, and extended his hand to me. Behind where he stood, a large floor to ceiling window looked out at the Pensacola Bay Bridge. Impressive, to say the least. So, this is what $500 an hour could buy.

"Mr. Ludefance."

"Mr. Dolaberitze. Thank you for taking the time to see me."

First impressions? He was a giant of a man. At least several inches taller than me, he gave the presence of both an imposing and intimidating person, not only in size, but in his tone of voice. I immediately surmised him to be a cultured man, both polished and aristocratic in manners. His thick, black mustache fully covered his upper lip, and matched his dark, bushy eyebrows and dark eyes. His high cheek bones and long face reminded me of a Caucuses prince of Georgia.

"Please, have a seat."

I settled myself opposite him, placed my Mac laptop on the table, and opened Pages to my notes.

His ever-efficient secretary spoke up.

"Do you need me to stay, Mr. Dolaberitze?"

"Mr. Ludefance, would you care for coffee or tea?'

"Coffee with cream, please."

She poured from the silver coffee urn, adding just the right amount of cream, and set it in front of me.

"That will be all, Dina."

She quietly left the room and closed the door.

"Now, Mr. Ludefance, before we begin, I'll reiterate that everything we discuss will be confidential and stay strictly between us. I'm a firm believer and respect lawyer-client privilege. I also record all interviews. Is that going to be a problem for you?"

"Not at all."

Speaking in a clear, articulate voice, he clicked on the recorder.

"December 11th interview with a new client, Jacques Ludefance, in preparation for his upcoming interview with the FBI. Mr. Ludefance, if you'll introduce yourself and give a brief background."

"My name is Jacques Ludefance. I'm 44, divorced, a retired naval pilot and my current occupation is private investigator in Santa Rosaria, Florida."

"Address?"

"I don't have one."

"Of course, of course. We'll come back to that. Now, if you'll start from the beginning. And, don't hold back. I need to know everything that happened and everything you did, even if it was unlawful. I need to know in order to prepare for your upcoming interview."

Unlawful? What did he already know? I closed my eyes and remembered as if it was yesterday.

"I was having an after-dinner beer on the outside deck of Bayside Restaurant in Santa Rosaria. An Asian woman, carrying a brown envelope in her hand, sat down heavily next to me. She pushed the envelope towards me and in a barely audible voice said, 'Can you help me, Mr. Ludef...' Before she could finish, she fell off the stool and lay dead on the wooden deck."

I opened my eyes, looked up at Dolaberitze and knew I had his undivided attention. His mouth was open in utter surprise and he was staring straight at me. Guess this was a first for him. He closed his mouth and cleared his throat.

"Go on."

"The bartender came around and checked her pulse and shook his head. Before calling the sheriff's department, I folded and slipped the envelope into my jacket pocket and took some pictures of her with my cell phone."

"And the woman?"

"Was later identified as Lillian Holler. Jonathan Holler's wife."

"Did you turn the envelope over to the sheriff's department?"

"No, I didn't."

"Why not?"

"Because, I'm a PI. Obviously, she sought me out and wanted me to investigate something."

"What was in the envelope?"

Opening my backpack, I took out the infamous brown envelope and unceremoniously slid it down the table to Dolaberitze.

"You'll find the Hollers' marriage certificate, birth certificates for their two sons, off-shore bank accounts, and a photo of a dead girl with her throat slit and an unidentified man, who I now know is Jonathan Holler, standing over her body. The only item missing is twenty-grand. It's in a safety-deposit box at Wells Fargo. It's my conclusion that it was payment to investigate her husband, Jonathan Holler."

Dolaberitze clicked off the recorder and picked up the envelope. He carefully examined each item, then placed everything back into the envelope, and clicked the recorder back on.

"Continue."

"Lillian Holler supposedly died of natural causes. The sheriff's department had nothing to investigate, but I did."

"What do you mean by, 'supposedly died of natural causes?'"

"I'll explain when I come to that part."

Clearly frustrated, he waved me to continue.

"I started to investigate Holler, to stalk him without his knowledge. I wanted to find out everything he was involved in, both legitimate and illegal. And, there was plenty. A friend of mine works at the Pentagon and he sent me what was on record."

I stopped again, pulled out all the e-mails from Colonel Scott and slid them down to Dolaberitze. He clicked off the recorder and took his time reading each e-mail, shaking his head as he flipped pages.

"You didn't think this was enough to take to the Feds?'

"That was all past history. Let's just say, I have a very inquisitive mind and I wanted to know what he was currently up to."

"Undoubtedly. Go on." He clicked the recorder back on.

"My next step was to plant someone in Holler Enterprises and find out what he was exporting and importing. I persuaded a friend of mine, Katy Ozener, to apply for a job in shipping-handling department. We beefed up her resume, and she was hired."

"Explain."

"Katy had a mere five months of an experience as a shipping clerk. So, we added a few years, and I gave myself as her former boss, listing a fake name, company and telephone number."

"First minor offense, Mr. Ludefance. Falsifying employment records."

"Right. Anyway, Katy was caught taking pictures of the invoices. Cutting to the chase, Katy texted me those invoices. Holler's company, which supposedly exports used machinery to Southeast Asia, is, in reality, exporting parts to C130 aircraft."

I pulled out the copies of the invoices and slid them down to Dolaberitze. Off went the recorder. His pile of evidence was getting thicker. The recorder clicked back on.

"You have evidence here that Holler is exporting parts to C130 aircraft, and you still didn't go to the FBI?"

"I wanted to know what he's importing."

"Continue."

"Katy was scared and wanted to quit, but I persuaded her to stay on, and help me in one more job."

"Which was?"

"I wanted to get inside Holler's estate located behind Holler Enterprises and find out what else was going on. I bought two walkie-talkies and had Katy stand guard outside and keep in radio contact while I was inside. If I was to get caught, I'd instructed her to call Sheriff Lawson at the Santa Rosaria Sheriff's Department."

"First felony offense. Breaking and entering. So, what did you discover, Mr. Ludefance?"

"A large warehouse filled with illegal drugs from China and a stash of stored weapons, along with a studio set up for filming porno movies. I took pictures of everything I could and got out of there when two Dobermans started chasing me."

"Slide the pictures down, Mr. Ludefance."

He clicked off the recorder and took his time looking over all the photos. I think even he was shocked by what the photos showed. He clicked the recorder back on.

"Please continue with your next escapade."

"As you've seen there, Colonel Scott sent me the names of two of Holler's buddies during his military years. I decided to pay each man a visit and see if they had any further information on Holler. I called Katy to boat-sit for me and I first flew to Los Angeles to see if I could meet with Kevin Bradford. He now owns his own company making aluminum for aircraft. Bradford's impression of Holler wasn't of the highest caliber and he was surprised to hear that Holler had his own business. It was always his thought that Holler wasn't cut out to be a business man, but rather a bodyguard to some businessman. Then, I flew to Dallas to interview DeAngelo Gonzales. Mr. Gonzales was not as cooperative as Mr. Bradford. Some kind of trouble with the IRS. But, I have ways of extracting information."

"And, just how is that?"

"I invited him to a local restaurant that happened to be his own. Got him drunk, basically kidnapped him and pressured him to talk."

"Pressured him how?"

"In my motel room, using hot water, cold water."

"Second felony- kidnapping and torture. Did he disclose anything useful?"

"He did. Holler and Gonzales worked together during the Bosnia conflict. Evidently Holler and some Serbian guy worked together to get passports for young girls and bring them into the US. Once here, they would hold the passports. They kept the girls in a secluded ranch house somewhere in Texas and made porno movies. Holler ended up serving five years, which corroborated what Colonel Scott had sent me."

"Good God. I'm a seasoned lawyer, but I can honestly say I don't know if I even want to hear what happened next."

"You probably don't, but I'm the one paying you a hefty fee."

Chapter 46

"Let's take a break, Mr. Ludefance. I'm sure we both could use a little time. I won't even charge you for it."

He called Dina and asked her to have some sandwiches delivered. I was relieved to have the time and some breathing space. All too soon, it was back to business. The recorder clicked back on.

"Let's continue, Mr. Ludefance."

"When I returned from Dallas, Katy was gone. To make a long story short, her body was found floating by the Santa Rosaria Bridge. Holler's goons had gotten to her while I was gone."

"I'm sorry to hear that. And, you presume it was Holler's goons? Do you have proof?"

"No. It just makes logical sense. Get Katy out of the way and scare me off in the process."

"I'll assume the sheriff's department interviewed you?"

"Yes. A Detective Harvey Langi. He kept harping on my relationship with Katy. So, I told him about doctoring Katy's resume, helping her get the job at Holler Enterprises, and her copying the invoices. He wanted to know why, and I admitted I was investigating Holler and his dirty business. When I told him about the invoices for military parts being shipped to Southeast Asia, he had the same reaction you did. Why didn't I go to the FBI? Told him the same thing, I told you. I wasn't ready to."

"Mr. Ludefance, let's be perfectly frank. If Holler is as dirty as he appears to be, your actions with Katy resulted in her murder. Yet, you continued on. You must realize that your living on the edge has led to dire results."

What could I say? I was still grappling with the guilt. I couldn't look him straight in the eye.

"Yes, I'm responsible for her death. And, no, I'll probably never be able to clear my conscience. Yes, I...I wanted more. I wanted it all before I took everything to the Feds."

"What did you do next?"

"After Katy's funeral, I wanted to find out more about Lillian Holler. I know her husband owns most of the massage salons along the Panhandle. It didn't take long to find a masseuse who had known her. Sofia, who's a Vietnamese national, set up a meeting with one of the cooks that works on the Holler estate. The cook identified the dead girl in the picture as Lillian's cousin, Duyen and that it was Jonathan Holler standing over her body. She also told Sofia that there were two other bodies buried on the estate."

"So, we know the identity of the dead girl in the picture as well as her murderer. Three murders, total."

"Yes. Also, through Sofia, I was introduced to another girl, Lila, who operated one of Holler's massage salons. In reality, she is nothing more than a high-priced whore. In order to get her to reveal more information, I was ready to pay her $2000 to go out with me, hoping to learn more about Lillian, but also about Holler's operation. For my stupidity, I was rewarded with being drugged, beaten and left in a swamp. Through a burn phone I'd hidden in my pants pocket, I was able to call Sheriff Lawson. He found me through GPS. I took me over a month to recuperate."

"You didn't press charges?"

"No. I didn't want it to become public knowledge. Only Sheriff Lawson, his wife, and Deputy Tucker know about the incident. Instead, I planned a most interesting revenge. I kidnapped Lila, took her to a rented cabin up near Blue Water River and used the same method I had used on Gonzales. I recorded everything she confessed to me. Including the fact that she had given Lillian Holler an undetectable drug which caused her internal bleeding and death."

I pulled my last piece of evidence, the tape of Lila's confession, out of my backpack. Dolaberitze didn't bother to turn the recorder off.

"Third felony offense- kidnapping and torture. On the other side, first-degree murder of Lillian Holler. I'm sure there's more?"

"Right. I called Holler, told him I had a valuable piece of merchandise that belonged to him, and that I would exchange it for two hundred-grand. We exchanged the money on Santa Rosaria Bridge. During the exchange, Holler tried to shoot Lila. I shot back, knocking his gun into the water and managed to escape with the money and Lila. During our getaway, we became involved in a police chase through Pensacola and back through Santa Rosaria."

Dolaberitze held up his hand.

"That was you? Let's add a few more felonies, why don't we. Where is this Lila now?"

"I drove her to Atlanta and bought her a one-way ticket back to Vietnam."

"At least we have her testimony on record. I assume your boat being blown up is next?"

I took a few moments to gather my thoughts. I didn't want to bring my dad into this, but he was my alibi.

"I was in New Orleans for a few days. My father has Alzheimer's. My sister and I felt it was time to place him. When I returned, I found things disturbed and the tiny pieces of wire. Suspicious, I called Sheriff Lawson and convinced him that Holler had planted a bomb on my boat. It was his call to contact the bomb squad. They flew in by helicopter from Bay County and did a complete check of everything except the gas tanks. As they were about to make that check, the bomb detonated, taking my boat with it."

"Anything else?"

"Other than I'm homeless, and have committed multiple felonies?"

That elicited the first smile I'd seen on his face. But, it quickly disappeared.

"Here's the tricky thing, Mr. Ludefance. It's my educated opinion that FBI already suspects you of planting the bomb. Doesn't matter that you were in New Orleans. Doesn't matter that you think it was Holler. What matters is how well we present all this overwhelming evidence to them. We need to convince them that the bombing was revenge for your investigating and trying to expose Holler. I want to schedule another meeting, to go over exactly what you can and cannot say during that interview. I assume the FBI hasn't scheduled it yet?"

"No, not yet."

"I need some time to digest everything you've given me tonight. As soon as you have a scheduled date, call and make an appointment. As far as payment for my services, we'll settle when this is all over."

"Of course. Thank you."

It was after midnight when I finally left. Eight hours of nonstop remembering. Eight hours at $500 a pop.

Chapter 47

Agent Johnson called the following week advising me my formal interview was scheduled for December 27th. Nothing like mixing all of this up with the holidays. Guess it's true. They never rest until their man is caught. I had every intention of making sure it wasn't me.

At ten o'clock Friday morning the 22nd of December, I was at standing in front of Dolaberitze's receptionist. God, she looked so much like Lila. That same flawless skin, large eyes, round nose, and sexy lips. The same perfectly matched white diamonds sparkling in her ears. Today she had parted her hair in the center, half pulled to one side, half pulled to the other. She looked up at me with her welcoming, inviting smile.

"Mr. Ludefance? How is your day going?"

"It's going as well as can be expected, thanks."

In the space of a second, my mind raced over the obvious sexual innuendos she was giving off. Her beauty reminded me of Lila, but she wasn't Lila. She wasn't an escort girl. Somehow, though, thinking of her as Lila got everything all mixed up in my mind. I was beginning to think I must have some kind of a fixation with Asian women. She snapped me out of my thoughts.

"Mr. Ludefance? Mr. Dolaberitze is in his office waiting for you. It's the second door on the left."

I walked down the hall and entered his office, just as opulent as the meeting room we had been in during my first meeting with him. Dolaberitze was standing behind his mahogany desk talking on the phone and indicated for me to sit down. The man is truly a giant and, with his imposing personality, there's no way I'd want to ever be cross-examined by him. He finished his conversation, reached across the desk, and shook my hand. He sat in his chair, leaned back and looked me straight in the eye.

"I've made notes as to what you should reveal in your testimony to the FBI and what needs to be left off the table. Generally, what happens is you'll be asked to give an opening statement of the events as they happened. Then, come the questions. The purpose of which is to tear apart everything you've just told them. They're going to try and catch you in either a lie or contradicting yourself. So, it's of great importance to stick to what areas I've Okayed."

"I'm listening."

"To the FBI everyone is guilty of something. Your job is to take the spotlight off yourself and put it squarely on Jonathan Holler, where it clearly belongs. So, with that, let's begin. Of course, you'll start with your initial meeting with Lillian Holler, including the envelope and all its contents, and your reasoning of why she came to you and why you began your investigation into Jonathan Holler.

"I don't want you to mention anything about your friend who works in the Pentagon, and the information he e-mailed you. Same goes for Bradford and Gonzales. No need to mention you met with either man. What information they gave you only corroborates what Colonel Scott sent you. As you said, that's all past history, and you need to concentrate on all the evidence you discovered about what he's currently involved in.

"I'm not happy about it, but since you were interviewed by Detective Langi, you're going to have to tell them everything about Katy."

"I was afraid of that. So, that includes breaking into Holler's estate."

"Yes. We're going to balance that with the photo evidence of that you found. Illicit drugs, a stock-pile of military weapons, and filming porno movies doesn't go over well with the FBI. You'll tell them about meeting with the Vietnamese cook, the death of Lillian's cousin, Duyen, and the fact that there are possibly two other dead girls buried on the estate. I'll guarantee you, when they make their raid, she'll be one of the first swept up and put into protective custody."

"What about Lila?"

"Kidnapping Lila must not, under any circumstances, be discussed. If it came to light, kidnapping and torture to get information would be very serious charges against you. Even criminals have constitutional rights. You'll say that you met with her several times, and over the course of those meetings, persuaded her that, not only was her life in danger, but she could be arrested and jailed for her illegal activities, including a massage salon that fronted for an escort service. She finally agreed to a taped interview, after which you drove her to Atlanta and put her on a plane to Vietnam. The saving grace with that is, the FBI can't interview her unless they to go to Vietnam, find her, and extradite her back to the US.

"After that, it gets very tricky. I don't want you to divulge the extortion of Holler, or the fight on the Santa Rosaria Bridge. I've had someone look into it, and there's no mention of it either publicly or privately. As far as the car chase, it's public knowledge that the chase occurred, but neither the Pensacola police nor the Santa Rosaria Sheriff's Department has any concrete evidence that it was you, nor were they able to obtain a license plate number. They'll grill you on it but stick to the story you gave Lawson. By the way, where is the car?"

"I have it hidden."

"I see. I won't ask where, but, I will ask what you plan to do with it. And, I will ask about the probability that it will be traced back to you."

"Simple. I've extended the lease with the rental company, explaining my car is out for repairs. Since, like you said, the authorities don't have a license plate number, and I used a fake ID to rent it, there's no way they can trace it. When I'm ready, I'll return it."

"Fake ID? I won't even ask. And, that brings us to the bombing of your boat. Right now, they're suspicious of you. However, after all the evidence we turn over, along with the fact that Holler is a demolition expert and you have an alibi, I think they'll turn that thinking around."

"Mr. Ludefance, no matter how you slice it, it's bologna. My job is to make sure the FBI doesn't pursue pressing charges against you for any of the illegal activities you do reveal. I can't guarantee you that they will, but, we're trading your hard evidence and information on Holler. I'm banking on the fact that they'll be more interested in taking Holler out. We'll just have to go with that. I'll be bringing with me all the evidence we plan to turn over. The rest will remain here in my safe."

"Right."

"So, your interview is scheduled for next Wednesday, December 27. I'm assuming it's their offices on West Romana Street? Do you have the time?"

"Yes. 9 am."

"Let's meet at, say, 8:30, in the lobby. Until then, I suggest you try to relax and enjoy Christmas. Have any plans?"

In reality, I hadn't even thought about Christmas, but made a spur of the moment decision. More than anything, I knew I wanted to be with my family.

"I'm going home to New Orleans to visit family."

"Just make sure you're back by Wednesday"

With that he stood, and shook my hand, and I was dismissed.

On the way out, I stopped at the receptionist's desk.

"By the way, I don't know your name."

"It's Lee."

"Lee, you have my cell number in case you need to contact me for any reason."

As I smiled and gave her a wink, she smiled back, clearly understanding the invitation.

"On Thursdays I work half of the day."

"Well, you have my number, Lee."

I walked out a happy man. The only downer was another two hours at $500.

Chapter 48

Later that afternoon, I called both Deloris and Margeaux to let them know I'd be coming home for Christmas. It lifted my spirits to hear the pure joy in their voices. Even if my father didn't recognize me, I needed to be there, not only for Deloris and my sister, but for me, as well. No one knew how much longer Dad would be with us, and at this point every moment with him seemed like a gift.

After a quick call to the facilitator of the place Dad was staying, I was informed we were all invited for Christmas dinner.

A quick trip to the mall was next on my list. Funny thing, though. It didn't turn out to be the quick trip I thought it would be. My first stop was Sephora. Because I believe that perfume is such an individual experience, and I wanted my choices to be perfect, I spent over an hour agonizing about which scent of perfume to buy for Deloris and Margeaux.

After the perfumery, I stopped by Godiva, then Hickory Farms for a large basket filled with cheeses and smoked meats, and finally, *Beyond the Grape* for several bottles of high-end wine. My final stop was a kiosk offering gift wrapping, where I had each gift wrapped in silver and blue Christmas paper with large silver bows and gift cards. On the way back to the cabin, I stopped at a local nursery, picked up a gardenia plant for Dad, and gassed up my car.

With all these stresses, I was feeling both overwhelmed and a little emotional. Then my sister's fear about us ending up being Alzheimer's patients started to diffuse in my mind. Would we? Did it really matter? I still held firm in my belief that all we needed to do was look after our minds and our bodies. As for me, I knew I had plenty of work to do in that department. But, in the end, whatever happened, happened. Worrying about it wasn't going to make any difference, and I forced myself not to think about it.

Back at the cabin I packed my roll-aboard with the essentials; my shaving kit, sweats and a change of clothes, literally all I had left. Everything was ready. All I needed was a good night's sleep, but that good night's sleep just was not to be. After tossing and turning most of the night, I finally gave up, made myself a pot of coffee, and took a cup down to the dock. Sitting in the quiet of Saturday morning, I tried to calm my mind and not think about anything beyond Christmas with my family.

Just after 9 am, I locked up and hid the key. For a moment I entertained the thought of driving the rental car. Perhaps it would be a good idea to put some miles on it, but then the thought of it possibly being recognized from the car chase, changed my mind. Even though I had rented the most unobtrusive make and car, a beige Toyota, there was no sense in entertaining further troubles, and I abandoned the idea.

It was the same route, the same towns, the same scenery, and because I'd had little sleep, numerous stops for coffee to keep me awake. A little over three hours later and I was home again. As I pulled into the driveway, Deloris opened the front door with a big smile on her face.

"Jack! It's so nice to see you! Merry Christmas!"

She opened her arms wide and hugged me.

"Thank you for coming to spend Christmas with us."

"I wouldn't have missed it Deloris. I called and talked with the facilitator and he told me that we're invited to have Christmas dinner there with Dad."

"We were planning to visit your father, but I didn't know they provided dinner."

"It is. Christmas dinner is on the house and all we have to do is show up. I was planning on taking us all out for dinner, but I think this works much better."

"I agree. I don't think your Dad would have done well in a restaurant. Well, get your things and come on in the house, Jack."

It took me two trips to retrieve my roll-aboard, backpack, Mac laptop, and all the Christmas packages. As I was setting the gifts under the tree, Deloris came out of the kitchen.

"Oh, my! What have you brought us?"

"It's Christmas, Deloris."

She tried to hide her tears.

"Would you like a cup of coffee?"

"No thanks, I think I've had enough coffee for one day. But, I won't say no to some of your delicious soup, if you have it."

"It won't take long to make it. Besides, Margeaux likes it, too. You just relax, and I'll get it started. Margeaux's on her way. She just needed to finish up some work."

I sat at the kitchen table watching Deloris prepare her special Cajun soup. While she was cutting the vegetables, we carried on talking.

"Jack, what about your mother? I thought of calling her to go see your father, then I thought maybe I shouldn't."

"Deloris, being with my Dad makes you our mother. Besides, I've never had a good relationship with my mother. No, I don't want her with my father. It will only bring memories that I don't want to think about again. I can still hear her voice in my head. When she and

Dad used to fight and she'd up and leave, she'd always tell me, 'You're a boy. You should stay with your Dad.' When I was eleven, she took off for good with some French man."

"I'm so sorry, Jack. Then, I'm glad I didn't call her. Oh, some news I want to share with you. Margeaux has a new boyfriend."

Before she could tell me more, I heard the front door open.

"Hello! Where is everyone?"

"We're in the kitchen!"

"Jack! I'm so glad to see you!"

She hugged me and kissed me on the cheek.

"Hello sis. You know I wouldn't miss spending Christmas with you! So, little sister. Deloris tells me you have a new boyfriend?"

"Yes! And, I'm really in love!"

As she started to get the dishes to set the table for dinner, Deloris stopped her.

"You two, go talk in private. I'll manage here."

"No, Deloris. We don't want to exclude you, you're our family. So, how about my big brother? Does he have someone?"

I thought of Lee, and told my little fib.

"Yes. I am seeing someone."

Margeaux came and put her arms around me.

"I'm not letting you go until you tell us all about her!"

"Nothing to tell. I met her at my lawyer's office. But, that's enough about me. Tell me more about your new boyfriend."

Margeaux and I talked on while Deloris stirred her soup, the delicious aroma filling the kitchen. After dinner, I excused myself and turned in early, my weariness catching up with me. But, it was to be another restless night. I dreamt that I was piloting the prowler and having a conversation with the tower. I could hear the voice saying, "You can't land this! It's not a Hornet. We'll not let you get away. You must make the loop before landing."

I woke up, soaking in sweat. What did that mean? I still had some unfinished business back in Santa Rosaria with Jonathan Holler?

Christmas Eve, I took my sister and Deloris to a Cajun restaurant for dinner. In my book, nothing beats Cajun, and, being in Florida, I missed the tastes and the aromas of all the spices. Monday, morning, we exchanged our Christmas presents over many oohhs and aahhs and enjoyed a delicious omelet Deloris prepared for us.

Early afternoon, we all piled into Margeaux's car for our trip to see Dad. I was apprehensive of how the afternoon would unfold. But, in reality, it didn't matter. The important thing was, we were all there together, as a family.

Dad was dressed up and sitting in his chair in his room. Holding the gardenia plant, I went in first, walked over to him, bent down, and hugged him with one arm. Then, I gently placed the small gardenia plant in his lap.

"Merry Christmas, Dad."

He looked up at me with no inkling of recognition, then he looked down at the gardenia, and started to caress the tiny, unopened buds.

"My gardenia. I cut it back. But you see, it's growing again."

Deloris and Margeaux had walked in and were standing right beside me. We all were taken aback and amazed with his few simple words. Was there still some of Dad left in there somewhere? In turn, Margeaux and

Deloris hugged Dad. He responded to both, with a weak smile.

When one of the aids came in to help Dad to the dinner table, he refused to let go of the gardenia, so it joined us for Christmas dinner. And, what a Christmas dinner it was. We sat at a festively set table, now complete with gardenia centerpiece.

Along with two other ladies, an elderly resident and her daughter, we enjoyed a delicious turkey dinner with all the fixings. The turkey had been prepared by an Indonesian cook, who, instead of traditional stuffing, had filled the bird with cooked rice. Unusual, but delicious. After desert and coffee, it was time to say another goodbye.

This goodbye was very difficult. Would I see my Dad again?

Chapter 49

On Tuesday morning, I took my time on the drive back east. Each mile brought me closer to Santa Rosaria and my meeting with the FBI in the morning. I'd done a pretty good job of not thinking about it over the holidays. But, now, I had to think about it and prepare my statement. I kept reminding myself, no slip-ups, and no contradictions. There was absolutely no room for error. I didn't want to end up the focus of an FBI investigation when it needed to be directed at taking Holler down.

Rather than going straight to the cabin, I stopped off at the mall and picked up a ready-to-wear suit, new shirt, tie, underwear and shoes. Couldn't very well wear the same jeans and shirt I'd been wearing since I'd lost my boat and all my belongings.

Arriving back at the cabin, I decided to do some research on how the FBI handles interviews. I was pretty much set in what I was going to say, but I wanted to be prepared as to what the procedure would be.

Googling, I found a website called, "techdirty." According to Tim Cushing, the author of the website, FBI agents always interview in pairs. One agent asks the questions, while the other writes up what is called a "form 302 report" based on his notes. The "302 report," which the interviewee does not normally see, becomes the official record of the exchange. He also stated that any interviewee who contests its accuracy, risks prosecution for lying to a federal official, which is a felony. And here is the key problem that throws the accuracy of all such statements and reports into doubt: FBI agents almost never electronically record their interrogations; to do so would be against written policy.

Thank God, I had a savvy lawyer who would be by my side during the interview. I realized now, he was going to be worth every penny. Otherwise, I wouldn't trust the FBI two-man interview system. It was too easy for them to either falsify my statement, or heavily editorialized the transcript.

That afternoon, Lee, the receptionist from Mr. Dolaberitze's office, called.

"Mr. Ludefance? Mr. Dolaberitze asked me to call you and remind you of your meeting tomorrow with the FBI. He'll meet you at 8:30 in the lobby."

"Thanks, and Lee? Do me a favor. It's Jack. You can call me Jack."

"Okay, Jack."

"Are you still off on Thursdays?"

"I leave work at noon. Why?"

"I was wondering if you'd like to meet me and have a drink and dinner this Thursday."

"Are you asking me out?"

"Okay. You can put it that way, I guess. I'm asking you to go out with me. That is, unless you have a boyfriend…"

"I have a boyfriend, but I'm not sure how serious he is about me."

"While he's making up his mind, I'd like to fill in for him, and see where it might lead. Kinda sad, really. He doesn't even know what he might to lose."

"You certainly have a way with words. Yes. I'd like to get together. This Thursday?"

"It's a date. I'd like to take you the East Bay Inn for dinner."

"I'd like that, Jack."

The softness in her voice told me all I needed to know.

"Do you want me to pick you up?"

"Umm...no. I think it's better if I meet you there. I don't want my roommate to suspect anything."

"Fair enough. I'll see you at around seven?"

"Seven at the East Bay Inn."

Chapter 50

Wednesday, December 27th. My day of reckoning with the FBI. Here I was, a man who lived on the edge. A man not afraid to wrestle with alligators. But, the Feds? This was a whole different ballgame. Could I, would I come away unscathed?

I found the building on West Romana, a dreary, old-fashioned, square, four-story high rectangular box, complete with tiny windows. It was, in my opinion, an ugly building and I thought the architect must have had an odd sense of humor when he designed it. I noticed a black sedan parked in front and assumed it must be Dolaberitze's. Pulling into the parking garage, I found a spot near the door to the lobby. Entering the dreary space, I walked over to the lawyer who, hopefully, was going to save my ass.

"Good morning, Mr. Ludefance. Are you ready for today?"

"Ready for this to be over."

"Of course, of course. And it will be. As I said in our last meeting, I have all the evidence that we are going to give to the FBI. All you need to do is to give them a factual, statement of the events. The evidence backs everything up."

He made it sound like a piece of cake. As we approached security, I let Dolaberitze enter first. He opened his briefcase, explaining what was contained it. The security guard checked each item and then directed him through the scanner with no issues.

I had brought my backpack and my Mac laptop bag. I took out my computer as requested, and my backpack, Mac, and laptop bag went through without any issues. But, when I went through the scanner, it buzzed.

"Sir, go back and take all contents out of your pockets."

He handed me a small tray.

I put my cell phone, wallet, and keys into it.

Again, the scanner buzzed.

"Step aside, sir."

This wasn't the way I wanted this particular day to start.

As he waved the wand, it buzzed at my lower leg.

"I have a pin in my ankle."

It never occurred to me that it would be a problem. Never had been in any airport I'd ever gone through. But, today of all days.

He lifted by pant leg and waved the wand up and down until he was satisfied I wasn't sneaking anything nefarious into the building.

Entering the elevator, we rode in silence up to the fourth floor, where a stern-faced receptionist directed us down the hall to an interview room. Agent Johnson was dressed in what appeared to be the same pin-stripe suit he was wearing the first time I'd met him at the marina. He and another agent both stood as we entered. The second agent was also dressed in a suit, maybe 5-foot-ten, with a round face and belly. Agent Johnson greeted us.

"Mr. Dolaberitze, Mr. Ludefance. This is Agent Antonia. He'll be writing down your statement and then your answers to the interview questions."

"Can't the FBI afford a voice recorder?"

I couldn't help myself, I had to break the overwhelming gloom in the room. It didn't go over too well, though. Johnson gave me a look that could kill.

"This is how we do it, Mr. Ludefance. We always interview in pairs. In this case, I'll be asking the questions, and Agent Antonia will be taking notes. Now, if you gentlemen will be seated, we'll get started."

My lawyer and I sat side by side at one end of the table, with Johnson and Antonia at the other end.

"Hopefully, we can finish this up today. Mr. Ludefance, I'm going to have Agent Antonia swear you in."

Antonia stood, picked up the Bible, and then walked over to me. I stood, raised my right hand and took the oath, after which he returned to the other end of the table. The table was so wide that if I was to consult with my lawyer, as long as we whispered, the agents wouldn't be able to hear the conversation.

"Before we begin, do you have anything to add Mr. Dolaberitze?"

"Yes. As Mr. Ludefance gives his statement, I will be passing down evidence corresponding to the events."

"I see. And the nature of the evidence?"

"Paperwork, photographs and digital recordings."

"You do know the evidence will become property of the FBI?"

"Of course."

"And?"

"And, in exchange for the evidence, I'm requesting that my client be absolved of any wrongdoing."

"Wrongdoing?"

"Yes."

"That request will be taken into consideration."

"Agent Johnson, the evidence that will be turned over is more than enough to direct an investigation that will lead to the take-down of Jonathan Holler for numerous illicit actives."

"As I just said, Mr. Dolaberitze, the request will be taken into consideration. You may begin, Mr. Ludefance."

I began with the details of that fateful night and the encounter with Lillian Holler. When I finished, Dolaberitze stood and walked the envelope down to Johnson and Antonio. They examined the contents carefully, whispering at times, but didn't ask any questions.

"Continue, Mr. Ludefance."

Next, I gave a detailed statement of everything that transpired with Katy, starting with helping her get the job at Holler Enterprises, and finishing with her death. Again, Dolaberitze stood and walked the file folder of photos from Holler's business, and from my late-night escapade inside the Holler compound.

Johnson and Antonia looked through the stack of photographs, then looked up at me.

"Mr. Ludefance, normally we would have you continue with your statement, but the severity of these events require that I ask you some questions before we go any further."

Dolaberitze and I looked at each other.

"What are your questions, Agent Johnson?"

"Mr. Dolaberitze, let's start with the fact that your client made a deal with Katy Ozener to obtain information regarding Holler's export business and report back to him. Is that correct?"

"You are correct."

"Which is spying."

I put my hand on my lawyer's arm.

"I wouldn't put it quite that way."

"What way would you put it Mr. Ludefance?"

"Look. I'm a licensed private investigator. It's my job to collect information. It's my job to find out, in any way I can, if someone is conducting unlawful business. It's perfectly legal for Katy, as my assistant, to report to me about whatever she finds."

"You're stretching your job description. You enlisted the help of a young girl, to spy on a legitimate company, and that girl is now dead. In addition, you illegally entered the Holler compound. Breaking and entering is a felony. You must know that any evidence, no matter how overwhelming, that is gathered as a result of illegal activities is typically not admissible in court. You may be a licensed PI, but you aren't above the law, Mr. Ludefance."

Now it was Dolaberitze's turn to speak up.

"Agent Johnson, we've discussed this with the understanding no charges would be brought against my client in lieu of evidence he is providing."

"No, Mr. Dolaberitze. I'll repeat what I said previously. The request will be taken into consideration. I could, in fact, have your client arrested right now."

"Then perhaps we have no business left to discuss. Do what you must. But we are done here."

Dolaberitze stood as if he was ready to walk out.

Oh, God. Please let this be a fake out.

"Wait. Just wait, Mr. Dolaberitze. First of all, you don't just walk out on an FBI interview. Second, it's my job to ask pertinent questions. Your client is factually guilty of breaking and entering. I need to know where we stand."

"Then at least hear the rest of what my client has to say and look at the rest of the evidence we have to present before you exercise your supposed legal authority. My client risked his life for the valuable information against Holler, which you now have possession of."

For several minutes Johnson and Antonia conferred in hushed voices. But, in the end, Dolaberitze won out and after a much needed lunch break, I was permitted to finish my statement. Everything my astute, larger than life lawyer had wanted me to convey. Up to the point my boat was blown up, that is. In turn, he turned over the rest of the evidence to Johnson, including the digital recording of Lila's confession.

The digital recorder peaked their curiosity. Johnson pushed play. We heard Lila's voice, and, in her own words, all her damning information about and against Jonathan Holler. When the tape ended, he looked up at me.

"Let's be blunt here, Ludefance. How did you convince her to spill the beans?"

"The truth. She knew too much, and because of that, Holler would eventually have killed her, or had someone else do the job."

"And, she's now in Vietnam. Out of our reach. How convenient."

"She's safe from Holler and his goons, Agent Johnson."

"Right."

"What more do you want?"

I stood up. I was angry, and let it show. My lawyer, obviously frustrated, tried to calm me down.

"Agent Johnson is just doing his job. Sit down Mr. Ludefance."

Glaring at Johnson, I sat back down, still fuming. Johnson continued.

"That brings us to the bombing of your boat."

"It does. I'm not a demolitions expert, Agent Johnson. But, Jonathan Holler is."

Johnson and Antonia conferred for several minutes, before Johnson made his next statement.

"Mr. Dolaberitze, at this point I must remind you, I didn't make any agreement with you regarding not charging your client. That is beyond my authority. I will consult with my superiors and we will meet again this Friday afternoon. I'll call you with an exact time. That's the best I can do."

Chapter 51

Although my dealings with FBI weren't over, I began to feel some relief. They had the evidence to bring Holler down. The question was, would they come after me in the process?

On the way back to the cabin, I stopped at Domino's and picked up a large pepperoni pizza. It was after four when I finally returned to the cabin. First thing I did was grab a Samuel Adams, open the bottle and drink half of it down, and then dug into the pizza. Next, I called the cabin owner and asked to extend another week. He explained that he could give me one more week but wouldn't be able to do any more extensions after that, as he had committed to another customer. I now had less than two weeks to find a new home. Which reminded me that I hadn't yet filed an insurance claim for my boat.

Relief and exhaustion had kicked in, and I slept late the next morning. It was after eleven when I finally fixed some breakfast of warmed up pepperoni pizza, salad and a cold beer. I called the insurance company, gave them the details, and the agent told me they needed the police report. One more thing to take care of. I knew that FBI still suspected me of the bombing, and I wasn't sure of how it would all be resolved.

My next call was to the East Bay Inn. I booked a corner table in the restaurant and took a gamble and booked a room on the top floor.

The afternoon flew by. Before I knew it, it was 4:30 and I was hungry again. I thought about my date with Lee at seven, so I decided on a sandwich and beer to tide me over.

Arriving early, I was seated at my requested table, nice and private. I had just ordered my first beer when I watched Lee walk in, look around, and smile when she saw me.

"Have you been waiting long?"

"No, I just arrived a few minutes ago."

Over a leisurely dinner, we talked mostly about Lee and her parents. It turned out working for Dolaberitze was only a temporary job. She was studying to become a lawyer. I had a new-found respect for her, could see her in several years taking on clients of her own. I did share with her my navy years and becoming a PI. It was, by all accounts, a relaxing and an enjoyable evening. More so than I expected. I really liked this woman. She was not only beautiful, but intelligent. After dinner, she asked for a take-home bag and we walked out into the lobby.

"I've booked a room for tonight."

"A room? So, you think I'm going to sleep with you?"

"I don't think. I know."

"Then give me a moment to get my overnight bag."

Ha. She could play cute all she wanted, but she had come prepared. Tonight, was a forgone conclusion. What was left to the imagination was how good it would be for both of us.

Closing the door, I pulled her into my arms, kissed her long and hard, then entwined my hand with hers, and walked her towards the bedroom. Both of us were hungry for sex, and the night didn't disappoint.

When I woke the next morning, she was already dressed. She leaned over and gave me a long kiss goodbye. For her it was another day at work.

For me it was knowing that this afternoon, I would learn my fate.

Chapter 52

Friday afternoon Dolaberitze and I were back at the FBI office. The interview room door was wide open. Johnson and Antonia were waiting on us, both wearing their best poker faces.

"Have a seat, gentlemen."

We sat opposite each other as we had on Wednesday.

"Mr. Ludefance. We've discussed at length with our superiors, your statement and interview, and reviewed every piece of evidence you've turned over. Pursuant to their decision, we intend to proceed with a further in-depth investigation of Jonathan Holler. Mr. Dolaberitze, your client is free to go."

Short and sweet. A sudden giddiness overtook, and I couldn't resist.

"So, you are going to bust Holler?"

"We're definitely going to pursue that avenue. We've had Holler under scrutiny with regards to his massage salons businesses, but, being a respectable business man in the community, we've held off. Kind of difficult to pursue someone who's considered a pillar of the community and donates to so many charities."

"In other words, you turned a blind eye?"

"Are you questioning the FBI, Mr. Ludefance?"

I entertained the thought of throwing out a few expletive words, and a "what about Hillary Clinton," but Dolaberitze interrupted.

"My client is free to go, Agent Johnson?"

"As far as we're concerned, we're done. There will be no charges brought against your client. He is, as they say, free as a bird."

"What do you mean free as a bird?"

"Look, Mr. Ludefance. Don't push it. We're overlooking a few felonies that you've committed. If I were you, I'd go home and forget about all this."

"At least let me be part of the bust."

"Under no circumstances would we will allow you to be a part of anything more concerning Jonathan Holler."

"But, I've read about other cases where the informant participated in the bust. Why not me?"

"Mr. Ludefance, if we allowed you to participate, you'd end up in deep trouble, if not possibly dead yourself. We are actually entertaining the idea of putting you into the witness protection program, and all that entails, including changing your identity and relocation. You really think Holler's people are going to leave you alone? You've managed to open up the proverbial can of worms. It's going to take months before we have everything in place. And, there's no telling where this will ultimately end, or how many years it will take to unravel everything in the courts. Add to that the fact that you'd have to come back and testify in any court cases that came out of this. Take my advice. For now, just go home and think about taking up another career. If you decide to continue as a PI, just be thankful we aren't going to report any of your activities to the licensing commission."

Chapter 53

A new year brought with it gloomy, chilly days. I'd survived the FBI interview, and thank God Dolaberitze had gotten me out of the malfeasances I'd committed. It wouldn't have been pretty had they decided to go ahead and charge me, and I knew now he'd been worth every penny I'd paid him.

With all the evidence I'd presented, albeit some illegally, they had enough to move forward on investigating Holler. He would finally be taken out. I couldn't get past the disappointment of not being a part of the bust, and it really began to bug me. I wanted to be there, see the look on his face when his perfect world collapsed.

On the other hand, I could only hope the FBI wouldn't pursue their idea of putting me into a witness protection program. Sorry, not for me. I'll take my chances. It's how I've always lived my life. Why stop now?

I needed some time and space to just do nothing. Decompress. The cabin was the perfect place. But, in less than a week, I'd have to find another home. I'd enjoyed being here, away from everything, and especially the idea that no one knew where I was, not even Lawson.

As far as the car, the rental company wasn't giving me any problems. My explanation of my car repairs taking longer than anticipated was accepted without question. At some point, I knew I had to return it, but, I'd neither had had the time, nor did I want to have to take another taxi from the airport back to the cabin.

Another Saturday. Another gloomy day. I hadn't heard from Lee again. Didn't like the thought of our night together as a onetime thing, and I contemplated giving her a call.

Wandering outside, I took a deep breath of moist, damp air into my lungs. The weather forecast was predicting a hard freeze through Tuesday. Returning to the warmth of the cabin, I decided to stay in and just be lazy for the day.

After making up several roast beef sandwiches, I pulled a Samuel Adams out of the fridge. Ready to enjoy my lunch, I was surprised when my cell phone rang.

Judge Hendrix? I honestly didn't think I would hear from her again.

"Debra? What a pleasant surprise to hear from you."

"I did say I'd call back and check on you. How did your interview go with the FBI?"

"Grueling, but it's over. It's still nice to hear from you."

"Actually, I'm calling to ask a favor, Jack. I need a date for tonight. I bought two tickets to the Pensacola Opera. My husband promised to drive over, but, now at the last minute, he's backed out. I know it's presumptuous, but I was hoping that you would like to go with me."

"Debra, I'm delighted with the invitation, but I don't know a thing about opera."

"There's really nothing to know. It's a matter of enjoying beautiful music, and incredible voices, all with good company by your side."

"How can I refuse that?"

"I know a lot of men who would rather go see a football game. But, my guess is, any man who can send beautiful flowers to a woman is a romantic man at heart and has room to improve in his enjoyment of cultural things."

"Right again. But, I'm also thinking of perhaps ending the evening in a more intimate way."

She hesitated only a moment before responding.

"That depends."

"On what?"

"On how the evening progresses."

"Fair enough. What's the name of the opera?"

"Carmen. It's one of my favorites. It's set in southern Spain and tells the story of the downfall of Don José, a naïve soldier who is seduced by the wiles of the fiery gypsy Carmen. Don José abandons his childhood sweetheart and deserts from his military duties, yet loses Carmen's love to the glamorous matador Escamillo, after which José kills her in a jealous rage."

"Love, sex and death. What could be better? I'm already looking forward to it. What time should I pick you up?"

"Let's see. The curtain goes up at 8 pm. I'd like to be there a little early, so that we can enjoy a glass of wine. What about 6:30? Oh, and Jack. Dress appropriately."

"You mean, a tuxedo?"

"No, not that fancy. Just something dressy will do."

"It's going to be cold tonight, just to warn you."

"How do you know that?"

"Been checking the national weather. We're in for a hard freeze through Monday."

"Thanks for the heads-up. I'll pull out my fur coat. Don't often get a chance to wear it in Florida."

"Great. I'll be at your house at 6:30."

"See you then."

Dressy? I didn't even have my favorite pin-stripe suit. It blew up with the boat, along with all my other belongings. And the one I'd bought for the FBI interview wouldn't do. Groaning, I knew a quick trip to the mall was unavoidable. It wasn't on my list of favorite things to do, but, then, what man enjoys shopping? Especially for clothes? I couldn't avoid it any longer. Nor could I continue wearing the same two pairs of jeans, shirts and sweats. It was time to replace my wardrobe.

Several hours later, I returned with packages overflowing with enough to get me by for the next ten years. Several pairs of casual pants, jeans, casual shirts, turtlenecks, shorts, t-shirts, sweats, underwear, socks, sports jacket, and, a new blue pin-stripe suit, complete with shirt and tie. While I was at it, I picked up a new and larger roll-aboard.

After a shower and shave, I put on my new suit, pale blue shirt, and tie. Not bad. I packed my smaller roll-aboard with a more casual pair of pants, turtleneck, and sports jacket, along with my sweats and clean underwear. A man could only hope.

It was 5.30 when I left to pick up Debra. To tell you the truth, I was feeling a little over-confident. She'd called me. I thought about how good I felt being with her. Although not completely gone, the nostalgia over my wife had pretty much faded. When you love someone and lose that person, it's hard to forget.

The reality for me is, Debra is a woman I could share my life with. Yes, she's married, but, we're both adults, and I'm sure she knows what she's doing. Maybe her marriage isn't going that well, or she's lonely being separated from her family, or maybe it's just simply that she doesn't want to go the opera alone.

It reminded me of a movie I once saw, "Bridges of Madison County," with Clint Eastwood and Meryl Streep. A famous National Geographic photographer is on assignment in Iowa to film their covered bridges. He meets a farmer's wife, they fall madly in love, enjoy three incredible days together, and then he is gone. My wife made me watch it, but, I never let on how it had affected me. Men aren't supposed to feel that way. Streep was later interviewed about how real she looked during the intimate scenes in the movie. She said, "For one day, you just make yourself fall in love with the character."

I reasoned that if Debra wanted to enjoy the night without feeling guilty about it, perhaps she should. Maybe her marriage was strong enough to handle a little spice. If her marriage was in trouble and heading nowhere, then perhaps that left things open for me.

Why was I second guessing Debra's behavior?

Was I trying to justify it in my own mind? I needed to stop and just enjoy the evening. Whatever happened, happened.

When Debra opened the front door, she took my breath away. She was dressed in an elegant, form fitting, short, red dress, with a ruby necklace and earrings to match, and held her fur coat over her arm. I immediately knew from the look on her face, she didn't like my suit. Too much? Too little?

"I brought a more casual outfit with me, just in case."

"Were you expecting that I'd disapprove of your attire?"

"I don't know what to think. But, you're obviously not thrilled with my suit."

"Very intuitive man. But, it's judges that shouldn't be transparent."

"You're not. I'm just an extra-intuitive man."

She laughed, and her eyes sparkled.

"Show me your other outfit?"

I returned to my car, clicked open the trunk, and returned with my roll-aboard. She pulled out the turtleneck, casual pants, and sports jacket.

"Ahh, this is much better. Why don't you change in my bedroom? We still have plenty of time."

I thought it was a hint of how the tonight might end. There was no denying the sexual tension between us. I was tempted to take her into bed right now, but quickly discarded the thought. I told myself to be patient and not blow it. Besides, we couldn't be late for the opera. I stuffed the suit, shirt and tie back into the roll-aboard and returned to the living room.

"Much better. Ready? And, Jack, thanks again for rescuing me."

backpack, Mac, and laptop bag went through without any issues. But, when I went through the scanner, it buzzed.

"Sir, go back and take all contents out of your pockets."

He handed me a small tray.

I put my cell phone, wallet, and keys into it.

Again, the scanner buzzed.

"Step aside, sir."

This wasn't the way I wanted this particular day to start.

As he waved the wand, it buzzed at my lower leg.

"I have a pin in my ankle."

It never occurred to me that it would be a problem. Never had been in any airport I'd ever gone through. But, today of all days.

He lifted by pant leg and waved the wand up and down until he was satisfied I wasn't sneaking anything nefarious into the building.

Entering the elevator, we rode in silence up to the fourth floor, where a stern-faced receptionist directed us down the hall to an interview room. Agent Johnson was dressed in what appeared to be the same pin-stripe suit he was wearing the first time I'd met him at the marina. He and another agent both stood as we entered. The second agent was also dressed in a suit, maybe 5-foot-ten, with a round face and belly. Agent Johnson greeted us.

"Mr. Dolaberitze, Mr. Ludefance. This is Agent Antonia. He'll be writing down your statement and then your answers to the interview questions."

"Can't the FBI afford a voice recorder?"

I couldn't help myself, I had to break the overwhelming gloom in the room. It didn't go over too well, though. Johnson gave me a look that could kill.

"This is how we do it, Mr. Ludefance. We always interview in pairs. In this case, I'll be asking the questions, and Agent Antonia will be taking notes. Now, if you gentlemen will be seated, we'll get started."

My lawyer and I sat side by side at one end of the table, with Johnson and Antonia at the other end.

"Hopefully, we can finish this up today. Mr. Ludefance, I'm going to have Agent Antonia swear you in."

Antonia stood, picked up the Bible, and then walked over to me. I stood, raised my right hand and took the oath, after which he returned to the other end of the table. The table was so wide that if I was to consult with my lawyer, as long as we whispered, the agents wouldn't be able to hear the conversation.

"Before we begin, do you have anything to add Mr. Dolaberitze?"

"Yes. As Mr. Ludefance gives his statement, I will be passing down evidence corresponding to the events."

"I see. And the nature of the evidence?"

"Paperwork, photographs and digital recordings."

"You do know the evidence will become property of the FBI?"

"Of course."

"And?"

"And, in exchange for the evidence, I'm requesting that my client be absolved of any wrongdoing."

"Wrongdoing?"

"Yes."

"That request will be taken into consideration."

"Agent Johnson, the evidence that will be turned over is more than enough to direct an investigation that will lead to the take-down of Jonathan Holler for numerous illicit actives."

Chapter 54

We arrived with time to spare. As we walked into the historic Saenger Theatre in downtown Pensacola, Debra took my arm. I fleetingly imagined her as my wife. Hey, you never know how things can turn out. After presenting the tickets, we entered the intricately detailed, high-ceilinged lobby. The architecture was old world Spanish, with thick carpeting, and magnificent chandeliers. Our seats were, comfortable, ideal third row, center, upholstered in red velvet.

After settling in our seats, there was still time before the opera started. I stood up and asked, "What would you like to drink?"

"I take either red or white wine."

I returned to our seats with two glasses of red wine. I had fleetingly thought of ordering a Samuel Adams but thought I should join in her good taste. The lights dimmed, the Pensacola symphony orchestra began playing the opening, and the red velvet curtains rose slowly on Act 1. I must admit, it was impressive.

After Act 2, during intermission, I walked up to the bar and ordered two more glasses of wine. We enjoyed sipping slowly and immersed ourselves in the music and the story. In the space of several hours, Debra had made me an opera lover.

As we drove back over Pensacola Bay Bridge, and the dark waters of Pensacola Bay, I gathered up my nerve. It was now or never.

"I don't suppose you'd consider coming back to my cabin?"

"I didn't know you had a cabin."

"I'm renting temporarily, until I decide where to settle next."

She took her time answering. We were almost back to the turn-off for her home when she answered.

"I'm curious to see your cabin. But, what you're really asking me is to spend the night with you."

"That crossed my mind. Am I that transparent?"

"I'm a judge, remember? Yes, to both questions. If you don't mind, can we stop at the house, so I can pick up a few things?"

"Of course."

After turning onto 67 North, I made sure to obey the speed limit, and pay attention to the turn off. How many times had I missed it before? Not tonight. By the time we reached the dirt road, fog had settled in. Thankfully, I'd thought to leave the porch light on. As we walked into the cabin, I watched her face. She was impressed. I took off my sports coat and removed her fur coat, setting them both on an overstuffed chair.

"The master bedroom and bath are on the left, if you'd like to get comfortable. I'm going start a fire, then make some coffee for us."

She took her overnight bag and purse into the bedroom and closed the door. By the time I brought the coffee into the living room, she was coming out wearing the same sexy caftan she'd been wearing the night I made a fool of myself. I didn't intend to make a repeat performance.

She first sat opposite me, then came over and sat next to me. The roaring fire and the rich, hot coffee relaxed us both. The silence continued a little longer. There were no words exchanged.

None were needed.

Besides, what would we have said?

I put my empty coffee cup on the table, took her cup from her, pulled her to me and kissed her. It was a long, deep, mutual kiss, and foretold of what was to come. I got up, took her hand, and walked her into the bedroom. Then I wrapped my arms around her, pulled her close and we locked in another long, blissfully wonderful kiss.

Lifting her in my arms, I set her gently on the big bed. She watched me as I stripped of my turtleneck, slacks and underwear. Sitting on the bed next to her, I slowly unbuttoned the caftan. There was nothing underneath but her beautiful body. I engulfed her in my arms, and moved one hand to her breast, cupping it gently.

We shared another deep, longing kiss. I moved my lips from hers and began kissing her neck, then slowly moving down to her right breast, then her left breast. I kissed them softly, gently, caressing each nipple between my lips. Moving down further, I rubbed my face with a snuggling movement against her warm belly.

I felt her quiver in my arms. Something in her stiffened in a moment of resistance, then she relaxed into the exquisite physical intimacy. Gently I laid her on her back, kissing and caressing her all over her body, until she was moaning with pleasure. I kissed her navel, and with both hands, gently parted her legs.

That triangular shade was waiting. I went down on her red opening, spending time there, enjoying her ecstasy, enjoying it as much as she was. Slowly I moved back up to her belly button, her breasts, then to her mouth. She was shivering from excitement and ready.

I moved myself aside, in full erection. As she laid me on my back, her right hand captured my ready manhood. She bent down and wrapped her lips around me. I could barely stand it, trying with all my strength not to come. When she had her fill, she lifted her head, taking a long breath. I pulled her up and laid her on her back again, and she opened her legs in anticipation.

She held me firmly, guiding me to her opening. I thrust myself into her and began a slow rhythmic movement. We moved as one, our bodies becoming moist with sweat. I couldn't hold it any longer and she rode it with me all the way to the end. After that sweet moment of release, we clung to each other as if there was no tomorrow.

Right now, this was all there was. The two of us together. There were no words. None were needed. We both fell into a blissful sleep.

A little while later, I woke up feeling cold. Debra was still sound asleep, curled up next to me. I covered us both up, wrapped my arms around her, and fell back asleep.

Sometime during the middle of the night, I took her in my arms again and drew her to me. Half asleep, she curled up with her back against me, becoming ever so small in my arms. She had let go, and with no more resistance from her, I sensed she had melted into a marvelous peace.

My whole body was alive with intense, yet tender desire for her, for her softness, for the penetrating beauty of her in my arms. Softly, ever so softly I stroked the silky slope of her back, then down, down between her soft warm buttocks, coming nearer and nearer to her opening.

I was completely consumed by wanting and I felt her melting into that same wanting. My manhood was rock hard against her leg. She felt it and raised herself up on her upper thigh. Then she turned onto her back, parted her legs, and invited me in once more. She quivered as I entered her and lost herself, as I did, in the shear ecstasy of being together.

It was mid-morning when I woke up and heard the shower running. I got up, put on my sweats, and went into the kitchen to make some coffee. She walked in to the room, wrapped her arms around me, and kissed my neck.

"Breakfast?"

"Sure. What do you have to make?"

"How about an omelet?"

"Sounds wonderful. If you cook, I'll clean up."

"Deal."

Over breakfast, we talked of mundane things, just as a happily married couple would. And there I was fantasizing again. Reality came flooding back when we heard her cell phone rang.

"Excuse me, I need to get that."

She came back into the room distracted.

"Everything okay?"

"My secretary. Reminding me off my full case-load tomorrow. I need to get home and organize my files. Do you mind driving me back?"

"Of course not. But, I have a favor to ask."

"Sure. You rescued me last night. What can I help you with?"

"Would you mind driving my car?"

"Where to?"

"I need to return a rental car to the airport."

"A rental car? I'm sure there's a story there, somewhere. Okay. No problem. I'll just follow you, then you can take me home. Sorry about this Jack."

"Let me ask you a question, Debra. If your secretary hadn't called, would you have stayed the rest of the weekend?"

"Yes."

They always say, timing is everything.

Chapter 55

As the days went by, I became more and more perturbed with the thought of not being a part of the upcoming Holler bust when it happened. I'd come this far, and I wanted to finish it. I kept after Lawson to tell me when the bust was going to take place, but he remained evasive. With time on my hands, and no new cases, I was, to say the least, extremely bored.

In addition, I was now down to only a few days before I had to vacate the cabin. Time to get moving on finding a place to live. Funny how the mind clicks in when you need it. I remembered a client I'd had last year, just after I'd moved from New Orleans. Remembered the case in detail, but for a moment, his name escaped me. But I didn't try and push it.

Sitting out on the dock, it finally came to me. Vance McGruder, a very wealthy man. He'd made his fortune, like so many Texans, after oil was discovered on his property near the Texas-Oklahoma border. Flush with money, he and his wife, Patty, moved to Southern California, and bought a house in Malibu overlooking the ocean.

His wife had inherited a sweet little two-bedroom cottage in a quiet subdivision just north of Highway 88, close to the Santa Rosaria Bridge. For sentimental reasons, she refused to sell it, and also didn't want to rent it out.

Vance had hired me to investigate his wife to find out what her activities were whenever she came and stayed in the cottage. It was one of the easiest cases I've ever had, and I actually felt guilty taking his money. After several months of following her during her visits, I reported back to him that his wife was not having an affair. During her stays, her daily schedule was pretty much the same. After a morning walk on the beach, she spent her afternoons at either Starbucks, at one of the local spas, or working in the garden at her cottage. Whenever her lawn man came, she worked right alongside him.

Vance was happy, and I was a few grand richer.

I started putting the pieces together. I had to accept the fact that I didn't want to buy anything right now. My hundred-grand wouldn't go very far, even here, and, besides that, I wanted to wait and see if I still had the where-with-all to continue with PI work. Patty had a cottage that would be perfect. All I had to do was convince her to rent it to me.

After locating his number, I made the call.

"Vance McGruder."

"Vance? This is Jacques Ludefance, Santa Rosaria, Florida. You hired me last year."

"Yes, of course. I remember."

"I recall you telling me your wife didn't want to rent her cottage out, but I was wondering if she might make an exception and rent it to me?"

"That's fine with me, but it's my wife who's adamant about not renting it. It's purely sentimental reasons. So, I'd have to check with her and see if she would agree. Personally, I would rather have someone reliable stay there as opposed to it sitting empty. Plus, we pay the lawn maintenance company $260 a month."

"I'd still need someone to do the lawn work, but let's say I pay that fee plus another $500 a month? Would that be agreeable to you?"

"How long do you want it for?"

"Let's make it a year lease, or until I find something to buy."

"I'll speak to my wife and get back to you next week."

"Hate to pressure you, Vance, but I'm under a time-crunch. I need to find something in the next few days."

"I'll see what I can do. Either way, I'll call you back this evening."

"Thanks."

In the end, Vance was able to persuade his wife to lease the cottage to me. He e-mailed a simple lease agreement and sent the keys by overnight Fed-ex. Once again, I heard the complaint about how hard it had been to find the cabin.

For the first time in over two years I had a new home. And, with the exception of the few weeks at the cabin, I was back on dry land. For a small cottage, it was large on living space with an open living-dining room, large eat-in kitchen, two-bedrooms, large bath, Florida room, a one car garage and sat on a half-acre of landscaped yard. Along with that came a security system and a land-line phone. It could easily rent for a thousand a month, and I wouldn't mind buying it somewhere down the road. It was, of course, fully furnished, many of the items family antiques.

It was an easy move. Just my car, my two roll-aboard suitcases, my new clothes, backpack and Mac laptop, and I was home. After putting my sparse belongings away, I called several people, including Lawson, to let them know where I was and gave them the land-line number, just in case.

Now, what do I do with myself? I still wasn't sure if I wanted to continue as a PI, but the thought of finding a new career was daunting.

I was officially in limbo.

Chapter 56

Should I call Lee? Or, should I call Debra?

Calling Debra won out.

"Debra, it's Jack. Any possibility of getting together this weekend?"

"Actually, Jack, I was thinking of giving you a call, but you beat me to it."

"Is everything all right?"

"Yes! Fine!"

I didn't argue, but, from the tone of her voice, I knew something was cooking, and whatever it was wasn't good. What the heck. I jumped in with both feet.

"Listen, I've got a new home, a little cottage I'd love for you to see."

"No, Jack. Why don't we have dinner...on me? We need to talk."

"Sure. When?"

"Friday, 7ish? Why don't you pick the place?"

"What about the East Bay Inn? I don't suppose you want to talk about it, now?"

"Not on the phone, but we'll talk over the dinner."

"Friday at 7."

To say the least, her call disturbed me on many levels. I'd had such high expectations. I now realized how foolish I'd been.

Diversion. Not always the best remedy, but I needed it right now. And I had nothing else to do. No upcoming cases. Nothing. Grabbing a cup of coffee, I perused the internet for some sign of inspiration.

Since I spent so much time there, perhaps a Starbuck's franchise? That idea quickly went up in flames. At 350 thousand dollars, it was way out of my price range, and I couldn't picture myself as a boss. I had to have something that kept me on the edge, but out of trouble. I closed down my computer, and grabbed a Samuel Adams, ready to drown my troubles.

Friday night came all too soon. Debra and I sat across from each other in a comfortable booth at the back of the restaurant. I'd chosen it so that we could have quiet conversation, and we managed to make it through dinner with small talk. After the waitress cleared away our dinner plates, we ordered coffee, and I waited for the proverbial ball to drop.

"Jack, I don't know how to say this, but to just say it. You've been very good to me, and you're one hell of a man, but I can't do it. I'm not like that. I don't know how I allowed myself to be in this situation. I'm not saying that I didn't enjoy it. It was very exciting to be with you."

"Debra, just tell me what the problem is."

"It's all…it's all mixed up and crazy. It wasn't me, really. I don't know how to tell you. I'm not like that. I'm married. I have two young sons to raise. I don't even know how I could have been so ……silly. I think it was because of being lonely here, and my husband cancelled out on the opera. And, you're being so God-damned charming."

She looked sideways. I put my fingertips under her chin, turned her head, and made her look at me. I looked into her eyes until she flushed and twisted her head away again. She meant it. This *was* a good bye. I felt the disappointment. But, unlike the dinner with my wife, I didn't feel the knots in my stomach. In a way, my instincts had been preparing me.

"The problem is that I'm married, and I don't want us to continue to see each other."

Her eyes went dead. I knew then, there was no way to ever get her back.

"Jack, I do want to thank you for everything. I feel so sorry about… about giving you the wrong idea, and a lot of false hopes, and…"

"This is a good bye then?"

She hesitated and lifted her chin a half inch.

"I d-dread it Jack. I'm so terribly sorry. It just keeps reminding me of something I'd rather forget."

Jack, the great lover, the eternal optimist. This was the one woman I wanted to keep. The one woman I could see a future with. Maybe it was for the best. I didn't even know her now. This Debra wanted to forget the other Debra. The Debra that had made love with such passion. And, if I knew her like I thought I knew her, she damn well soon would.

So, Jack, shake hands with this good woman. Say good bye, and try not to see the evident relief she's trying to hide.

I asked for the bill, but she had already instructed the waitress. We left the restaurant together, and out on the parking lot I extended my hand. She hesitated, then hugged me, and I could see that she was crying. Tears for what? It was over.

I walked away, not feeling anything.

Chapter 57

With Debra gone out of my life, I felt a void; an emptiness I didn't know how to fill. Being in limbo wasn't a good feeling. And, like other times before in my life, I had no idea where I was headed.

The only positive, and I had to keep reminding myself, was that I was through with the FBI. There would be no witness protection; no indictments for any of my not quite so lawful actions. My overpaid lawyer had been worth every last penny.

February came and went. The days passed, one by one, melting into each other, never differing. Each morning I got up and had breakfast, sometimes on the front porch, sometimes on the back porch. Next, came a shower and then off to Starbucks to do some internet work. I did some research on the Santa Rosaria County Sheriff's department and found out that there were more than two hundred deputies under Sheriff Lawson. I used any excuse I could find to call Lawson and ask for the update on the Holler bust.

In early March I finally called and asked Lawson to have lunch with me at the East Bay Inn. We sat down, and both ordered hamburgers, fries, and Samuel Adams.

"So, what's the latest?" I asked.

"Swamp, you need to forget about the bust, just forget it. Why don't you get it?"

"Look, Hiker, it's not so much that I want to be involved in the bust, but you and the FBI need me. You have to understand, if Holler escapes, I'm in trouble. Guaranteed, he'll come after me for sure. It's my life we're talking about."

"Like I said, let it go Swamp."

"I don't want to let it go. I don't want to look over my shoulder for the rest of my life."

"Look, from here on you're on your own. So, stay out of trouble."

"What's that supposed to mean?"

"It means, Ludicrous, I can't cover your ass any more. That's what it means."

"Look who's talking."

"Excuse me?"

"You figure it out."

"No, I want you to tell me."

The rage was building inside me.

Who the hell are you, Hiker?

"Ask your wife."

"What the fuck are you implying, you bastard."

"I'm not implying anything."

"Then what's my wife got to do with it, huh? You have some secrets with my wife?"

"You're always three steps behind on everything. We've known each other a long time. Been through a lot together. I didn't and wouldn't ever have an affair with your wife, stupid."

"Then what the fuck are you talking about?"

"Alright. I've had enough of your slowness. I'll tell you."

"Please do."

We stopped talking as the waitress arrived with our burgers. As soon as she left, the intense conversation carried on.

"How exactly do you think you got elected to sheriff of Santa Rosaria County?"

"I was duly elected, pal. Don't try and tell me it was because of you."

"Oh, contraire. It was very much because of me. A few weeks before the election, I found out Holler was trying to frame you, pal. If I hadn't interfered, you wouldn't be sitting there wearing a sheriff's badge."

"Tried to frame me how? And exactly how is Linda involved in it?"

"Come on, Lawson, you know how hard Linda and I canvassed for your election. She knew everything that was going on. I told Linda not to say anything to you because you didn't need to have any doubts in your mind while you were campaigning. Holler was about to have a story run in the NW Florida Daily News about how corrupt you were and even went so far as to have pictures photo-shopped of you and one of his whores. Thanks to a friend of mine who worked on the paper, I found out about the plan."

Lawson just stared at me.

"It wasn't easy to get the story squelched. I had to go so far as to threaten the editor that if he ran with the story, he was going to have one big fat lawsuit. Big enough to close the paper down. I explained to him about Holler's business, and who he's connected to, and finally was able to persuade him not to go with the story. If he'd run it, you'd have been a history. You see Hiker, even if it wasn't true, if the story had run, the damage would have been done. No way would you have won."

Lawson continued to stare at me. I picked up my burger and started to gobble it down; wasn't chewing, just swallowing. That's what happens when I'm angry but satisfied. Lawson still hadn't said a word, but I was enjoying my food, the beer, and the look on his face.

"Are you going to eat or just stare at it?" I barked through a mouthful of fries.

He lifted his fork and knife and started to cut his burger.

"Come on Hiker, you hardly use a utensil while you eat, why now?"

He put down the fork and knife, grabbed the burger, and took a large bite.

Neither of us spoke for the rest of the meal. I ordered coffee for both of us; one black, one with cream. I know how Lawson takes his coffee. Lawson asked for the bill.

"Don't worry. I got this one, buddy."

There was still that look on his face as he looked straight into my eyes.

"Thanks, Jack."

He hardly ever uses my real name, let alone saying thanks unless it's serious.

"Forget it. No apology needed. We both cover each another's behind, just like our navy days. So, when's the bust, Hiker?"

"Don't push it, buster."

But, there was a smile on his face as he said it.

Chapter 58

Another two months passed with no word on the Holler bust. Two months of virtually doing nothing other than obsessing about Holler. Despite my obsessing, I was happy in my little cottage, thanks to Vance McGruder who had persuaded his wife to rent it to me. Even so, Holler still dominated my every waking moment. A job did come in from Destin, but I turned down. Nothing was going to interfere with my being a part of Holler's take-down, even if Sheriff Lawson thought otherwise. I'd only had that one lunch meeting with Lawson, and, although we got into a heated argument, it did end to my satisfaction.

It was 9 am on a sunny morning in early May. While I was getting out of the shower, I thought I heard my cell phone ring. I grabbed a towel, wrapped it around my mid-section, and rushed to the kitchen.

"Hello!"

"Jack? This is Charlene from the Sheriff's Department. Deputy Tucker just radioed me to call you. The Holler bust is about to go down. He thought it would be a good idea for you to come down to the office."

"Thank you, Charlene. Yes, I'll be there as soon as I can. But, why Tucker? Did Sheriff Lawson okay this?"

"Sheriff Lawson, along with a dozen of his deputies, Pensacola Police Department, ATF, and the FBI all getting ready for the bust. I don't know if I was supposed to tell you, but before he left, I heard a heated argument between Sheriff Lawson and Deputy Tucker."

"An argument?"

"Tucker argued that they should somehow let you in on the bust. Sheriff Lawson finally agreed to it and told Tucker he should get in touch with you. That you and

Tucker should work outside of the bust and if needed, trail Holler."

"Trail Holler? They think he might somehow evade the take-down? That puts a wrinkle in the works. Where's Tucker now?"

"I don't know, but I can radio him to meet you here."

"Yeh, do that."

"Oh, and one more thing, when you get here, Tucker has the authority to swear you in and give you a badge."

"That's the best news I had heard in a long time. Thank you, Charlene!"

In under fifteen minutes I was dressed, had made a fresh pot of coffee, and gulped down a cup as I ate a slice of cold, left-over pizza. I strapped my gun in my shoulder holster, the gun I'd gotten from Lila was hidden in the inside pocket of my khaki pants, and I had taped a knife to my ankle. I almost forgot. I grabbed Lila's pepper spray and put it in my side pocket.

I was about to pick up my cell phone when it rang again. "Unknown Caller." Assuming it was Tucker, I picked up.

"Tucker, I'm ready and on my way. Charlene briefly informed me what's going down."

"Good. Then you know what we talked about?"

"Vaguely. You can fill me in with more details when I get there. See you in a few."

I hurried to close and lock all the doors, except the front, and pushed the alarm button "on." I knew I had 80 seconds to get out the front door and lock it. As I started to open it, I suddenly remembered I'd forgotten my binoculars. I rushed back through the kitchen to the garage, grabbed them off the shelf, and went back to the front door to lock it. As soon as I opened the door, I heard the piercing whoooouu, whooouuu. The damn alarm system went off. Apparently, while grabbing my binoculars, I'd used up all my 80 seconds. I quickly cancelled the alarm, waited a few seconds, and then turned it back on. As I was opening the front door, the house phone rang, and I rushed back in to answer it.

"Hello?"

"Good morning. This is James with ADT Security. We're responding to an alarm that just went off at your location. We have to verify if everything is alright, sir."

"Everything's fine. I pushed the alarm on, then realized I'd forgotten something. Apparently, I'd used up all my time before I was able to complete locking the front door."

"Sir, I have to ask you for your pass code."

"Code? What code! I don't have a code!"

"I'm sorry, sir. If you can't give me the code, I'll have to alert the police to check things out."

"As I just said, I don't know the code. I'm renting this place from a man by the name of Vance McGruder. Actually, his wife owns it. Can you check with them?"

"Okay, sir. What is your full name? I'll call and verify with the owner. Please stay on the line."

"Look. I'm a hurry. I've got to leave. Surely you can settle things with her?"

"Sir! In that case we must call the police. They'll be there within ten minutes. You'll need to speak to them."

"Alright! My full name is Jacques Ludefance. Don't call the cops. I'll wait."

I put the house phone on loud speaker and set it on the kitchen counter. Mentally I rechecked everything I had on me. But, I still had this nagging feeling I'd forgotten something. Holler's photo! The one of him standing over

Duyen's body. Damn! Damn! Damn. That photo was one of the pieces of evidence that had been turned over to the FBI. Checking my files, thank God I found another copy.

I thought I should call Tucker and let him know that I was running late, but since I didn't have his number, I called Charlene.

"Charlene, this is Jack. Would you please let Tucker know I'm running a little late? If he could meet me at my house that would be even better."

"Of course! I'll let him know."

After giving her the address, I disconnected, turned and went over to the low cabinet on the other side of the kitchen where I keep a bowl of mixed nuts. I grabbed a handful and gobbling them down, started pacing, and then grabbed another handful of nuts. Typical Jack, I eat when I'm frustrated or excited.

"Hello?" came a voice from the house phone.

As I grabbed the phone, I tried to swallow my mouthful of nuts.

"Please hold on," came out sounding like, "pzz ld mm."

"Hello? Mr. Ludefance?" came the voice again. "Is anyone there?"

I swallowed hard and answered, "Yes, I'm here!"

"Yes, sir. I've cleared everything with Mrs. McGruder and it seems she forgot to give you the pass code. Sir, from now on you'll have a new code."

"Fine! Just give me the code!"

"Sir, you'll need to make up a code and give it to me. It must be a word with not more than three letters; something easy to remember."

I was exasperated by this point, but what could I do? I gave him the first word that came into mind.

"That will do. Have a wonderful day, Mr. Ludefance."

Chapter 59

Have a wonderful day? Yes, sir. I'm planning on doing just that. As I hung up the phone I heard a knock on the front door. I opened it to find Tucker.

"Tucker. I'm ready to leave."

"Actually, Mr. Ludefance, we need to plan what we're are doing."

"Mr. Ludefance?? Since when did I become Mr. Ludefance? Tucker, it's either Jack, Swamp, or Ludicrous. Take your pick."

I wanted to ask what was with the attitude, but thought better of it.

"Come on in. There's coffee in the kitchen."

While I was handing Tucker his coffee, I pulled out the picture of Holler and Duyen, ready to show it to him. I knew he hadn't seen it, but he needed to know what we were up against.

"Sorry, you take cream and sugar? I don't have sugar, but I have cream."

"Cream will do."

I let him finish adding cream. As he took his first gulp, I held up the picture of Holler standing over the dead girl's body. He took one look and spit out what was in his mouth.

"Tucker, I'm sure you know, Holler's a very cunning bastard. He's got no empathy for anyone. He'd sell his own mother in second. That's why we can't under estimate him. I wouldn't put it past him that he's got ears in the sheriff's department. I'm telling you, he probably knows about the bust. Charlene even mentioned that you and I might need to work outside of the bust and trail Holler."

I had to give Tucker credit for a quick comeback.

"You trying to take the lead on this, Jack?"

"Not necessarily, but I have some ideas, if your open to listening."

"Go ahead."

"Can you contact Pensacola Airport to see if Holler's private jet is there?"

"What else?"

"I tell you as we progress."

While Tucker was making his call to talk to security at Pensacola Airport, my cell phone rang. Recognizing Lawson's number, I picked up.

"Lawson. What's up?"

"Ludicrous, is Tucker there with you?"

"Actually yes, he's talking to Pensacola Airport security right now."

"Good, so you've worked out what to do then."

"We're in planning right now, after we find out if Holler's private jet is at the airport."

"You're going to need to speed it up. I was just informed that a helicopter took off from Holler's estate. I've requested Pensacola Police to put a tail on that chopper, but the chopper seems to be heading towards Mobile."

"Mobile! Holy shit. Lawson, we'd better get moving. Can you contact Mobile Airport security?"

"I'm ahead of you. I've already done that, but it could be just a diversion. It could land any place."

"Then we need to cover all the small airports in the area."

"In the meantime, keep me informed."

"Ten four."

Not ten seconds later, as Tucker was signaling me, my phone rang again.

"Lawson, can you hold on? I think Tucker has something."

I turned my cell phone to speaker.

"What's up, Tucker?"

"I just spoke with Pensacola Tower. The chopper was heading towards Mobile and was almost there, but it just made a U-turn. It's not heading back toward Pensacola, but heading northeast, destination unknown."

"Lawson, did you hear what Tucker just said?"

"Yes! I've instructed Pensacola Tower to track until it leaves their jurisdiction."

"Wait, wait Lawson. I think I know where the chopper's heading."

"Don't keep me in suspense. Where the hell is it going?"

"Bob Sikes, near Crestview."

"How can you be so sure?"

"I'm not. But, it's the only possible explanation."

"I'll ask one more time. How do you know all this?"

"Lawson, there's no time to argue. The short answer is Holler usually keeps a medium size jet at Pensacola Airport, which I am guessing belongs to the big boys. But, he also keeps another small jet at Bob Sikes for himself. It came up when I was doing all my research. That's where he transports his whores to other cities."

"Look, Swamp. I don't have much time. You and Tucker make sure to follow him."

"But, wait Lawson! I need you to arrange for a helicopter to get us to Crestview!"

"You know the department doesn't have a chopper. Neither does Pensacola."

"Rent one! There are private companies at Pensacola who rent out choppers. Look, Lawson. You have more weight than either Tucker or me. Call Black Helicopter and arrange a chopper for us. We need to get to Bob Sikes before Holler takes off in his jet. Better yet, have Charlene arrange the phone call and then you talk to them."

There was a pause, longer than I'd hoped for.

"Lawson, there's no way Tucker and I can reach Crestview in time by car. Have the chopper pick us up at that small touch and go strip just east of Santa Rosaria Bridge. It's the closest and quickest way. We can be there in under ten minutes."

"I'll call Charlene. One of us will get back to you."

Within five minutes he called back. A chopper was headed to pick us up. Tucker went out ahead of me and was waiting, engine running. I had everything I needed, turned on the alarm, and locked the house. As I got in, Tucker turned to me.

"What now?"

"I need to swear you in."

"You can do that while we're waiting for the chopper."

Turning onto Highway 88 we immediately encountered heavy traffic.

"Accident up ahead."

"Oh, shit. Not now. We're so close to that touch and go strip."

"No worries."

Chapter 60

Tucker hit his police lights and siren, and we careened down the middle strip of 88. After Santa Rosaria Bridge, traffic cleared, and Tucker did a hard right onto the field where the chopper was already waiting for us. That was one hell of a service, I must say.

I was about to get out of the car when Tucker yelled, "Wait!"

"Not now, Tucker! We've got to get going!"

"I'm swearing you in!"

Over the roar of the choppers propellers, he gave me the oath.

"It's abbreviated, and I'm not sure of all the words, but it will have to do. 'Do you Jacques Ludefance solemnly swear to perform with fidelity the duties of the office to which you have been appointed, and to which you are about to assume, and that you will faithfully execute the office of deputy sheriff to the best of your knowledge and ability, agreeably to law.'"

"I do!"

"You are now a deputy sheriff of Santa Rosaria County."

He handed me a badge and I affixed it to the pocket of my shirt.

"Tucker, are those the exact words or you did you make them up?"

"Close enough. It's what came to mind."

The private chopper set down just long enough to pick us up. The pilot looked back at us, gave us a thumbs up, and we were airborne, as Tucker and I were still buckling ourselves in. In less than fifteen minutes, Bob Sikes came into view with its small terminal, tower, one taxiway and one runway.

Just before touchdown, Tucker turned to me with a scowl on his face and yelled above the roar of the chopper.

"One question, Jack. That *was* you I was chasing, wasn't it?"

My answer was a simple smile.

"I knew it!"

He turned away and looked out the open door as the chopper started to set down.

"I hope Lawson has already called airport security."

"I don't think they have elaborate security."

The chopper bounced once as it hit the tarmac. I noticed three individuals were approaching a waiting jet.

"Tucker, we've got to block the jet somehow!"

As we jumped down to the tarmac, the pilot shouted after us, "Do you want me to wait for you guys?"

Tucker shouted back, "Affirmative. Wait for us!"

We rushed toward the small airport terminal. While Tucker went inside, I checked the airport vehicle in front. No keys. Rushing in after Tucker, I demanded the keys for the car parked outside. A bald-headed man behind the counter looked from Tucker to me. Tucker quickly displayed his badge and explained the situation, and the guy threw the keys my way.

Sprinting back outside, I got in, turned the key and headed out toward the jet. As I drove down the runway, I saw Tucker in another vehicle close behind me. The jet was already making its revs and started to move down the runway for takeoff. As it sped up, I drove straight towards it. Crazy, but it was the only thing I thought would stop the jet.

As Tucker caught up to me, another vehicle seemed to appear out of nowhere and covered the rear of the jet. The jet slowed down and stopped. I exited the car and pulled out my gun, pointing at the jet, which was now surrounded by Tucker and two security officers who also had their guns drawn.

One of the security officers with a microphone shouted, "You're surrounded! Come out with your hands up!"

We waited for what seemed an eternity before the door slowly opened and the stairs were lowered. The pilot exited first, followed by one of Holler's bodyguards, then Holler, then his other bodyguard. As the last bodyguard started down the stairs, he pushed Holler into the first bodyguard, who in turn, lost his balance and fell onto the back of the pilot.

The domino effect left all three men sprawled on the runway, one on top of the other. As they tried to untangle themselves, the two security officers surrounded them.

At that same moment, I saw the second bodyguard raise his hand, his gun pointed straight at my forehead.

What they say is true. In less than a second, my whole life flashed before me. In that same second, Tucker took aim and fired, grazing the bodyguard's shoulder.

In the next instant, Tucker had the injured bodyguard on the ground, cuffed, and Mirandized.

While one of the security guards called for an ambulance, Tucker and the second security guard cuffed the other bodyguard, Holler and the pilot, then Mirandized them.

I approached Holler and looked into his eyes and did not say a word.

"This isn't over, Ludefance. You still don't know who you're fucking with."

"Maybe not. But, as long as you and your bodyguards are in the slammer, and I guarantee you'll be there for a very long time, I'll sleep very well."

One of the security officers said, "We'll take them back to the terminal and meet you there."

Tucker and I drove the vehicles back to the terminal and waited for security and the handcuffed men to arrive.

"Are we going to take them back with us in the chopper?" I asked Tucker.

"No. You can go ahead back with chopper. I'll stay until the ambulance and proper transportation for the other three has arrived. Hey, Jack, here's the keys to my squad car. You can drive it back to your house, and I'll pick it up later."

"Tucker?"

"Yeah?"

"Thanks."

"Your one of us now, Jack. We watch each other's back."

As I climbed back in the chopper I shouted to the pilot, "Santa Rosaria Sheriff's Office!"

Chapter 61

As the chopper approached Santa Rosaria, I had second thoughts. I unbuckled my seatbelt and approached the pilot.

"I've changed my mind. Can you drop me off at Holler Enterprises? There's a chopper pad on the estate behind the front buildings. It shouldn't be hard to spot."

He gave me a thumbs up, and changed course. From the vantage point of the chopper, I could see the estate was completely surrounded. With the FBI, ATF, Pensacola authorities and Santa Rosaria authorities there had to be at least several hundred. It was quite an impressive sight.

As the pilot set the chopper down on the pad, and I jumped down. Everyone near the pad turned to stare. I yelled above the noise as the chopper lifted off the pad and departed. Flashing my badge, I asked, "Where's Sheriff Lawson?"

"He's inside the main house."

I turned and strode toward the mansion, noticing along the way men digging in a spot I assumed was where the two girls were buried. From one of the buildings I'd broken into, in what seemed to be an eternity ago, I saw agents carrying out cardboard cartons. Past the barns, men were loading horses onto a horse van. They certainly were wasting no time.

It was one hell of a busy site.

Walking into the large, two-story foyer of the mansion, I encountered a hub of activity; a sort of controlled chaos. Turning left I entered the large, expensively decorated, formal living room, where several Holler's house staff were being interrogated by the FBI with the help of translators.

"Anyone know where I can find Sheriff Lawson?"

"Check the kitchen! Back of the house!"

I wove my way back further into the maze of people and found Lawson in the immense kitchen interviewing one of the cooks through an interpreter. As soon as he saw me, he stood up and strode over to me.

"Swamp! How'd it go? Where's Tucker?"

"Tucker's back at Bob Sikes with the prisoners waiting for an ambulance and proper transport. He told me to go ahead and take the chopper back."

"Ambulance? Explain that one."

I gave Lawson a quick recount of what had happened.

"He did the right thing, but you shouldn't be hanging around here. How'd you get in, anyway?"

"I had the chopper land on the pad, and they let me in when I showed my deputy badge."

"Go on home, Swamp. If you stay here, there will only be more trouble. You don't want to confront Agent Johnson."

"You're right on that, Lawson. I just wanted to make sure they exhumed the bodies of the two girls."

"They've found one, but still looking for the other girl's body."

"I think I have an idea where it might be."

"Where? And how do you know?"

"Several months ago, I had an interview with one of the cooks. Through an interpreter she said something about a 'faah corner.' I don't know which corner, but it does narrow it down."

"Come on. Get out of here. And avoid Johnson, if you can."

"I'm going, and I will."

I took a few steps, stopped, and turned back.

"Hey, Lawson!"

He turned toward me.

"You're welcome!"

He looked at me and tried unsuccessfully to stifle a big sneeze.

"Damn allergies," he mumbled.

I walked out of the house, back into the bright sunlight, and pulled out my sunglasses. It may have looked like chaos, but every person here had a specific job to do. On the front steps, one of the agents was talking to his superior, asking for geological equipment to search for the other body.

It brought back the memory of talking to the Vietnamese cook who, through Sofia, had talked about the sick girls on the boats and how, if they died, their bodies were tied to concrete blocks and they were dumped overboard. That and how there were two girls buried on the estate, 'one girl buried faah corner.' Her words still haunt me to this day.

Walking back through the maze of people towards the front of the estate, I saw agent Johnson in the distance talking with several other agents. I knew Lawson was right about not letting him see me. It was time to get the hell out of this wretched place. The FBI would find the other girl's body. It was their job.

When I reached the front of Holler Enterprises on Highway 88, I approached one of the deputies on duty, and showed him my badge.

"Listen, I need a ride back to the touch and go strip just east of Santa Rosaria Bridge to pick up Deputy Tucker's car."

On the way he introduced himself and asked, "You were in the navy with Sheriff Lawson, right?"

"Yeah. How'd you know that?"

"You're a star, pal. Every deputy in Santa Rosaria knows who you are."

"What can I say-"

"By the way, what kind of name is Ludicrous? We keep hearing Sheriff Lawson call you that."

"It's a long story."

He stopped the car right next to where Tucker had parked his car.

"Thanks for the ride."

"Welcome. Really, what is it with the Ludicrous name?"

"Ask Sheriff Lawson."

Chapter 62

I drove Tucker's squad car back to the cottage, took my car out of the garage, and put his vehicle in. No need to garner attention or questions from the neighbors. Opening the front door to the cottage, I heard the beeeeeep of the alarm. After turning it off, I called Charlene and gave her a message for Tucker.

Realizing how hungry I was, I thought about ordering a pizza, but let that idea slide. I'd had two slices for breakfast. Thought about going out but didn't want to. I wouldn't mind having a McDonald's big mac, but they didn't deliver.

After a quick Google search, I found a Chinese place that did deliver, and ordered shrimp fried rice, beef broccoli, garlic chicken, and six egg rolls. Yeah, I was that hungry. After paying the delivery guy and giving him a five-dollar tip, I dug in. There wasn't much left, but what there was, I repackaged and put in the refrigerator.

After settling on the couch, I remembered I hadn't read my fortune cookies. I was surprised at one that read, "Someone is romantically thinking of you." Well, it certainly wasn't Debra. Then, Lee came to mind. Should I call her? It had been several months, but she kept popping into my mind. While I was debating whether to call her or not to call her, I fell asleep on the couch. Chinese food has a way of doing that.

When I woke, it was 11:27 pm. After getting into bed, I had trouble falling asleep again, and when I finally did, it was a restless sleep punctuated with a number of vivid dreams.

In one of the dreams, I was carrying a heavy bag and walking along a city street where a number of art works were displayed. From the bag I took out a hacksaw and placed it on the sidewalk. I started walking again and then remembered to go back and pick up my hacksaw. I thought about cutting down all the branches hanging low over the fence. They were hanging from a poisonous tree and dangerous.

In another dream, people were trying to sell me dark art, and I started running from them, believing they had to be bad people. I've always believed that dreams are the brain's way of making sense out of confusion, and I let them be.

I woke up again at 3 am to heavy rain, the sound echoing off the metal roof of the Florida room. It continued raining all morning until mid-afternoon, which was fine with me. I had nowhere to go, and nothing to do. Time to decompress after yesterday's events.

Tucker came by in the late afternoon to pick up his squad car and filled me on the latest happenings. The Holler estate was still being processed and would be for several days to come, but the rain had slowed things down considerably. There was a plethora of evidence to process and had to be done carefully and correctly to make the case against Holler air-tight.

I asked about the other body. He informed me that the FBI had located it and both bodies were currently at the medical examiners in Ft. Williams, after which they would be given proper burials.

Sadness at the horror of it all descended over me, and I spent the next few days trying to find sense in it all.

Chapter 63

Late Friday afternoon, I received a call from Lawson. It was about time I heard from him.

"Lawson? What's up?"

"Don't 'what's up' me."

"Alright! What have I done now, Lawson?"

"You didn't do anything. It's just the way you talk. Like a teenager. 'Wassup.'"

"You know what they say, I've always been young at heart."

"Why don't you act your own age? You're a grown man."

"What's eating you? What do you want Lawson? You're the one who called me. I figure you want something."

He paused. I really think he wanted to say something, but, as usual, either couldn't admit it, or couldn't say it.

"I'm at Bayside. I thought you might want to come down and we could have a couple of beers."

"Sure, Lawson. I still think you want something. By the way, I haven't had dinner. You paying for that as well?"

"Sure. Dinner's on me."

"Well then, I'll be there in a few minutes."

When I pulled into the parking lot, I noticed a few other deputy vehicles. Actually, I counted more than ten. This certainly triggered my curiosity. Why did Lawson want me here?

Walking into the restaurant, I found it full to the brim as it always is on a Friday night. I didn't see Lawson or any of the deputies in the main dining room, so I proceeded out onto the back deck.

"There he is!" One of the deputies shouted. They were packed into several tables over by the water. Several of the deputies had gathered their high stools around Lawson's table.

Lawson turned, saw me, and signaled for me to come sit. As I walked over, one of the deputies grabbed another stool. Several empty pitchers of beer scattered the table, with another two pitchers being delivered by one of the waitresses. She poured beer into large glass mugs and handed me one, and I had a tough time not staring at her obviously oversized breasts.

"Have a seat, Ludicrous."

One of the deputies turned to me and said, "Ludicrous? What kind a name is that? I've always wondered about that."

"Ask the sheriff," came my standard reply.

"Yep, I gave him that name. It's a long story and I'll tell you in a minute."

While I was gulping my beer, Lawson stood up.

"But, first I have something important to tell you guys. Now! All of you here participated in the events of the past week. Both the local and national news have been giving us, along with Pensacola police, the FBI, and the ATF well-deserved praise for our success in busting a so called well-respected businessman who turned out to be a notorious criminal, operating under our noses. But, in reality, the success rightfully should go to this man, who happens to be a friend of mine."

Lawson paused and put his hand on my shoulder.

"Actually, he is more than a friend; he is like a brother to me. I will say this, you can choose your friends, but you can't choose your blood brother. Case in point, my own brother, whom I haven't spoken to for over twenty-three years. I guess I traded my own brother for this man whom I spent quite a bit of time with in the navy. We've remained friends to this very day. And, like real siblings, we have disagreements, even arguments. Sometimes we even get on each other's wrong side, but we've never let that get the better of us. We always have come to each other's rescue when needed."

He stopped for a moment and raised his glass mug of beer.

"That is why I believe the success of this take-down really belongs to this man, who stubbornly, doggedly worked his ass off to bring about Jonathan Holler's arrest and in bringing a criminal empire down. Yeah, along the way he sometimes bent the rules which we, as law enforcement officers, can't. Was it worth bending the rules and sometimes getting in the mire? I think in this case, absolutely, yes! A toast to Jack Ludefance!"

Glass mugs of beer clinked in the air.

"You ask about the nickname. Well, I'm gonna tell you about it. Ludicrous here used to have a boat named, *THE LUNA SEA*, which you all know was blown up by Holler. I thought the name Ludicrous went quite well for the owner of *THE LUNA SEA*."

He smiled and waited as the deputies all had their moment of laughter.

"So, what else makes Ludicrous, sorry Mr. Jacques Ludefance, tick? He doesn't live by the rules, but rather on the edge. See his scar? He got it wrestling with an alligator. By the way, what other man do you know that would keep an alligator as a pet? Other than a man who prefers to live his life dangerously?"

Another toast went around the crowd.

"I'll wrap this up by saying that it all started here in this very restaurant nearly a year ago, when the sheriff's office received a call from Ludicrous saying that a woman had just died. That woman turned out to be the wife of Jonathan Holler and she had come here asking for Jack's help. He didn't fail her. Remember that. He very nearly lost his life, but he didn't fail her."

The cheers and clapping went on for several embarrassing minutes. Several times through his speech, I almost asked him to stop. But, it sure was a nice feeling to know I had a friend like Lawson that I could always count on.

Without friends, what is life?

Epilogue

You may wonder, did I ever call Lee? It took me several more days, several aborted attempts of picking up my cell phone, starting to dial her number, and then hanging up.
But, in the end, yes, I did call her.
And that is a story for another time.